Donna M. Gershten was born in eastern North Carolina and later lived for some years in Sinaloa, Mexico where she ran a fitness and community centre. She returned to the United States, received a master of fine arts in creative writing from Warren Wilson College, and began to publish short stories in literary journals. Gershten now divides her time between the Huerfano Valley in southern Colorado and Denver. *Kissing the Virgin's Mouth* is her first novel and won Barbara Kingsolver's Bellwether Prize for Fiction In Support of A Literature of Social Change.

Acclaim for *Kissing the Virgin's Mouth*:

'A beautifully written, lyrical novel . . . the kind of book you inhale in one breath and can't forget afterward'
Barbara Kingsolver

'Gershten's sensuous first novel is lit from within by its imaginative, outspoken narrator'
Elle

'A triumphant piece of writing – full of genuine affection for its characters . . . a wild ride of a tale . . . an honest and gusty effort at writing across borders'
The Village Voice

'Full of passion and courage. Reading a book like this – like eating a meal that's not only healthy but also delicious and prepared by someone you love – is not only one of life's great pleasures but also food for the soul . . . Gershten has created a heroine who is utterly human, maintaining a delicate but sure-footed balance between fragility and strength . . . *Kissing the Virgin's Mouth* does indeed set a standard for defining a literature of social responsibility'
Washington Post

'Most of Magdalena's stories are about beginnings or endings – turning points. Gershten's novel, unlike most, leaves us wishing for even more of what happened in between'
Los Angeles Times

'Sensual and ironic, dramatic and sensitive, Gershten's insightful cross-cultural novel astutely weighs the inequities between men and women, rich and poor'
Booklist

'Gershten writes powerfully, carefully choosing words that create atmosphere and portraying characters that are tangible and have depth. This deeply moving work should find a place in the fiction collections of both academic and public libraries'
Library Journal

'Moving . . . This spirited novel, the first recipient of Barbara Kingsolver's Bellwether Prize for a work of socially or politically engaged fiction, will ultimately win over most skeptics'
Publishers Weekly

'Brilliantly written . . . richly poignant . . . Gershten's novel reflects contemporary Mexico; a modern fairytale based on the reality and aspirations of today's Mexicans'
San Francisco Chronicle

'It is (Magda's) voice – straightforward, fallible, grateful, sensual – that provides much of the pleasure and immediacy of *Kissing the Virgin's Mouth*. Through her observant and practical eyes, we glimpse some of the ardent contradictions of Mexican society'
The Santa Fe New Mexican

'Gershten's spunky heroine . . . (is) one of the toughest, smartest, most vulnerable and endearing heroines in recent fiction'
Arizona Daily Star

KISSING THE VIRGIN'S MOUTH

A Novel

Donna M. Gershten

BLACK SWAN

KISSING THE VIRGIN'S MOUTH
A BLACK SWAN BOOK : 0 552 99978 4

First publication in Great Britain

PRINTING HISTORY
Black Swan edition published 2002

1 3 5 7 9 10 8 6 4 2

Set in 11/13pt Melior by
Phoenix Typesetting, Ilkley, West Yorkshire.

Black Swan Books are published by Transworld Publishers,
61–63 Uxbridge Road, London W5 5SA,
a division of The Random House Group Ltd,
in Australia by Random House Australia (Pty) Ltd,
20 Alfred Street, Milsons Point, Sydney, NSW 2061, Australia,
in New Zealand by Random House New Zealand Ltd,
18 Poland Road, Glenfield, Auckland 10, New Zealand
and in South Africa by Random House (Pty) Ltd,
Endulini, 5a Jubilee Road, Parktown 2193, South Africa.

Printed and bound in Great Britain by
Cox & Wyman Ltd, Reading, Berkshire.

for Malinche,
for Magdalen
for all the whores in history

I have begun to teach Isabel the important things. Just as I taught my hija. Feel gratitude. That's what I told my little five-year-old cousin yesterday when she found a coin in the grass. Wrapped her fat fingers around a peso, eyes bright. Say thank you, I tell her, like this: I kneeled beside her, pretending the peso was inside my tight fist and I closed my eyes and filled my heart and kissed my fist long and firm like a mother who finds her lost child, like a father saying good-bye. She did it too. Thank who? That is not important.

Some people think I am religious.

I am not.

I believe in gratitude.

KISSING THE
VIRGIN'S MOUTH

I thank the dark Virgin, morena like me . . .

There are many who will tell you that the dark-skinned girls, las morenitas, have got no chance. But when I was a girl, I noted the Virgin de Guadalupe, her with the important job of taking care of all the pueblitos, and standing in every home with candles and all the respect, and her own day of Guadalupe with people crawling across the zócalo and up the cathedral steps on raw knees and singing themselves ronca all night long in the square. She did okay.

I arrived to this world through the splitting little monkey of my mother and I bloodied the hands of Tía Chucha. The name they gave me when I was born was Guadalupe Magdalena Molina Vásquez. My mother and aunt called me Chupita, Little Sucker, me always after the breast; Mexican family and friends call me Magda, and my American husband called me Maggie. My saint's name is Guadalupe, so in a way, though I would have been slapped for saying it, I am tocayas with the virgin, we share a name, we are both dark, but I never took her virginity to heart.

In my life, I have added two names and subtracted two from my own and now I am back to my original: Guadalupe Magdalena Molina Vásquez. Vows of love and chimney smoke, the wind soon blows away.

*   *   *

I returned to the place of my birth, to Teatlán, and to my own name thirteen years ago. Mami and Chucha, the ones who called me Chupita, are dead. Now, in the golden zone of Teatlán, the resort city in Sinaloa, in México, I sit in the chair of Tía Chucha on my roof in the good light of the morning sun. The chair is the same. The roof is of a different house. Mine.

When Tía Chucha died, I chipped the mortar that secured this wooden chair to her roof and brought it to my fine house in Las Gaviotas in the golden zone, three blocks east of the sea and just west of Las Gaviotas Tennis Club that contains the shrine to the porcelain miracle, Niñito Jesus. People ask where I reside, and I enjoy saying, 'Just west of the miracle baby Jesus.' Those from Teatlán know the shrine of the porcelain miracle, and those who are not, smile blankness. I mortared Tía's chair far from the dirty barrio to my own roof in the Las Gaviotas neighborhood, where rooftops of the rich are angled and tiled in rounded terra-cotta instead of leveled cement, where only the smallest section of roof – enough room for a water tank, a clothesline – is flat. Here in the golden zone, there are gardens and sea breeze and little need for rooftops. Only servants climb the spiral iron stairs to lift the heavy circle lid from the tank and jiggle the black rubber bulb inside so that the pump will draw water up into storage. But I come here. I have mortared Chucha's chair to the roof to face west, just as she did, toward the Sea of Cortés. I come here out of habit, because it is in my blood to do so. A roof is where my mother died, where my tía escaped, where my father made tejuino corn drink, where I learned to dance. I come here to remember. To feel gratitude. To see.

The magic of the roof I discovered when I was no bigger than the tip of a little finger – maybe five – when my mother sent me to pull down the laundry from the line so that no one would steal it in the night.

'Make many trips,' she said. 'Fill the basket only a little, bring it down, and empty it on my bed. Then return for more.'

Labor was my family's wealth. We had enough bodies and power of muscle to use them extravagantly. We could afford five trips to retrieve laundry. We could afford twenty trips through the house and up the stairs and back to make a washtub of tejuino.

I remember so clearly standing on the flat concrete roof of our house forty-five years ago in el barrio Rincón. The basket sat at my ankles, and I stood behind the curtain of my family's clothes for a moment and felt the pride of a job before I tugged with both hands at the hem of my sister's skirt. It fell to me, and a surge of happy success came as I captured the stiff cloth and contained it in the basket. I sidestepped and pulled at once both legs of my brother's trousers and they too fell to me. Pulling down the skirt and pants revealed Tía Chucha sitting still in her straight-back wooden chair in the last light. She faced the direction of the ocean, her hands limp in her lap. Tía Chucha did not turn her head when I greeted her, or answer when Tío or Abuelito or my cousins called to her from below, 'Tía, Vieja, Pocha, Mamita . . .' Aunt, Old Lady, Ruin, Mother. They each called her by a different name, and each wanted something: a shirt ironed, a drink of water, to slap her for not answering their needs, permission. She sat very still, staring toward the ocean, though she could not see it. From our roof in el barrio Rincón, rebar emerged from the flat cement like the stalks of dead plants. The only ocean visible was one of rooftops where skirts and trousers snapped from clotheslines, where dogs lived and where their shit dried in the sun and scattered in the wind.

*   *   *

Now, from Chucha's chair mortared to the roof of my fine house, I try to see into the groomed gardens of my neighbors. No more do I have the clear vision. Even with my eyeglasses, my sight lacks the sharp focus of youth, but that it not important. In the quiet hours, I can hear the ocean waves. Every day I slowly push my glasses up on top of my head so that strands of hair are pinned away from my face, and I see smears of young green – bougainvillea just budding – or deep green – gardenia or mandevilla. Pedacitos of debris dance across my vision like the floating black ash of burned paper. Ragged pieces of a life. My friends, I call them. My sins. I inhale the scent of jazmín, of blossoming limón, or the sweetness of madreselvas en flor. I lift my chin and know that close by, overripe guavas are wasting on the ground.

Someday I may have to find a path through my house by the feel of the walls and furniture under my palms. The soles of my feet will give attention to the tiniest change beneath, electric to the danger of grit or moisture, and the high polish of marble tiles that delights me now could become a threat underfoot. Perhaps I will grip the iron banister of the circular stairs outside, cool in the mornings, hot in midday, and lift a foot in search of the metal mesh of the next stair step so that I might climb to my roof.

From Chucha's chair, I remember in pieces. Blind Mami, Tía, mad Abuelito, Papi el huevón, the prisoner, my poor husbands and amantes: each is a piece and a step in the story of how I came to live in plenty – a fine tejas roof over my head, good food in my belly, money in the bank – in the golden zone east of the Sea of Cortés and west of the porcelain Jesus. I thank them all. I sit facing the sea with my back to my neighbor, Jesusito, and with memories and lessons of life, I beam

14

my gratitude toward Cortés. All the time, I sharpen the vision of memory. And all the time, I await blindness.

Five blocks away, just north and west of my roof, my business sits between Bing's Ice Cream and Teatlán T-shirts across from Las Gaviotas Hotel and Señor Silver.

LUPA'S JUICES.

Lupa is my own special name for the dark Virgin, Guadalupe. No disrespect intended. She knows. I speak with Her daily. On Her altar in my sala, my Virgin Guadalupe stands on burgundy velvet with golden milagritos and candles shining at Her feet. La Virgin. My Lupa.

Most customers do not notice the connection between the Virgin and the name of my business. Some think I am Lupa.

The sign for my business is wooden, painted on each side, bright grass-green with yellow letters, bananas and guavas and pink watermelon, a blushed mango. It hangs from a stand in the sidewalk. Tourists must walk around it. They cannot miss it. LUPA'S JUICES, it says, and below that, 100% PURIFIED WATER and then SAFE CLEAN FOOD. That brings them in. Tourists are very frightened of the little parasites that do the breaststroke in Mexican water and food. With my imagination and a little bleach, I purify everything, and my customers don't get the shits, or if they do, they blame it on some other restaurant. No animalitos, no bichos in their bellies. They like clean, and so do I.

There are many ways to arrive here at the golden zone.

As one of my customer tourists, you come from the belly of a plane at the airport forty kilometers away and step onto the platform of diamond metal mesh at the

15

top of the stairs on wheels into the first gentle bath
of warm, moist air. You descend, smiling, into the
warmth, and in a herd move across the hot asphalt
toward the small airport building. Inside, you walk
down wide hallways toward the customs officials.
Through the windows, you see the tops of coconut
palms. A man older than you holds himself in the top
of the palm, pressing the trunk between his knees. He
squeezes it in the bend of one elbow, just the way he
walks with his friends when they have drunk too
much. In his free hand, the old man holds a machete
and chops away at the broad brown leaves at the stem
of the green coconut. You have the same feeling you
do when an elderly woman is a waitress, when the old
must do the work of the young.

The heels of hard-soled shoes echo against the cool-
but-not-so-clean tile floor. You stand in line and begin
to feel nervous – the Spanish words, the stern, bored
faces of bureaucrats with starched brown shirts too
tight over bellies. You are quickly waved through
the business of immigration, but not so quickly that the
heat doesn't start prickling behind the knees, under
the stockings, and a tear of sweat trickles down the
center of your back; not so quickly that the winter coat
carried over your arm doesn't begin to chafe and irri-
tate and feel ridiculous.

In groups of two or ten or forty, you reload into taxi
or van or bus to ride past mango groves and ranchitos
of limes, and you think it is quaint and lush and
beautiful in its simplicity. Then you pass the stinking
fish fertilizer that embarrasses the driver so that he
winces and hopes your nose doesn't notice. You ride
through Villa Unión, the town where my mother was
born, slowly through deep dirt holes in the thin
asphalt. And your body rocks, waist moving separately
from pelvis, and you laugh an uncomfortable laugh –

this is not what the brochure looked like – and small children press snotty faces and grimy hands against the taxi window and say, 'Meester, meester, mo-ney,' and the driver sounds his horn and waves them away with the flip of one hand and stares straight ahead. Maybe the driver feels embarrassed again, this time because he can sense you are nervous and wondering why you have come because the ride is now slow through a dirty, noisy city that is one concrete box after another. The ride is not so pretty or interesting or quaint anymore.

But then the taxista comes into the golden zone and turns his head to see your reaction to the coconut palms and working traffic light and the suddenly smooth paved roads and bright hotels against which the sun glints, and he smiles proudly, presses his back into the seat and lifts his chin, steering his taxi or van or bus with the palm of one hand and swinging his vehicle into the shaded cobblestone entrance of the hotel. You forget the trip from the airport as soon as the tires touch the cool shade.

West of the hotel, from a lounge chair under the shade of thatched palm palapa behind a rope fence draped like the one in movie theaters, on the white-sand beach that is combed with a rake more often than my hair, you watch red and purple and green para-chutes above the calm Sea of Cortés. Other tourists float seated through the air just below and ahead of the parachutes and above and behind speedboats and their bare legs hang – some crossed properly at the ankles, others kicking at the air. The sun is high, its sharp light ricocheting off the whitecaps of the waves. Cheerful brown men in sparkling white uniforms duck their heads and trays under the thatched palapas. '¿Margaritas? ¿Nachos?'

You think *Paradise.*

This is not how I arrived here to the rich golden zone of Teatlán, where I mortared Chucha's chair to my rooftop.

South and east of the tourist shade palapa on the beach, beyond the golden zone road, beyond the terracotta roofs, beyond the groves of coconut palms, there is an estuary where newborn shrimp larvae dance their crescent jerk, where flamingos fly with their pink necks and bellies almost touching the water, and where white egrets strut the shallow waters on skinny legs with eyes sharply focused for the movement and shadow of snake or eel. And that is beautiful. But beyond that, even farther south and farther east near the docks, beer factories and canning factories and concrete box houses crowd out all green and breeze – that is el barrio where I grew, el barrio Rincón. Where Chucha's chair once sat.

I arrived to el barrio through the splitting little monkey of my mother. The walls of her vagina squeezed my juicy self into a blinding light and I bloodied the hands of Tía Chucha. Chucha lay me screaming on my mother's belly with the greasy cord still connected, and slowly sank both her hands palms up into the bowl of water beside the cot. Vibrations of Mami's silent weeping quivered through her jellied tripe and through my new self. Standing over Mami and me drying her hands on her apron, Chucha also cried. She cried for new life. She cried for us all. And her tears fell onto my back and rolled down the curve of my ribs onto my mother's loose belly.

I grew just east of where the taxista drove slowly into the dirty city and felt embarrassed. It could have been my great-nephew pressing his snotty face to the taxi window. The tourist would not know of my house or my life in my barrio center there, just as for my first

18

years, I would not know of the places from which they traveled, of the route from the airport, or of the golden zone, of the promise and gleam of cleanliness.

My Martina, my hija, Martina Guadalupe Jones Molina, arrives to the golden zone by the route of tourists but not with the mind of one. She has traveled the route too many times between Idaho and Teatlán. Media gringa, she is comfortable in both places and belongs to neither.

Between semesters last Christmas, Martina came to Teatlán, as she usually does, and we walked together through the streets of the town center, her with her twenty-one years of firm youth that cannot be disguised even in the unflattering one-sex American clothes, and me not so bad either, and the men called from their cars and from the tops of buildings under construction, sucking teeth, groaning, 'Ay, mama-sotas, qué buenas están,' and I enjoyed it, feeling like a woman.

The men said the same words as always. Teatlán has been a coastal port since the 1500s and our ways have never been so formal as those of the cool north or of central Mexico. Men have called out to women walking since I can remember.

My Martina walks with her head held so proud and an argument ready in her throat. She argues with the ways of the world. My passions focus on smaller things – food on the table, the safety of my own.

Perhaps Martina thinks her life more sophisticated than mine, more civilized, more complex – elevated above the scrape and crawl of my barrio. May she always believe that. May my hija's life be lucky and prosperous enough for her to continue believing. But if something drags her down to hunger and fear – divorce, disease, locura – she will find that the fall is

19

not so far as she thought. And then she will want to know how to use all the tools, even the tools she now thinks beneath her. Then she will need most to feel gratitude – fierce gratitude. Then she will need to remember all I taught her.

A car pulled up beside us and the passenger said, '¿Dónde vas, mamacita?' to Martina.

She ignored him. I watched and walked beside her. Her loose unisex shorts hung from her hips like a worn hula skirt, the curve of her waist and her belly button peeking out just below the small faded T-shirt. She had applied makeup American style, to look pretty but not to look as if she had on makeup.

The man was a fatty with shining skin and hair.

I am inspired by the assurance of ugly men.

The car rolled slowly along. El gordo hissed spit behind his teeth, which bit deep into his lower lip. 'Qué buenas están,' he said, this time including me.

'Y qué pendejo es usted.' Martina imitated the growl of his words. She cursed him in the formal, in her accent media gringa.

'She needs a good man,' the passenger said to the driver.

'What do you think?' Martina addressed them directly. 'That we'll be so charmed by your wit and intellect that we'll hop in the car with you?'

Gordo answered by half closing his eyelids and circling his lips with his tongue.

In frustration, Martina stopped, and with hands signaling her curses, yelled, 'Agarre un palito y coma shit, pendejo motherfucker!'

Martina with her own ways in the world. She had things so easy that she has to make them hard.

The man clutched both hands over his heart as if shot in the chest. 'Ay, how I love a woman with fire,' he said. The car sped away, the horn honking.

20

Martina's pupils were large and dark. 'Those fuckers,' she said in English.

I took my daughter's arm. 'Grab a stick and eat shit, you idiot motherfucker?' She makes me very tired.

With poison, one drop is enough. A raised eyebrow and disdainful look would have been much more powerful, but my Martina thinks everything must be said aloud.

'Women would never be so, so . . . intrusive, so . . . irrespetuosos.' I could tell by the inward focus of her eyes that she pressed her brain for English and Spanish, for words to give meaning to injustice. *Injustice* to her is a word in a schoolbook.

Martina nodded as if she'd remembered just the words she had searched for, the title of the lecture that would follow. 'Contaminadores del universo.'

She stopped and turned as if to accuse me. 'Who fouls the streets with their piss?' She swept an arm to point to the walls, to the curbs. 'Men.' Martina nodded in agreement with herself and pointed to the sky as if they lived there. '¡Contaminadores del universo!'

I followed her erratic pace as best I could. It was like dancing with el mendigo, Jorge, who had a rhythm that was only his own. She started, stopped, sped forward, and slowed to a stroll.

'Do women start wars, knife each other in the streets, stick guns out of the windows of cars and shoot people?' Martina stopped and opened her arms wide to an answer. She turned to me as if I'd missed a cue.

I did not satisfy her with an answer.

'No. Men do,' she answered for me. 'Contaminadores del universo.' She was the impatient maestra answering for a dull student.

Martina walked backwards a few paces to face me while moving. 'Do women vomit drunk outside cantinas?'

21

'Women are not allowed in cantinas,' I said.

She glared at me, demanding the correct response. 'Los contaminadores,' she insisted. 'Admit it, Mami. Say it.'

I had vowed not to argue with Martina, but I felt myself heating. My heart fast, my thighs tight. I could not quiet my tongue. Qué simple, mi hija. 'Contaminadores, you want me to say? Contaminadores?'

'That's a start, Mami.'

Hateful daughter.

'You want me to curse them, hija? Will I curse men?' I spoke with my lips close to her cheek. 'Sometimes. But not at the demand of a spoiled daughter. I will not join your rally.'

The owner of the dulcería stepped into her doorway, holding a piñata up like a lantern. A doña sweeping the sidewalk slowed the strokes of her broom and bent an ear toward us to better hear our drama.

'Coward!' Martina spit the insult on my cheek.

'Call your mother coward?' I squeezed her wrist hard. 'There have been times when those who you call "contaminadores del universo" have saved my life. No, hija, pendeja mía. I will not curse men so easily.' I wanted to sink my teeth into the muscle of her shoulder. To break skin and to scar, to mark my words into her flesh, to make her feel. I spoke through a hungry, tight jaw. 'Listen, pendejita. I thank the contaminadores del universo. I celebrate their weaknesses, their generosity. I light a candle to the small cracks in their power. I kiss their cheeks.'

I seized Martina's face between my palms and kissed her hard rough on the cheek before she could pull away from me, then turned and walked fast past the dulcería with the señora in the doorway hugging the piñata to her chest, past the doña sweeping, shaking her head, eyes to her dust.

'Saved you?' Martina yelled after me. 'Ple-ease.' Her voice stretched high and cracked hysterical. 'You prostituted yourself to them all.'

I turned and faced Martina's direction. As if to avoid bullets, the doña struggled down the curb into the street and the dulcería owner stepped back into her shop.

My words were slow, each aimed and measured to harm. A raised eyebrow. A disdainful look. 'And what does that make you, hija?'

Martina thinks I am at fault for the wrongs of the world, for the powerlessness of women. She said that once: 'You perpetuate the powerlessness of women.' Stood right beside Chucha's chair and said that.

I had said something in passing about the Sea of Cortés. Martina corrected me. 'Call the sea El Golfo de California – anything but Cortés. Do not honor that murdering conquistador, Mami. Words have power. Words are political statements.'

Martina corrects my words as if what comes from my lips will change what is. 'Cortés was just a man, hija,' I said. 'Like any other man. And his Indian whore, Malinche, that everyone loves to hate? She was a woman. Like any other woman. Trying to survive.'

That's when Martina said that I perpetuate the powerlessness of women. Nineteen years old. Then she cried and ran quick *bang-bang-bang-bang* down the circular metal stairs like twelve years old.

So serious, my Martina. Like her father, she reads about how to be in the world. Her father read books about everything, even about how to be a good person, a better parent, how to talk to a wife. Martina studies how to be Latin, how to be a woman.

After Martina was born, on the good days, her gringo father, Robert, and I would stand over the crib and say,

23

'Look what we made.' Mira, lo que hicimos. We laughed with our arrogance. Our pride.

Parents are arrogant by nature. Acting God.

Some days, I would stand over Martina's crib and cry, and my Robert said I had the post-having-a-baby depression. He read that in a book. The book said that I wept for all the changes and sacrifices in my own life, but the book was wrong. I wept for my hija, for her life to come.

Before I gave light to Martina, Robert studied books to learn how to be a father.

He read to me. 'Listen, Maggie.' Robert traced the words across the page with his fingertip. '"Parents must form a consistent philosophical standard and a commitment to basic rules in order to form a sound and secure foundation for the psychological development of the child."'

I was grateful to have a husband who even before her birth loved his child enough to read many books. With Martina pushing at the walls of my panza, I too had begun to worry for her well-being, but in a different way.

Robert tapped his finger on the shiny magazine. '*Consumer Reports* says, Maggie, that the front-loader Snugli may force too much curve into the developing spine of an infant.'

Robert wanted to raise our child scientifically, in the best and most modern ways. I loved him for that. He worried about the angle of our child's spine. I worried for a way to give her spine enough strength to survive any angle.

As Martina had grown in my belly and came closer to knowing the light of day, so did the idea that I must pass everything I knew to her. If I could pass everything to her, she could begin with what I had endured long to learn. She could begin with strength. I became crazy obsessed with the idea that her salvation depended on this miracle: the transmission of my soul's knowledge to her.

The idea seemed even more potent after Martina's birth. When she had lived three months, while I was watching her lie in her crib, I felt my hands swell and burn, and I was sure that it was all of my life and history that filled them. The moment had arrived, and I placed my hands palms down like the wings of a bird folding around my child's sweet belly and chest and back. At first her arms and legs circled out from her round gourd of a belly and she seemed pleased, but then she began to kick and jerk. It was too much for Martina. She screamed a cry unlike her hunger or colic or unhappy cries, as if I had plunged her in fire.

Robert came running. 'What happened?' He braced his hands on the rail of the crib.

I could not answer. My life swirled through my own belly and heart and then pushed through burning and paralyzed hands to my daughter.

Robert put his face close to mine. 'What are you doing to her? What is wrong?'

Though mi vida, mi hija, my child was screaming death and fear, I could not take my hands from her skin. I could not.

'Let her go, Maggie,' he said.

I responded in gibberish.

Robert thought it was Spanish. 'English, Maggie, English.' His voice was loud, close to my ear.

All my soul, I thought I said, but it was not English or Spanish; it was pure urgency, a growl to give my Martina the secrets of survival.

Robert pried my fingers from her body, lifted Martina to his chest, and turned to the window. Over his shoulder, I could see Martina's red face. She cried and hiccuped and cried more until she calmed and began to suckle his T-shirt. 'Hospicio Cabañas,' it said across the back below a faded print of a man spiraling upward in flames, a mural from the museum in Guadalajara where we had met.

I scared my husband and my child and myself that day. Robert did not know what I was trying to do, and I could not explain it to him. After that time, he sometimes watched me as if I were a danger to our child. I think he was suspicious of 'primitive superstitions,' and I could tell by the looks he exchanged with his mother that they had discussed it.

I am a practical woman. I threw away the idea of passing my soul's knowledge to Martina in one jolt. Instead, I set myself to the work of spooning knowledge to my hija as she was able to digest it – first milk from the breast, then mush from the jar, then bistec to chew. Robert said that I terrorized Martina with ugly stories. He told me and I told myself that there was no need for ugly truth, that my girl would never know the stab of hunger, the stink of shit in the streets, that she would have the best snuggly carrier and the strongest spine, but I could not depend on that. I taught Martina all along what little bits I could.

Perhaps my words still whisper in her ear.

I thank the blindness of my mother . . .

My beginnings began before I was given light.

Women's lives fall like saints and devils onto the backs of their daughters.

The young woman who will be my mother, María Candelaria Vásquez Ramos, is seventeen years old; her sister, Chucha, nineteen. They stand at the border of Villa Unión, the dim pueblo between the airport and the golden zone where tourists become nervous. Only the year is 1946. There are very few tourists. No airport. No golden zone. By the dirt road that is now the highway, the young women stand together beside and a little behind their father, waiting for the truck to Teatlán.

The man who is my mother's father, who will be my abuelito, José María Vásquez Amado, leans on a bent walking stick. One leg of his trousers is rolled to the knee, and on the brown skin of the ankle and calf, oozing sores with moist white edges circle purple-red craters that refuse to heal over. He shifts his weight and moans.

Chucha smooths the material of María's skirt. 'Like this,' she whispers, and runs her palms firmly over the fabric, over her sister's thighs. 'Smooth the wrinkles to look nice at the Seguro Social.'

María Candelaria holds the handle of a basket that contains lunch: tortillas wrapped in a thinning gray cloth with big-stitched flowers embroidered on its edge, a shining orange-black pottery bowl of beans and another of manteca.

'And remember, the cloth to clean the dust from your shoes is beside the beans. The one to clean your face is next to the tortillas.' Kneeling in the powder dirt before her sister's feet, Chucha wipes the dust from the cracked leather of the borrowed shoes.

'Don't confuse the cloths, sister.' Chucha stands bosom to bosom close with her sister and holds the shoe cloth to María Candelaria's face before returning it to the basket and bringing out the other. With a light touch to the shoulder, Chucha signals María to step back out of their father's vision. The sisters are familiar dance partners. María lifts her chin up and smiles at the coolness on her face as Chucha circles over her sister's forehead and cheeks and chin with a damp rag. 'Soon you will see me and all my warts,' Chucha says.

María Candelaria does not answer, but lifts her hand to her sister's face and runs the side of her thumb in the hollow of Chucha's cheek before taking the folded square of cloth from her hand. With it, María pats her own forehead, holds it against the cords of her neck, then turns her back to sister and father so that they cannot see her reach through the neckline of her dress to press the cloth into her armpits. It is difficult to stay fresh in the damp heat.

'Stop your monkey grooming,' their father says without turning around. 'The truck is coming.'

Chucha takes the cloth, tucks it beside the tortillas in the basket, then holds María Candelaria's shoulders in each of her hands and kisses her forehead. 'May you come home with clear sight,' she says.

'Eres tú, hermanita?' María asks.

'Soy yo,' Chucha answers.

It is a question odd to ask face-to-face, but it is their own coded hello, good-bye, how are you, where are you, since their beginnings when the sisters first shared a cot and warmth and words in the darkness.

On the truck, the father does not speak much because he is a stoic man and because his leg throbs, and because, like everyone else, he assumes that María Candelaria is a little stupid. Everyone thinks she is media tonta but her sister, Chucha. It is because of Chucha that María has been to a doctor in the Seguro Social in the city of Teatlán. On this day, she will pick up her eyeglasses.

María's is a soft world, one without borders, edges, beginnings or endings. I remove my own glasses to try and create her undefined world. All is blurred to a dream of itself. Hers would be, I think, more like the melting light that slides down a wall when sunlight shines through old glass. Her world is a movement of colors, a world without detail. Standing at the roadside, she witnesses a graceful world of yellow tans and a fog of spring green nopal before a smudged row of cement houses, an easy dark green movement of guava and limón trees before an expanse of soft damp blue. Her sight is romantic, watercolors. Smudge and blush. No rusting cans or trash, no broken fences, no mange dogs. The face of her father, the faces of her family are featureless, only smears of brown, darker at the eyes, darker still on top of the head, a mauve blush at the mouth, two dark spots at the nostrils.

María Candelaria, the fourth child, is mostly unnoticed, blurred to others as they are to her. The family thinks her – when they think of her – slow, stupid, clumsy, but with a good heart. That's what they say about María in their little summary of her: 'María

Candelaria is media tonta, but she has a good heart.' It is only with Chucha's insistence that her father allows his fourth daughter along when he rides the bus to Seguro Social to have his sores inspected.

The man who will be my grandfather is a middle-aged man at this time. Over the years, these sores or sores like them will fester and weep, and angry red rot will travel from ankle to knee toward his precious member until the doctors amputate one leg, then another. After that, he will become my fat abuelito who sits in the front room of Chucha's house in Teatlán, calling out the window to me and my mother, to women who pass.

On the trip to Teatlán, though María sees none of it until her return home this day, she rides in the back of a truck that has a canvas canopy over a frame to shield rain and sun. A wooden plank runs along either side of the bed. Passengers – mostly albañiles riding into town to labor with concrete and rebar, some Indios, mothers – sit and face each other, knees almost touching. Some tie cloths over their mouths to screen out the dust; some sit on folded shawls to cushion the ride. María Candelaria thinks of the damp cloth in her basket and wonders how she might find the privacy to clean herself with it before Teatlán.

She thinks of Chucha. Of her smell. Soap and sweat. The sound of Chucha's whispers in the dark. Of her names. From Marta to Martucha, the little bad girl name for Marta, and Martucha, Chucha.

Chucha had changed since the Federales robbed her. That's what people said in their little summary of her: 'Chucha is not the same since the Federales.' Before, Chucha had told María Candelaria stories every night, the two lying in one cot. She had talked in the dark when others wanted to sleep. María Candelaria had liked best the stories about faraway characters who were just like her: a girl, the fourth child, wandering and tripping on cactus and rocks until she becomes afraid to step outside her house.

María Candelaria thinks about Chucha since the Federales, how she lies quiet and stiff on her back in the cot, how sometimes, but not often, she holds one finger of María Candelaria's hand tight inside her fist. How sometimes Chucha lifts one foot and lets her heel fall again and again on the taut cot, and how María waits, anxious for the next dull thud to vibrate through her.

The young woman who will be my mother sits and lets her eyes float over the blend of colors. She listens to the various conversations that cross paths between benches – the high, quiet, upward-lilting accent of the Indians going to market, the chopped slang of the young cholos. Most of the laborers are quiet, conserving strength for the day. Most stare across and beyond at nothing, though María does not know that. There is one albañil, however, who watches her, one who thinks her timidity is beautiful, who thinks her silence is feminine. He will be my father. He will change his mind. That is another story.

In the doctor's examining room, María sits on a stool, her hands in her lap, fingers worrying each other. A pink beige face bends toward her. *Too close, too close.*

'I'm going to put eyeglasses on your face,' he says, and he slips black frames over her ears, thick glass squares in front of her eyes.

María's eyes spasm behind the glass. She blinks slowly, squeezing her eyes hard shut and then opening them. The facial features of this fair man jump out at her. A nose. Her first. She cannot say it is a big or small or attractive nose. She has nothing to compare it to. María knows only that there is a feature protruding

31

from the middle of the head. There is a dark spot on his cheek, furious black hairs above his eyes. A chin. Short, coarse hairs shadow his jaw. His eyes have flecks of amber and brown. María gasps. Never has she seen a face so clearly before. She puts her hands over the glass for a moment. Her breath is quick as a bird's. When she slowly takes her hands away, she must turn from the clear vision of this face. María looks down at her own hands that lay against the faded pattern of her skirt — tiny margaritas, daisies, though she doesn't know that yet — and sees that the skin is brown, the nails are uneven with dark crescents beneath the white; cuticles are thick and ragged, dry, torn.

'I must go,' she mumbles. To speak to a person outside her family, to see his face clearly and closely gives her too much embarrassment.

The doctor thinks her ill-mannered, a little stupid. He adjusts the frames of the eyeglasses, pressing both arms against her temples with the bellies of his fingertips and then steps back and looks hard at the frames before shifting and pressing them again. His hands have black hairs curling up from the knuckles, his nails broaden at their tips to even white crescents.

María Candelaria finds the strength to speak. 'I must go,' she says again.

She touches the doctor's elbow lightly — so lightly — and slides down from the stool. Outside the examining room, just after the slow click of the latch, she turns to the door and says, 'Thank you.'

At the end of the hall, a hundred faces wait for a doctor or nurse. She looks at those faces as long as she can and drops her head to gather herself. The floor is made of tiny octagonal white and black tiles with greasy dirt thick between the ceramics. Grayed bubble-gum mounds at places, though she doesn't know bubble gum.

From the far corner of the room, her father calls for her: 'Hija, María.'

The man who calls her is gripping his walking stick to balance on one foot. The leg of his pants is rolled above his dry knee, a thick white gauze circles his calf and ankle, and his foot hangs helpless, inches above the floor. Her father is much smaller than she had thought. She walks toward him, keeping her eyes to the floor. Too many faces in the room, too many details.

When she reaches her father, she stands before him, her eyes still cast down. His pants are tan with darker stain circles, black curly hairs similar to the ones on the doctor's fingers grow from his uncovered leg, his foot is creased with dirt at his sandal straps, and his toenails are thick and rough as oyster shells. Everywhere, there is more than she can stand to see.

'Don't be tonta, María,' he says. 'Look at me.'

The young woman who will be my mother lifts her chin to see her father's face. His nose is larger than the doctor's; his skin, more brown and green and shinier, with deeper creases than the doctor's. Her father laughs at the strange expression on her face, and María Candelaria sees black holes where teeth are missing from the side of his mouth.

'Am I so ugly, hija?'

'Ugly.' She says it without meanness – a matter of fact, not cruelty – just the way everyone calls the crippled girl Cripple. Because she is. He is. And through glass that magnifies María's eyes too large, she studies the dark single hairs growing around the border of his eyes, the creased and shining skin that stretches pale to close over them, the large, oily pores on his nose. 'So ugly.'

Her father closes her braid inside his fist and pulls it down slowly, firmly, so that her chin rises to him

33

and past him and she sees the flaking plaster of the ceiling above. 'Ay, tonta, what can your eyes know?' He releases her braid and she sees the skin folds at the top of his nose, the corners of his lips pinched downward.

María Candelaria turns and offers her shoulder to her father. She cannot look at him any longer.

With his weight pressing on her, she slowly leads him to the truck, her eyes all the time cast to the tile floor and sidewalk and asphalt. Already she has seen too much of the ugly world. She conserves her vision and her hope for one thing.

I must go, she repeats inside herself.

I must go see the face of Chucha.

I returned many times to the Seguro Social office with my mother, riding not in the truck from Villa Unión, but on the bus from el barrio Rincón, and each time, Mami's glasses grew thicker and stronger and her vision somewhat better. Each visit, her eyes seemed larger and less real behind the glass. After each visit, she left the office with renewed sight, curious of the world, but she was quickly disappointed and made timid by that same sight, so that by the time we were riding on the bus toward home, her eyes were cast to the floor and feet of passengers.

Courage was taken from María Candelaria in her near-blind childhood. When there was noise in the streets of our barrio, she sent her Magda to see about it. 'Go, Magda, find out what is happening.' 'Go for tomatoes, Magda. Get a good price.' She was timid in the world outside her house, and sent me out to interpret it, to negotiate it, and I would go and return and sit at her table and tell her – that Silvia had been grosera to her mother, that the vegetable man had tried to cheat me, that el cine owner, Fat Chuy, was getting fatter.

One trip home from the doctor, seated next to me on the bus bench, Mami allowed me to take the eyeglasses from her face.

'May I?' I asked, pressing the fingers of each hand against the arms of her glasses to slide them away from her ears and face.

Mami's eyes sank, retreated into her head. She smiled.

I slipped the dark frames onto my face. My eyes throbbed and the world melted, and I looked toward the smear of my mother, who was looking at me, and wondered if in that moment our vision was near the same.

From the place of beginnings,
from the quietest place within . . .

I press myself deep into the stories that are Mami's, Tia's. Mine. To find gratitude, fierce gratitude, I go to the quietest place within, and revive sorrow.

In 1942, in Villa Unión, when the young woman who would be my tía was fifteen, los Federales robbed her right from the land of her father. They had heard of her beauty, of the magnificent blue-black and shining trenza that hung to her waist, of her long fingers, of her fair skin. Men on horses had come for her before. Twice her mother had hidden her in the oven and told the Federales that Chucha had moved to Teatlán.

One day Chucha was chasing the goat that had escaped beyond the nopal fence into the field where chile morón grew. Three men on horseback chased and corralled her without ever dismounting. By her braid and by her skirts, they pulled her over a horse's rear and rode away.

The man who would be my abuelito searched days for his Chucha. He found her bleeding and ruined in a barn only two miles from their home. She had lost her bones, he said. That's all he would say of that day. Many years later, legless in the window of Chucha's house, Abuelito would mutter, 'Chucha had no bones,' and we knew that he visited the time when he found his daughter crumpled limp in the straw. Chucha was his favorite and she remained so, though forever after that, he called her Pocha. Abuelito did not use the word the way most did. He used the word the old-fashioned way. Ruined. He said it without anger or sadness – a matter of fact, not cruelty – just the way we called Fat Chuy fat. Because he was. She was.

Five years later, Chucha married Pelón, who was not bald but named so since his birth, and they moved to Teatlán.

Imagínate. 1947. Olas Altas, old Teatlán in the years of my tía's youth, the original boardwalk along the Sea of Cortés. The malecón winds above and alongside the fine sand beach. A cobbled street separates the boardwalk from shops and restaurants. In the night, moonlight and street lanterns reflect in the whitecaps of the waves. Vendors sell from their carts: mangoes carved to resemble flowers on a stick, ears of corn with butter and chile and salt. To those who lived in the tight barrios miles from the shore in houses choked together on streets blocked and cemented from sea and breeze – to them, to Chucha – to steep in the mist and brisa was brief salvation. On Sundays, families and novios strolled the malecón, breathing for a day. Some things don't change so quickly.

During Carnival, el malecón was not the sweet calm family stroll of Sunday evenings. Streets were blocked and filled with people, pure bodies pushed together in a way that would be acceptable only between man and wife in their own bed.

El malecón at Carnival throbbed with life and death and sex. Las bandas of Sinaloense music stood every twenty meters. Dancers twined and circled the musicians and each other. Tuba and cymbal and trumpets of one band overlapped the music of the neighboring one.

The fair itself, rides, and the Palenque tent were not so crowded as the street. Chucha, recien casada and attending her first Carnival, stood beside the Ferris wheel while her husband watched the cocks fight inside the tent. A cousin operated the ride, and invited shy Chucha to stand alone on the wooden platform inside the makeshift fence that circled around the base of the engine of the wheel. Her cousin stood beside a long handle that slowed and stopped and started the wheel's circling, just where the seats floated down. He pushed the handle forward to disengage the engine and stop the wheel, then lifted the bar from the laps of passengers to allow them to step down, leaving rocking empty seats behind them to be filled with two new passengers ready with their yellow tickets. Tía Chucha said that she remembers thinking that if her cousin had not been observant, he could go on emptying and filling seats without ever pulling the throttle back to begin the ride.

Tía would never talk about the Federales, but she would talk in detail about this night. She spoke of it as if this were the night she was ruined.

On the small platform below the Ferris wheel, away from the line of waiting passengers, away from the crowd, the young woman who would be my tía watched the soles of small shoes circle down. She told me once that she remembered thinking about how the circles of worn leather were different on each person – some wore away their shoes under big toes, others under the balls of their feet – and how heels were worn to an angle, some on the inside and others on the

38

outside. She was pondering the patterns of wear, she said, when she felt someone tug at her long single braid.

Chucha thought that her husband had sneaked behind her, and without turning around, she said, 'No, mi vida, don't.' She never called her husband Pelón, but always mi vida.

The pressure increased slowly at first and then pulled her backwards. Chucha turned her head as much as the pressure allowed, but could see no one. From the angle of the tugging, there could be no one between the Ferris wheel and her. It was an awful knowing, Tía said, when she understood that it was something so large and powerful that had her.

There has been much speculation about how her hair became tangled in the engine. Some say the wind took it up to the gears, but I say it would have to have been a tormenta wind to move her thick trenza upwards. Others say her own black angel put it there. Others accuse a young drunk or a woman jealous of Chucha's beauty. All that matters is that it happened.

'Help!' Chucha shouted. 'Someone help me!'

But over the madness of Palenque, over the grind of the engine, no one heard her.

Chucha screamed high and constant. Her braid wound through the gears, pulling her closer to the machine. No one heard her. No one came. Chucha bent her knees to lower all her body's weight against the pull of the braid. She picked up her feet, then dropped to her bent knees, hovering inches above the ground as if she were a santa praying. Hair ripped in patches from her scalp, but still the machine pulled her closer. She brought her knees up to her chest and made herself as tight and heavy a ball as she could. Chucha no longer screamed for help.

The quiet cry. Sorrow too deep and hopeless.

Chucha said that she thought, I will die by my condenada braid one way or the other. It will be my death. And then the engine idled and choked or the ride for the group finished and her cousin pulled back the lever to stop the wheel. Chucha did not know what stopped the engine. Someone yelled from the crowd. Chucha looked up to see a man waving one arm above his head, running toward her, pulling his young son along behind him. There hung Chucha, with her knees tucked up to her chest, like a Christmas ball ornament.

The man and his son pulled the fence away, and others were soon there to help. Some kind person gently encouraged Chucha to straighten her legs, pushed gently at her kneecaps until Chucha unfolded at her hips, then placed light pressure behind her knees so that she unfolded again. A gentle voice. Tía says she did not recognize it as male or female, only its gentleness, its soft breath at her ear. 'Straighten your legs now, hija. It's safe to stand now,' the voice repeated until Chucha straightened. Her feet did not touch anything and someone hugged her hips and lifted her until the pressure against her scalp eased. Someone else brought a small wooden stool, and she stood again on her feet.

There was much discussion about how to free Chucha. Some argued to save the braid and slowly untangle it from the teeth of the motor; others, the owner of the ride included, argued for quick force. Her scalp was patched with circles of blood. Unknown hands pulled at her arms, her waist, her head. Some thought to reverse the Ferris wheel, reverse the damage, others to take the engine apart; others argued to pull hard at the count of three on the extremities of my aunt. I have been told that Chucha offered no suggestions, that she only cried throughout the discussion, softly from deep within her.

A crowd grew and swarmed around her. Mostly men were in the inner circles, women and children and late arrivers in the outer circles. The woman who would be my mother, María Candelaria, stood at the fringes. She could see nothing, and relied on the bits of information that passed through the crowd.

'A woman caught in the engine.'

'Caught in the engine.'

'In the engine' echoed and ricocheted through the crowd.

Young people jumped straight up in the effort to see. Parents raised their children to their shoulders for reports.

'Her braid.'

'Braid.'

'Her braid' waved through the crowd.

'She's almost bald,' a boy called down from the shoulders of his brother.

'Bloody.'

'Much blood.'

Someone yelled. 'It's the wife of Pelón.' And that vibrated through the crowd past María Candelaria.

'Dios mío.' María brought both her hands to her mouth. I know she did. She began to cry. She cried just the way Chucha cried. Softly, deeply.

From behind, María could hear her father.

'My Pocha,' he said, bumping his path through the crowd from the farthest outer circles toward the center. 'She has no bones,' he said, as if this would explain his right to move toward her. 'No bones,' he repeated in a voice cracked with pain.

'Cálmate, cabrón. You're drunk.' No one stepped aside for Chucha's father. One man elbowed him hard in the ribs.

41

María Cande heard his scream. She knew that he no longer moved forward, that his fists were clenched at his sides, that his head was dropped back on his shoulders and his mouth was lifted and wide open to the bright lights and stars.

'¡Pocha!' he wailed long, stretching the syllables to his favorite daughter.

I wish I could say that the woman who would be my mother saved Chucha, that for the love of her querida hermana she found her courage and overcame her shyness and near blindness, squinted through thick eyeglasses, elbowed her way through the crowd to find scissors, and then went to her most loved one and cradled Chucha's head and whispered soothing words to her. '¿Eres tu?' she might have said as she gently snipped and freed her sister's trenza from the engine. I wish that their father, the man who would become my grandfather, had been macho enough to sober his drunkenness and anger and move deliberately through the crowds to take care of his own hija.

The truth is, the sister of Chucha quietly wept and her father wailed. While some man sawed at the black gloria of my aunt with a dull knife, María Candelaria fell to the dust and wept among the bare feet and boots and fancy shoes of onlookers. Somewhere in the crowd, Chucha's father dropped to his knees and pounded both fists against the polvo, screaming. 'Mi Pocha. She has no bones. God help her.' And people in the crowd thought him another Carnaval crazy. A man doubled Chucha's hair over his blade turned toward the dark sky. In one fist, he held and pulled her hair down against the metal. In the other fist, he gripped the handle of his knife and sawed back and forth and back and forth, pressing upward through chunks of thick hair as if cutting a hemp rope. Chucha's neck and torso arched back, exposing her throat and breast to stars and lights and unknown men. Her bloodied hair fell away from her scalp.

I cannot even say that her long braid fell to the ground coiled like a thick and potent snake. No. What was cut free from Chucha's scalp sprouted matted and bloodied from the gears of the dark motor.

I thank the plátano that saved my life,
the prisoner who set me free . . .

It's important to know what you can do. Do something. Anything. I tell Isabel who has just come to me about the macho banana. I tell her all the stories I told Martina, and more. I tell her about the man in jail. I want to tell her what a woman can do.

El barrio Rincón, where I grew, was sometimes a stinking place where there was no water for months at a time, where in the alleys everyone would make shit when they couldn't wait to get to work or because they had no other place to go. The houses of my youth were stuck one to the next except for an occasional alley, but crowded as they were, nobody wanted a stinking alley path beside his house. When I had to go bad, I squeezed the cheeks of my nalgas to try to hold in my caca until I reached the school, walking in short little steps like the downhill-duck prize in the cereal box, faster, faster, praying, and always with an eye open for a piece of newspaper or something to clean myself with when I finally reached the toilet.

The stink in el barrio alleys, I can still smell. Still, every day, I wash my hair and scrub my scalp hard with my fingernails until I hear the squeak of clean. I am crazy for clean.

44

*　　*　　*

Until a year ago when she came to live in my house, Isabel lived in el barrio Rincón, but I describe Rincón to her as if she has never known it.

I want her to remember.

Isabel came to me from the puros pendejados of her father, Chucha's only son, my first cousin Rafael. That is not a story worthy of detail. The tonta mother of Isabel was hit by a bus and pendejo Rafa went to the house of the driver and knifed him in the heart.

Sometimes a woman must leave her daughter.

According to gossip, when the bus driver answered his door, Rafa stood rabid and drooling. 'For my wife,' is all he said, then plunged the knife in an under-handed arc beneath the ribs and through the heart of the driver. Pendejo. While his daughter, Isabel, crying, hungry and alone in the same house where I grew, while his mother, Chucha, moaned mortified from her grave, before his wife was in her grave, Rafa satisfied his selfish justice and fled.

A neighbor brought the news and Isabel to my door.

Me with almost fifty years, and a new daughter.

When I was near the same age of Isabel, in the same house where her father left her, I used to stare at a bowl on the shelf that contained a banana that I was forbidden to eat. I stood beneath the shelf looking up under the lacquered terra-cotta, chipped, color of dried blood, and I could see the scabbed tip of the plátano, the black and yellow curving just over the edge, teasing me, causing my stomach to pinch. It was the macho banana, the biggest and cheapest, though not the sweetest. The picture in my memory is in light filtered through dust, but the pinching in my belly is sharp and clear as midday sun.

We ate tortilla and fish, always tortilla and fish: the

45

food we could afford. My brothers and my cousin fished the ocean with nylon line and hook. They tossed out line and sinker salvaged from tangles found on the beach and wound around sticks; they walked the rocks at low tide in search of oysters; Mami and Chucha patted tortillas. Good food, but always the same food, and never enough.

In the year 1956, when I had six years, sitting at our table, four brothers and sisters, a cousin, elbow to elbow, I choked, a fish bone in my throat. I imagined it sideways like the sign Tía Chucha had shown me for naught; a circle with a line through it, only the bone line threatened my breath. Without looking up from her plate, my sister, Rosa, reached behind me and beat my back. Quickly, my mother stepped to the shelf and reached into the bowl while Chucha grabbed my wrist and stretched my arm straight above my head. Through my tears I saw Mami's fingers peel back and expose just enough banana to fit in my mouth, just enough to do the job. She did not speak, only touched the banana to my lips. It was cool, slick, and when I swallowed, sweet pulp pushed down the bone in my throat, clearing my throat, setting my mouth to longing.

The banana was used only for children choking. Lástima.

'Ya, hija?' my mother asked. Enough? She folded the banana skin over the end of the fruit.

Chucha released her grip and I lowered my arm to the table.

Mami held the closed banana close to her. The flowered material of her dress pulled tight against her breast, and there was a wet dark circle at one nipple.

A week later, I coughed a good show, opened my mouth like a bird, and as I tilted my head back to receive another piece, I saw Chucha standing at the stove with her arms crossed over her breast, and tears rolled

46

into my ears. I knew that with a lie I could taste the banana, press it between my tongue and the roof of my mouth so that its sweetness lingered. I could. I did. Perhaps I ate more than my share, perhaps I kept food from my family.

My hunger was bigger than my shame.

I began school soon after. The school and the jail were in the same building, a cement square similar to houses of el barrio except the school/jail stood two stories high with bare dirt lots surrounding it. Downstairs was the jail, one large cell with an office desk outside it. It was not the main town jail, only a place where barrio offenders were kept a short time or where real criminals awaited transfer. The second floor was one large schoolroom – grades one through four. An outside staircase ran up one side of the building.

The smell of male urine – concentrated, sick, strong – vented out one high window that was closed only by three vertical, rusted bars. If I climbed to the seventh stair step and then turned around and looked behind me, I could see down into the jail cell – a dirt floor, wood cots in the shadows.

Sometimes in our schoolroom upstairs, we heard muffled yells from below. 'Give no attention to that,' the maestro would say, 'the loco is back.'

But it was not always the loco. From the windows sometime, I saw prisoners being transferred, their faces bruised and bloody. Men beat each other on the first floor the way men will.

I often lingered behind on the step that allowed me to see inside the cell. One day a man called to me. He stood on his cot, but still I could see only his eyes and his dirty knuckles, each hand gripping a bar.

'Chica,' he called to me in a voice gritty and unaccustomed to whispering.

47

I stood still on the step, my back to the stairway, facing the criminal.

'You want a candy?' he asked.

His eyes and eyebrows were dark, his forehead creased with oil and dirt. I didn't answer.

One hand released a bar and then a burgundy disc flew from the window and made a little puff cloud when it landed.

'Go ahead,' he said. 'Get it before someone else does.'

Watching to see if other children were also late, I slowly stepped down the stairs and walked in the powder dirt where the red disc landed. I nudged it with my toe, squatted next to it, and moved it with one finger, then picked up the candy and put it in my pocket, glancing up all along at the window, afraid to take my eyes too long away from the hand on the bars.

With my fingers inside my pocket touching the gritty disc and my eye on the knuckles and eyes in the window, I slowly climbed the steps to my classroom.

'Be late again tomorrow,' the prisoner said.

Once past the seventh step, I ran to the top and entered the classroom breathless.

'Magdalena?' the maestro said while writing on the blackboard, his back to me. 'So nice of you to join us.'

That was Señor Gómez, a good teacher. The first sarcastic person I ever knew.

Through the morning lessons, with my eyes to Señor Gómez and the blackboard, I secretly touched the candy and formed a plan to wash and eat it. It had no cellophane wrapping, and was rough of dirt and lint from the prisoner's pocket save one slick edge newly chipped.

Don't take anything from strangers, Mami had warned me. She had knelt before me and squeezed my shoulders and shaken me a little as if she was mad, her giant magnified eyes wandering my face for guilt.

At lunch, after all had drunk, I took a dipper of water and secretly dropped my treasure disc in it. The dirt on it darkened, then dissolved, and the candy glistened burgundy. I drained most of the water to the ground and drank the shining circle left in the tin dipper. Cinnamon. Sharp, hot sweet cinnamon burst in my mouth.

The next day, I was late again. The same knuckles and eyes waited for me at the window.

'Like the candy?' the grit whisper said.

I didn't answer.

'I'll give you money enough for a kilo of candy if you come to my cell.'

I stood on the seventh step and looked all directions to see who might be watching, listening.

'Just go to the front entrance. The police official sits at a desk there. Tell him you're my godchild. Tell him your mother sent you.'

I ran up the stairs.

Men can be dangerous. I could hear Mami's close frog-eyed advice. *Ask Chucha.* But even with only six years, I already knew that Tía wouldn't talk about men.

During the lessons, I remembered the candy – how I had first pressed the disc against the roof of my mouth and then hidden it under my tongue; how it burned the taut connector that held my tongue in place; how it was both pleasant and unpleasant, hot, sweet; how the tips of my fingers were red where I'd touched it in my pocket. I remembered the promise of the prisoner.

The following day I lingered behind again, but the man was not at the window. I paused at the seventh step and then started up the stairs.

'You don't have to tell the official nothing,' the voice said.

I descended the stair to his level.

'Just wait until the guard crosses the street to pick up

49

his lunch, then walk in and get the keys from his desk drawer and give them to me. Simple.'

I ran from him.

'Two pesos,' he called after me. 'Two pesos I'll give you.'

Two pesos repeated through my lessons, but so did the sharp sting from my mother's wooden spoon with a hole in its center. Lesser offenses had resulted in circle welts on my thighs and back. Two pesos.

For the remainder of the week, I arrived on time to class with my classmates, ascending the stairs among the safety of their bodies.

The weekend passed with work and washing and play in the streets, but the promise of two pesos lingered. I'd never had my own money before. Two pesos would buy more than a kilo of candy. So much money. I remembered the candy disc in my pocket and imagined a larger heavier coin in its place. Two of them. My own.

It was easy.

The pendejo guard went across the street to pick up his lunch and I slipped in the office, walked to the square desk and opened the top drawer. There were the keys. I moved so quickly, so calmly. Don't ask me why or how. Instead of holding the potential punishment in my mind – a beating, a shaming, the disappointed eyes of Chucha and Mami – I saw only the coins. Clearly. I felt their weight in my pocket, my belly full, sweetness on my tongue, and I moved steadily, evenly toward my reward.

The prisoner stood quietly at the bars and watched me work. 'Good girl. That's right.'

He was small, dirty, dark, his hair black and oily, a wound scabbed over his mouth and chin.

Two other prisoners stood pressing themselves against the bars, yelling for me to hurry.

'Shut up. Let her work,' my prisoner said.

He extended his hand through the bars. I handed him the jangle of keys.

As he tested one key, another, and opened the bar door, I recognized the calm and efficiency of my own movements. The two other men exploded from the cell and ran from the jail in clumsy noise. My prisoner closed the cell door behind him and turned the keys to relock it. He moved quietly, quickly to the desk, replacing the keys in the top drawer, then opening the lower one. From it, he lifted a bundle – a jacket wrapped around a gun. He unfolded the fabric arms and lifted the gun gently from his jacket, turning it over and opening its chamber before pushing it under his waistband so that the dark handle arched over his belly. He smiled at me as he slipped his arms into the jacket and zipped it over the weapon; then reaching inside one sleeve, he pulled from an unseen pocket – one missed by the policia – two coins. My prisoner took my hand and closed my fingers as much as they would around the heavy pesos. He pinched my chin gently between his thumb and fingers and said, 'You're going to be okay.'

I followed him to the door, where he walked to the left and I walked to the right and to the right again to climb the stairs to my classroom.

I've wondered why no one thought to blame me.

No one did.

Two of the prisoners were in jail for debt. People said the third, my prisoner, was a murderer waiting for transfer. El Cochiloco. They called him the Crazy Pig, and people told stories about how he got his name: he killed five men, made the first four bury the one killed before him and left the fifth to the buzzards; he gave his money to orphans; he fed entire towns; he killed entire towns. Stories.

I chose the stories I believed.

In my life, when I have needed the calm intent and efficiency I first knew that day, it is my prisoner's soft encouragement that I hear. 'Good girl. That's right.'

Sometimes I think I can taste the macho banana, the hot sweetness of cinnamon.

Sometimes I hear him say, 'You're going to be okay.'

This is a story I told my hija again and again, hoping that she would understand the calm focus of purpose – the prisoner's way.

Where you place the eye, you place the bullet.

Robert said I encouraged poor morals with these stories. Martina agrees, though I think that she once loved them.

'You want me to break someone out of jail, Mami?' she teases. 'Steal some food from the poor?'

But Isabel listens. Isabelita. Six years old, and she has the clear vision that pierces through beyond where most intent sees, beyond doubt and fear and guilt, straight through to the heart of what she desires.

Perhaps she remembers hunger.

I light many candles to the power of sex.

Not so close that they burn the Virgin,
not so far that She is not illuminated . . .

I cannot remember not knowing about sex. Not understanding it. But knowing about it.

My knowing grew in stages. I first knew that sex was violent, then that it was shameful, that it was dangerous, then that it was tender, that it surrounded me, that it pulsed through the world, and then, the most painful knowing: that sex was all of these things at once, and that the pulse coursed also through me.

My first ideas about sex were that women and men fought and that fighting was sex. Though a simple and unsophisticated idea, it is as accurate as any explanation I have since been offered.

My own mother would pull against the shirtsleeves of my father to hold him back from leaving. 'Don't come home again if you go with her,' she'd cry. 'Don't go.'

My father would push her hands from his clothes, press her down into the chair and squeeze her shoulders tight enough to pin her there, his face a silent command just inches from hers. *Quiet yourself.* Then he would relax his grip and walk straight out the door.

I don't even remember when I first saw that scene or how many times it repeated. From the open windows and doors of the other houses, I often heard what I thought was sex: all the don't-gos and please-stays, the go-to-the-fucker-places and never-returns. I knew that with sex, sometimes couples hit each other or tumbled and struggled on cots and against the walls of the alley and under the guava tree. I had heard in the dark the jerks and grunts from my parents' cot. Sex was as common as piss and food; its musk blended with stale manteca and sweat and urine to form the aroma of our small house.

Sex in Moscow, Idaho was not in the homes like it was in el barrio. Idaho homes, with the separate sleeping rooms and shitting rooms and living rooms and cooking rooms – each with its own door. Who can know what occurs behind all the closed doors? There was a lot of sex in the television and in the movies and even on the billboards, but there was no strain or sweat or musk to it. Sex was inside the TV box or magazine advertisement or in the sexy voice on the radio, but it didn't seep into the clean painted walls and waxed floors there the way it did in my barrio.

Years ago in Idaho, Robert could not tolerate that I talked of sex with Martina. He could not remember that he was sexy when he was a child. Children know sexy. Martina knew sexy. As young as three, she lay on the kitchen floor with both hands tucked under her cosita and clenched her nalgitas. 'I'm pooping,' she once explained.

'What you're doing is playing with your cosita,' I said.

'Pooping.'

'Don't go crazy with that, hija,' I warned her.

Later she was more honest. With her arms tight to her sides, her hands tucked away, and her neck craning to look up from the floor, she was like a seal. 'Cosita,' she said.

'Yes, cosita,' I agreed, and as I chopped the pork, I advised her, 'It's a tool to enjoy and to use. There's a lot you can do with a cosita.'

Martina turned her head, lay one cheek against the linoleum and worked her pleasures.

My grandfather was a sexy man. An ugly man with crusty skin, legless from diabetes disease, and toothless, too, and from sitting so long and from eating manteca on tortillas, he had three belly rolls. That is what children in el barrio called him – tres panzas – among other names, though not to his face. Sex pulsed through him in a current I noticed long before I knew what it was.

Ugly doesn't stop sex.

Age doesn't either.

Abuelito lived next door in the house of Tía Chucha and Tío Pelón. He stayed in the front room, sitting up in a narrow bed beside the open window with his two stumps before him. From that window, he watched the sexy world of couples and cositas and huevos. Mami said that he was a 'victima de la naturaleza,' that sex made men stupid.

Abuelito sucked his gums as women and girls passed and commented under his breath about the size and shape and desirability of nalgas or chichis, or legs or ankles, about the cosita itself. 'Ay, what a large and squeezable ass – what precious little titties – how I would like to throw a wedding sheet over that!'

The women would hear him and mutter, 'Crazy old malcriado,' loud enough to satisfy themselves but not so loud to be ill-bred.

But somehow Abuelito knew what they said and he yelled, '¡Viejas hediondas! Filthy women!'

When Abuelito heard my mother scold me, he would call from his window, 'Send the malita, mi vida, to me,' and I went to him, stood shy in the doorway, blind from the daylight, waiting for him to tell me which one I was – the bad girl or his life. He, patting the bed beside him with his palm, said always the same thing: 'Siéntate, mi vida. Soy un hombre decente.'

Sit down, my life, I am a decent man.

Abuelito wore gray boxer shorts, the front usually gaped open. My fascination with his puckered, bruised stump ends and his pene in the shadows sometimes made it hard to keep my mind on his tales or my gaze on his face.

'La Llorona wailed outside my window last night,' he said. 'But I gave her fear, horse-faced whore, waving my stumps in the air in front of the window.' He narrowed his eyes and bent toward me from his waist. 'It was not easy. I lured her here, and just when she came forward in all her misery, I hurled my backside in the air and made blood spurt from these shiny stumps.'

He varied his story only in what shot from his stumps. Sometimes blood; other times, lightning; once, bubbles. White caked at the dry corners of his lips as he spoke of his actions against whores and traitors, all the bad women. I could see his tongue, swollen and cracked inside his mouth, roaming and circling in search of teeth, and I delighted and mortified myself thinking that it might escape.

Chucha was the only one who subdued Abuelito. He had called her Pocha since the time when the Federales robbed her. Ruined. He did not use it the way most did – to speak of Mexicans born in the USA. Abuelito used it in the old way. Ruined. Like fruit too ripe.

'¡Pocha!' Abuelito screamed his needs. He yelled from his seat at the window, abusivo, until Chucha, and only Chucha, stood near him.

Bring me water!

Bring me food!

Rub my back!

Tía Chucha entered the room in her quiet. When she chose silence, Papi talked louder, Abuelito mumbled and muttered. Only Mami seemed comforted. Chucha would wear silence like a holy rebozo, like God's judgment. Hers was a rubbery solid silence that you couldn't stick a fork in.

When I was twelve, while stirring tejuino on the roof, I could hear Abuelito at his window below.

'¡Pocha! Bring me warm water. Bring water for a bath.'

Chucha's black hair, her face, her shoulders, then her slender torso rose from the stairs. She moved with tranced grace across our roof to hers and stood at its edge just over the demands of her father.

'¡Pocha!' Abuelito yelled again. 'Puta madre ¿dónde estás?'

Third roof down, next to Chucha's, Rojo the red dog stood at the roof's edge and barked toward Abuelito. Rojo was as ugly as most dogs on the street that children tortured and adults ignored – short-haired, long-bodied, short-legged, tail curled to expose the gray butthole of a large dog, big as an old peso.

From her apron pocket, Chucha gently retrieved a chicken egg and held it between thumb and finger above her face to the light of the sun as if checking its fertility. Satisfied with the egg, she slowly extended her arm straight in front of her, holding it still between dainty fingers.

Do not, I thought. *I could eat that.*

Chucha stood a few moments, calm in this position.

57

Rojo barked.

Tía smiled and widened the space between her fingers.

The egg landed on the concrete just centimeters below the window of Abuelito. A distant sound, at once brittle and wet.

'¡Pocha!' Abuelito yelled. And waited for her response. Then again, '¿Pocha?'

He needed her to answer to know where she was.

She stood quiet.

Frustrated on his bed beside the window, Abuelito crossed into pure locura the way he sometimes did. '¡Pocha! ¡Cochina! ¡Abusadora! Someone is wasting food! Someone is trying to kill me!'

Abuelito ceased for a moment. I knew that he was wheezing and wild-eyed. In the brief and dangerous absence of his screams below, we could hear normal sounds – mothers scolding children, music from distant radios, the high whine of Rojo the dog, crying for the rich fat yolk of the egg. I could hear my heart beat high in my chest.

'Pocha, come clean this desmadre,' Abuelito called in a voice more civil. 'Come! Clean!' Abuelito yelled again.

Chucha stepped over the low wall that separated the roof of her house from Rojo's. The dog lay on his stomach, his front paws to the roofs edge, peering down, whining, wheezing, clicking scents high in his nose.

My tía sat down beside Rojo, her own legs hanging over. She must have considered her next actions – whether to leave her egg on the concrete to rot under Abuelito's nose or to clean it away. She sat with one arm around Rojo, leaning from her waist to see the sidewalk below. Rojo's drool strung down from the roof toward the street and it gave me asco to see her so close to the sex-mad mongrel, who went hysterical when a perra bled within a mile. His owners, afraid that he would leap off the roof after a dog in heat, tied Rojo with a short rope to rebar. From the end of the taut rope, Rojo would jump straight up, springing from all four paws like some sort of toy, up and down as if there were springs on all four feet. Rojo on a rope.

Chucha stood and brought her palms to her nose to sniff Rojo's stink, then wiped them down her apron, walked back to her own roof, descended the circular stairs and passed through the narrow house to Abuelito sitting at his window.

'¡Malcriada! ¡Vieja hedionda! ¡Malinchista! Black-cloud-that-walks! Clean up this shit! Bring me food! I need a bath!' Abuelito was high-pitched locura by then, but when Chucha brushed by him, with her bucket on her arm and a rag in her hand, he humbled. He quieted. That was always the way.

'Are you throwing rotten food?' he asked.

'No, 'Apá,' she said, and walked past him through the front door.

'Pocha, are you disrespectful to your father?'

Chucha scraped the clear gel and yellow into the tilted bowl with the side of her palm, and swirled the slick puddle around the sides before setting it aside to soap the cement.

'Bueno . . .' Abuelito spoke to her through the open window.

Chucha finished scrubbing the walk. 'It wasn't rotten,' she said, and still on her knees, she lifted the bowl under his nose.

Abuelito turned his head away.

Placing her weight on flat palms and knees like a swayed mule, Chucha stared at the place where the egg had fallen. A child could have climbed on her back to ride. She stayed in just that position without lifting her head, her bucket and rag and the bowl beside her. Abuelito stretched one hand out the window to touch her back, but she was beyond his reach, and he let his arm fall limp against the front of the house.

Tía sat back on her heels, and lifted the bowl. 'Do you want the egg, 'Apá?'

'No, mi vida.' Abuelito turned his head and pressed his cheek against the sill of the window.

Tía walked through the front door, past her father, through the narrow house, up the circular stairs and over the two roofs to Rojo on a rope. There she placed the bowl before the dog. In the end, she could not waste a perfectly good huevo.

When I was seven years old, I saw real sex, real close. It was late afternoon and I was carrying my baby sister, Kiki, in my arms, returning from the house of a neighbor. You don't see so much the American children caring for their younger sisters and brothers, but in my barrio the older children raised the younger. It took all my concentration to carry the lump of Kiki and walk at the same time. With her pressed to my chest, she covered nearly all of me and I could barely see over her head. My arms ached from her weight and I had to pee real bad and so I made my way to a narrow alley between two houses.

A few feet inside, I lay Kikita on her back and stepped away from her. She was a good quiet baby. I reached beneath my skirt, pulled my panties to my thighs, and squatted. Mami taught me to pee just like that, with your skirt draped all around, but I lifted the front of my skirts and dropped my head to watch the urine stream from my smooth folds, moving my feet and the hem of my skirt to avoid the stream. The dirt was hard and dry and the pee splashed at my ankles.

'Ay, no. Ay, no,' a woman said. I expected that someone was scolding me for wetting my skirt, for looking at my cosita, for laying Kiki on the cool ground.

Dropping my skirt to cover my privates, I looked up. My eyes adjusted to the dim light and I could see Silvia Trujillo's face peering above someone's shoulder. A man pressed her against the wall with his whole body. His pants were dropped to his ankles, both knees were bent, and the cheeks of his nalgas were clenched against Silvia. The back of her full skirt draped against the wall but the front was raised, exposing her brown legs. Silvia balanced on one foot; her other bare knee bent at the man's side. Though it was me she looked at, she spoke to him, and a moreno I did not recognize turned his head to see me.

Silvia said, 'Stop now, Oscar. We have to stop. Everyone will know, Oscar.' She tried to drop her free foot to the ground as she spoke, but each time she did, el Oscar would grab just behind her knee and in one rough motion, bend, lift and pin it back to his waist.

She squirmed beneath him, but el Oscar did not change, he did not pull up his pants. He turned his neck hard to watch me. I don't know why I didn't run. I just squatted there in the stench of the shit-and-piss alley, Kikita cooing in the dirt beside me. Then el Oscar, while looking at me, put one hand firm over the mouth of Silvia so that she could not turn her head to free her mouth and speak. He smiled at me and thrust his pelvis. Light caught on the wet slime of his teeth, and with his eyes focused on me, he thrust again, each thrust an independent motion; each, he began and ended for me. Each seemed to end with a silent pregunta: How about that? Or that? El Oscar held all of my attention – those teeth, those muscles of his nalgas and legs contracted in his efforts – and for a

61

moment, I forgot about Silvia. His rhythm quickened and Oscar tired of his game with me. He turned to Silvia and with his hand still over her mouth, he lay his forehead against her shoulder and hammered his pelvis on her until there was no rhythm. His nalgas spasmed, his knees looked as if they might collapse under him, and he groaned and dropped his hand from her face.

'Silvia lay her cheek against his damp hair. Looking at me, she said, 'Make her leave.'

Oscar turned only his head. 'Go,' he said. 'Now.'

I pulled my panties up. The wet hem of my skirt clung to the backs of my calves.

'Now,' he said in a forced whisper.

I could not make myself move.

'Vete,' he said again in a whisper louder and more malicious than any shout.

I gathered Kiki against my shoulder as best I could, roughly maybe, because she cried as if I'd pinched her, then staggered out of the alley away from the sex.

'If you tell, something horrible will happen,' he said to my back. 'Horrible.'

When I remember all of that now, I think that Kiki with her eyes just over my shoulder, through tears and the blurred vision of an eight-month-old, was the last to see el Oscar and Silvia tangled, fighting in that stinking alley, and how young she was to have seen it.

After I saw Silvia and Oscar in the alley, my ears tuned in a new way to what had surrounded me always, to the sex that was in the dust in the air. Almost anytime on the streets you could hear talk of chiles and huevos and cositas and changuitos – chiles and eggs and little things and little monkeys. Away from mothers and wives, children and husbands teased with all the pet names for private parts. The innuendoes and double

meanings blended with the hateful slimy smile of el
Oscar and became newly vivid and offensive to me. I
turned against sex with vengeance, the way little girls
hate little boys. Any child who suggested anything
involving sex – penises, balls, vaginas, anything – got
a beating from me.

Abuelito loved my fights. From his window, he sang,
'Dale dale dale. No pierdas el tino,' the song to
encourage the blindfolded child to strike and burst the
swinging piñata with a stick. 'Que de la distancia se
pierde el camino. Hit it, hit it, hit it. Don't lose your
touch. With distance, you'll lose the way.' Sometimes
he sang the whole birthday piñata song, sometimes the
Christmas one, sometimes single verses out of order:
The quietest girl. Becomes hotly excited. With your
eyes blindfolded and a stick in hand. Break the jar to
pieces without compassion.

Children in the barrio soon knew how to entertain
themselves. They had only to urge the ignorant or dare
the brave to say something so simple.

'Ándale.' I heard my cousin whisper to poor
Conchita León, 'Ask her. Just ask her, "How's your
cosita, Magda?" Or just say cosita. Just say it. It's funny
what she will do.'

'Cosita,' Conchita said with her head down.

I threw dirt in the eyes of my cousin Rafa, then
charged him and punched my fist into his neck, turned
and knocked poor stupid Conchita in the arm just for
being so stupid. I beat many tontos silly and was
beaten myself. The bigger kids punched me hard. My
mother beat me for fighting. She used the beating
spoon with a perfect hole in its center, and even
through my skirt and panties, it left purple welts on
my nalgitas and thighs that lasted days.

'What kind of girl are you?' she yelled. She gripped
my upper arm and, pivoting in place as I circled her,

struck my nalgas with her wooden spoon. 'Who will marry a fighting girl?'

From next door, Abuelito yelled, 'Send the malita, mi vida, to me.'

Mami ignored him. She continued her blows and her questions. 'What will become of you?'

With time, I calmed and stopped fighting, because it was a stupid thing to let others know what upset me, to give them power, and because my confusion dissolved my anger.

My mother, who grunted on the cot with my father, would not touch or even look at her own sex parts or the sex parts of her children. She stood us in a metal tub and washed us with the indifference and efficiency of washing dishes. The soapy rag traveled our necks, down our arms, over bellies, from feet up calves and legs, but when she reached our vital centers, she paused, turned her face from us, and reluctantly soaped through the cotton crotch of our panties or just splashed water up between our legs. She washed herself behind makeshift curtains, and peeking through the parted cloth, I saw her standing in the tub wearing her sagging underpants and a graying bra. Even years later, after I installed a private shower in my mother's house, she continued to bathe herself through the crotch of her panties. My mother, who grunted on the cot with my father, was shamed by cositas and beat me for hitting children who talked dirty about cositas. My grandfather, who muttered nasties from his window to passing women, cheered my fight against nasty talk out that same window and then inside his house, scolded me for my fighting.

My focus was narrow and simple when I was a girl. I saw one thing and then another. First, I concentrated on the violence of sex and that was all I saw. Later, my attention focused on something else. Just as I had once been obsessed with the fighting begging stinking alley violence of sex, I turned equal fascination to the love yearning sweetness of various novios who walked the malecón on Sundays, to the movie posters of Pedro Infante. Musk and grunt and names for private parts faded into the background, and I gave my full attention to tenderness.

Though I could not have told you then, I understand now that the tenderness was more dangerous than the violence, more mortifying than the shame. It aroused in my young body a hopelessness and yearning that threatened to eat me away from inside out.

It was impossible to connect the smile and the clenched nalgas of el Oscar in the same mind that held the image of gentle novios, whether in real life or on movie posters. I thought sex was one act and tenderness another. Think me stupid, but I was then about nine years old. There are grown men who still have not made the connection. It is the dangerous ones who use tenderness to their advantage – the ones who understand the seduction of a kind word and a gentle caress given far away from and as if it had no connection with the bed. They know the power of whisper and touch so light that the woman rises to meet it. Something as simple as gently lifting a crumb from the face, following the line of the jaw with the back of a finger. Maybe it is good that many do not understand the power and sex of tenderness.

It is my weakness.

I knew that I would not allow any nasty Oscar type to slam his bare nalgas against me in a stinking alley, but if someone were to stand quietly beside me, place an open palm lightly in the center of my back, kiss me

65

so slowly that I could feel the lips on my forehead long after they had parted from my skin, if someone were to attend to me in those tender ways . . .

It stirred me crazy in my heart.

From the window of my mother's house, I would watch young neighbors, Manfredo and Beatriz, linger in the shadows of evening. He stole shy touches, picking invisible lint from the fabric of her dress, tracing her eyebrow with his finger to slowly brush hair away from her downcast eyes, and I traced with my own finger an arc above my eyebrow; I gently pinched the fabric at my own shoulder.

In my body was a longing for gentle touch that extended the familiar hunger and thirst of my belly and throat into muscle and skin and heart. It was a yearning, a gnawing, a knot that would not relax. Mami had too many children to linger in her affections, Chucha was far away in her presence, Abuelito too dangerous and disgusting. In our cot at night, my hermana Rosa and I would tickle each other's back. I tried to demonstrate what it was I had seen, what I needed. With all my hands' attention, I studied her contours, using my full palm or one finger or one fingernail, but when it was Rosa's turn to touch, she lay bored on her stomach, her chin on one fist, and swept my back over and over in the same pathways that she could easily reach, her fingers absently repeating the same routes.

'Ya,' I'd say, and again I would demonstrate on her what I longed for: slowly pull a few hairs through thumb and finger from the scalp to end, trace the cords of her neck, lightly drag all fingers down the full length of her back and over her pompis, then trace one thumbnail over the same path. I waited for her to raise a shoulderblade or bend her waist sideways in anticipation, then surprised her with something different

– just the right combination of familiarity and surprise – but Rosa never seemed to understand what I wanted to give or to receive.

Even then, even so young, I knew that I was separate, different from my hermanos. Even then I knew that I would leave them. To find what I needed.

When I was thirteen years old, Tía Chucha appeared beside me on the roof as I lifted Mami's dress to the clothesline. 'Tomorrow, we will go with your mother to visit the Niñito Jesus,' she said.

The miracle little baby Jesus lived kilometers from el barrio Rincón on 32 Ibis Street in Las Gaviotas neighborhood within the fenced confines of the Teatlán Tennis Club. In the golden zone. I know the address because I still have the Niñito's prayer card with his picture on the front and his name and address on the back, and because his address is only two numbers different from my present one: 30 Ibis. He is my neighbor now.

Mami and Tía had only twice before visited the porcelain miracle baby in the Las Gaviotas Teatlán Tennis Club – once when Abuelito's legs were removed, once when Papi didn't come home for two months.

I watched Chucha's face as I slid a wooden pin over each fabric shoulder. She did not turn to me. Her fair skin glistened. Her hair was short, brilliant black, something to draw between fingers and squeeze inside your fist. Her still melancholy did not draw her features down; it did not pull at the corners of her mouth to create bitter folds. Instead, it made her more beautiful. Chucha was silent, at home and complete in her sadness, and that is what people had always wanted to destroy.

'Sister must go to the miracle Jesus for her sight,'

she said. 'It is worse.' Tía drew Father's pants from the basket and clipped the waistband to the line. 'Worse.'

I had not sensed Tía's presence on the roof until she stood beside me, but the surprise did not frighten, it did not even startle me.

'María Cande will go and pray for me, I know,' Tía said. 'She will pray for her husband and her children, but your mami will not pray for herself. Perhaps if she kneels near the miracle baby, perhaps if you and I pray, He will cure her.'

Mami's sight had grown progressively worse until there was no more a doctor could do for a poor woman.

Tía leaned over me and pressed her nose into my hair. 'Clean yourself well, Magda. Hair and everything.'

I was thirteen years old, already bled like a woman, I had hard proud breasts and long legs, men noticed me, I had seen sex. The Niñito Jesus was not important to me. But I'd never seen the golden zone.

My mother went nowhere alone. Always a child or a cousin or a sister accompanied her to the market or to the church. She needed a shoulder to hold and to guide her. Though her eyeglasses improved her sight, she had no perception of depth to step up the high walkways or over disturbed stones.

Mami stepped slowly and with difficulty up and down from the high walks. She was an old woman in many of her ways, and though she was not yet forty, people greeted her as doña. I, Mami and Chucha formed a short chain as we moved through the barrio toward the bus stop on the big avenue.

'Step down,' Chucha said while I stepped down.

'Step down,' Mami said.

Any movement or sound initiated from one rippled through each of us.

I was ahead and to the right of Mami so that she could have her hand on my left shoulder. Tía Chucha followed close behind. My mother was a shadow, the pressure of her palm, a voice in my ear. The print and weight of her hand, I can still feel in the skin of that shoulder; the breath of her comments still puffs in my ear.

She instructed me, 'A little slower, hija,' and our chain slowed.

She commented on her condition, on what she saw around her. 'I'm okay,' or 'Ay, it's long, this walk,' or 'Dirty cochinos live here.'

If there was silence too long, she spoke without turning to Chucha or Chucha to her.

'Eres tú, hermanita?' one would ask.

'Soy yo,' the other answered.

We walked through my barrio, past the homes, past the stinking alleys. My mother had the habit of muttering the names of the families as she passed. 'Rodríguez, Ramos, Trujillo,' as if accounting for them before she left. Sometimes she attached a label to the family names. García, the fishermen; Montevilla, the ill-breds; de la Cruz, those huevones.

When we were outside the familiar, Tía, silent until then, called forth the world in Mami's ear. 'A güera with bucked teeth . . .'

'Pobrecita,' Mami responded to Chucha's world. 'At least she is fair-skinned.'

'Plastic flowers in the window . . .'

'One day we will put plastic flowers on the grave of 'Amá,' Mami said.

'The carnicero who sells old meat.'

Mami nodded her head at the butcher as he passed.

'Doraluz in a pink dress.'

'Buenos días, Doraluz. Qué rosa tan linda,' Mami said as we passed a woman I did not know in a stained pink dress.

Past our barrio the neighborhood improved, the difference only that the stinking alleys disappeared and that the continuous cement wall, separated from the street only by the high narrow sidewalk, was more recently painted. Faded washes of blue or pink or yellow distinguished one house's boundary from the next. The colors overlapped at the vertical wavy edges made by handheld brushes, and colors blended to make a hanging thin braid of a new color to mark the boundary. Some neighbors shared the same house color and there was no line of separation between their residences, but still women knew where their home began and ended. Each residence had one window with iron protection bars, one wooden door that opened to one section of cement before it. On hands and knees, with worn bristle brush and hard soap, women scrubbed only the small rectangular section of sidewalk just in front of their domains, no more.

The walks were uneven, heaving in places, a combination of old stone slabs and concrete, narrow, wide enough for one person or two pressed together. Young men walked past us in the streets, easily hopping to the high walk – some as much as a meter up from the street – to avoid cars and bicycles, and quickly stepping down again to walk past Mami and me without a change in the pace. Drivers sounded horns at the pedestrians but did not slow for them. In Teatlán, the only traffic rule is the rule of Big. Whoever is bigger – trucks over cars, cars over bikes, bikes over pedestrians – wins.

At the edge of el barrio Juárez, entering Golondrina, a car slowed and a man leaned from the open window, bit his lower lip and sucked spit and air through his teeth. '¿Dónde vas, mamacita?' he said.

My fists clenched, though he was not talking to me, and I could feel Chucha tighten behind me, though he was not talking to any of us.

'Maleducado,' Mami said under her breath.

The passenger leaned far out his window toward a young woman, licked and chewed his lips.

The young woman walking toward us kept her eyes cast down, and I felt for her embarrassment. Then, with practiced grace, she stretched one side of her neck long to expose and offer it, and slowly lifted her arm and reached behind her neck to gather her dark hair in a mass and sweep it over one shoulder. The breast of the same side rose under her cotton blouse with the movement.

The three of us stopped and turned sideways to let her pass just as her hair relaxed over the double taut cords at the back of her dark neck.

'Ay, Dios,' my mother whispered with impatience.

Chucha was silent.

'Dios mío,' a voice echoed from within the nearest doorway.

Only blue cotton-covered knees and the tips of heavy black shoes protruded into the sidewalk. An old señora sat there in her chair, tucked away, watching the street. Her knotted hands came forward and braced one on each knee, and her gray head leaned into the walkway and into view.

'Malcriados.' She flipped her hand above her head as if swatting a fly.

The car rolled along beside the young woman and then sped around the corner. The señora's head and hands disappeared back into her doorway like an old sea turtle's.

Mami squeezed my shoulder to signal that we

71

should continue, and we passed in front of the old woman's doorway. Tucked in her niche, she mumbled about the bad manners of young men and the whorish ways of young women.

'Así es,' my mother agreed.

Her comments about the scene and Chucha's silence continued long past the señora's door. According to Mami, the young no longer had manners, they were sinvergüenzas. Without shame.

'You will behave,' she said.

And I answered, 'Sí, Mami.'

'You won't act like a puta.'

'No, Mami.'

But though my mother's words continued in my ear and the señora's in my memory, it was not the words of the señora or of my mother that called my attention, it was the image of the slow black hair, the bare neck, the lifted breast of the señorita.

We passed the Pacífico beer factory, walked through el barrio Puerto, which we called the Fly Colony – so many flies from the guts of so many fish – and we passed the lane where taco and seafood stands lined along the street.

Lazario Fuentes, the best taquero for tacos of carne asada, joked with a customer who stood waiting for his food just arm's length across from Lazario's grill and cutting board. 'You want tacos or tacas?' He laughed.

'Tacos for me, tacas for my little girl.' Tacas, without chile. That was the joke.

Mami had coins for the bus, a piece of candy for the baby Jesus, but altogether it was still not enough for one taco. The scent of grilled meat made me ache, made my throat contract, my mouth wet as Rojo the dog's.

Hiss and splatter, a rapid knock against wood, laughter, all in a rhythm fast as folk dancers' feet – it was a taquero's show. Lazario's hands were efficient, quickly pinching and turning thin strips of meat on the small grill, chopping cooked meat, scooping it onto the side of the cleaver and sliding it onto the small hot tortillas, cupping an onion in one hand, crossing its exposed face over and over . . .

Just one taco.

Beside Lazario, a silent round Indian woman with gray braids looped in a loose knot at her back patted a tortilla to its proper thickness, gently lay it on the flat comal over coals, and turned three others, pinching an edge between her fingers just as Lazario had turned the meat.

'Vegetables?' Lazario held shredded cabbage over the tacos, impatient for the customer's answer.

Mine was a silent scream of desire. Small brown shining pottery bowls filled with condiments – pale green watery tomatillo salsa; molcajete salsa with the black floating char of tomato and onion; salsa cruda, finely chopped fresh tomato and cilantro and onion and chile; curly mounds of purple onion slices that had been cooked with beets; chopped fresh onion, limes and cilantro – were lined in the center of the table. Without Mami and Chucha, I could have bumped hard against the well-fed customer and rescued the tacos for my own fierce hunger. The customer carried the plates to his daughter, who sat at a narrow table pushed close to the curb with her back to the street, and father and daughter curved their bodies around their food.

Give me one bendito taco.

Chucha reached past Mami and pinched the back of my arm. 'This is no time to think of food,' she said. 'Think of El Niñito.' Mami pushed one stiff finger into my lower back to try to make me move.

Primero es comer, que cristiano ser. First food, then Jesus.

73

We passed the seafood carts. The solemn owner held an oyster in his palm and with the flat edge of his knife found the weak opening, turned the knife over, pulled the top shell off, cut the thick connection and left the oyster loose in half its home. He set it on a plastic plate beside five others, squeezed lime over all, and pushed it over the top of his cart to a man who took it without words, turned his back to the cart, then lifted and tipped a shell to his lips, tipped his head back and sucked the oyster down whole.

'Don't stare, hija.' Mami spoke into my ear, a peripheral presence, the voice of conscience.

I wished that my own father sold something so profitable, so delicious.

The man tipped the same shell a second time to suck the remaining juice, then licked his lips in a way that had nothing to do with his food and all to do with me.

'Don't look at that desgraciado,' Chucha whispered.

'Don't,' Mami echoed.

Mami's hand pushed me to walk faster, and I knew without seeing that she and Chucha had dropped their eyes to the ground just as they knew without seeing that my eyes burned back at the desgraciado.

'Santo mío, Dios mío,' Mami spoke to God, to herself, for me to overhear. 'What trouble will she bring to herself?'

'Trouble,' Chucha echoed.

We continued past the seafood stands, past the cart with the machine that shitted out raw dough churros into a copper vat of bubbling oil. A woman lifted a long-handled colander full of gold brown links and shook off the excess grease. Holding the handle with both hands, she turned it, spilling them onto a sugar-covered board. Churros, tacos, ostiones. This was a cruel passage for me. I closed my teeth hard against each other, held my breath so that I would not inhale the aromas of grilled meat or fresh churros, and I pledged to myself as I always did as I passed good food – *Some day.*

At the edge of barrio Puerto was the the Central Market. The market, so full of noise and color on other days, was all gray metal, chain, trash and padlocks. Walls of corrugated tin and chain nets were pulled over storefronts to keep out Sunday thieves. There were no car bumpers to squeeze between, no tight-uniformed policemen to *bee-op* their whistles, no car horns, no competing radios – Sinaloense and mariachi and salsa and canciones de amor – no round señoras with bulging plaid nylon bags to bump around, no color of fruit or vegetable clothing. Only trash and gray and filthy scavenger dogs were left behind, mongrels with ribbed grease and mange-spotted sides pressed against protected storefronts, chewing oil brown paper, nosing orange peels and onion skins.

Two blocks past the Central Market, two blocks closer to the avenue that traveled along the shore from Old Teatlán to the golden zone, was Cine Maravillo. Cine Maravillo was set back from the other store-fronts, creating a cool semicircle of shade on shining marble around its ticket booth. Because there were no people waiting to enter or standing and talking about the movie they'd seen, we stopped there. It was the place to tuck away from the sun and crowds for a moment, a good place to rest, the most luxurious place we knew.

Under the awning of the theater, behind glass, inside two cases on the front wall, were the movie posters. This was el Gordo Chuy Beltrán's movie theater. I knew about Gordo Chuy Beltrán from people talking, from things I'd heard on the streets. He was the owner of Cine Maravillo. He was crazy for Pedro Infante. That's what people said in their little summary of him:

75

'Gordo Chuy is crazy for Infante.' The posters inside one case changed as the movie did, the others stayed the same, always with the same black and white photographs: Fat Chuy, when he still had hair, shaking hands with Pedro Infante, and four photos, each from different Infante movies, all with a loopy autograph of El Infante himself.

Mami took her hand from my shoulder and moved so close to the glass case that her nose touched.

She squinted behind her thick glasses at the photos. 'Chucha, are these still of Señor Infante?' she asked.

'Sí, hermana.' Chucha studied the pictures over her sister's shoulders.

Mami took small sidesteps to position herself inches before each photo. She stopped before my favorite, the one with Pedro in jail. I had never been to the theater, I didn't know Mr Infante's movies, but this was one photo that I would study while resting in the shade of the awning. Through the bars, Pedro Infante held the hand of a serene woman in an old-fashioned high-collar dress.

'Is it the picture of the woman?' Mami's sight was memorized from the times when her eyeglasses had served her.

'Sí, hermana. A woman with Señor Infante.'

My mother blinked before the photograph. Her fingers were next to her face, touching the glass lightly as if touching the picture might help her better see it.

'Is he kissing her hand?' she asked.

'He is.'

Pedro's eyes were closed, and the serene woman's hand he pressed to his lips.

I had invented stories around this picture. Pedro Infante was in jail for protecting her honor, or he was a scoundrel that she could not resist; she was his mistress, the one he truly loved. These were the

76

love stories I knew from the streets of my barrio.

A head and torso of a woman appeared in the ticket booth that was centered in the alcove. Her hair was stylish. Her lips, red. She scowled at us, raised her index finger, wagging it back and forth in the no-no-no-don't-touch signal for children. The underbelly of her upper arm draped and swung like a hammock with the movement. She must have been the fat wife of Fat Chuy.

'Who is that waving?' Mami waved at the woman. 'Should we greet her?'

Chucha and I pushed and pulled Mami away from the theater until we reached the top of a hill that descended to the avenue. Looking down the last narrow street, I could see a small square of the ocean in sunlight. I longed to break out of my mother's and Tía's pace, to run to the open air, but as we descended closer to the sea, Mami and Chucha grew smaller, tighter on my shoulder, their steps stiff and short, hesitant. They cared nothing for the wide sky and sea, nor did they want to see the golden zone. Mami and Chucha had turned their attentions to their visit with the miracle little baby Jesus. Here, close to the avenue, their pilgrimage began en serio.

Behind me, mumbles escaped Tía's silent prayers. 'Sight . . . hermanita . . . vision . . . forgiveness . . . grant her.'

Mami fingered a candy in her pocket – a single sweet offering for Jesusito – and listed her requests. 'I will ask El Niñito Jesus about the tejuino business . . . about Uncle's amputation . . .'

'Mami, ask for your own eyes,' I said. I wanted to snake my fingers into her pocket and liberate that candy.

My prayers were not in words. They were the clear aroma of grilled meat, the rush hiss explosion of moist churro dough lowered into crazy bubbling hot oil; they were my strong young legs pulsing to run to the avenue that would take us to things never seen. To the golden zone.

Mami continued her list. '. . . for the crazy ways of Rigoberto . . . to bring my husband home . . . the sadness of La Chucha.' She talked to no one, but in my ear, she gathered her prayers.

We boarded a blue bus, the cheapest one, and traveled only far enough to grind the gears once through a change before stopping for passengers who waited in front of the open air restaurants of Olas Altas, the oldest part of Teatlán. The bus jerked forward again and we moved toward new Teatlán – toward wide asphalt, new cement and rebar, toward banks and hotels and restaurants and bars. If we had continued through the entire route, we would pass through the newer businesses, through the golden zone, past the wetlands, north to coconut palm groves and empty beaches, toward Los Cerritos, the little hill beside the rocky shore where the poor searched for oysters and fished and swam on Sunday. I did not know that route then.

One long bench ran along each side of the bus, so I stared at the faces and feet of those seated across from me. There were feet that revealed whole lives on the blue bus: the plump bare feet of a little girl, tender as rising dough; the dense feet of albañiles, grayed by the daily dust of cement, tire tread laced onto their callused soles; a señora's feet with wide cracked heels that crushed the back of her best red pumps.

Those who cannot look you in the eye will judge you by your feet. I always told Martina that. I will tell Isabel. Keep your shoes well maintained and clean.

The bus filled in four stops and my view to the other bench was blocked by the bellies of adults and the faces of the children standing in the center aisle. A small boy stared up at me and held onto my thighs innocently with light hands, wedging himself between my knees for support. My muscles weakened beneath his innocent touch. His mother ignored him, her nalgas to his head, near my face, and I could smell the rancid manteca of her kitchen.

From her pocket, Mami took the worn prayer card she had saved from her last visit to the miracle baby. On the front was a picture of the porcelain Jesusito lying on his back, pale and naked, knees bent, one foot up in the air so that his privates were not visible. His head with a cap of light brown curls was frozen in a position lifted without support. His eyes focused upward, his elbows were bent, and on both hands, littlest and next to littlest fingers were folded down, the other two, index and middle, were straight, just like the big Jesus' hands are in every picture. The miracle little baby Jesus lay on light blue satin, and the shadows of one hand and his head were black beside him. With her head bowed, Mami muttered into the worn prayer card held on her lap. A secret conversation.

Chucha, her back erect, her focus internal, hummed low in her chest. I knew the verse she often sang over and over: 'Lloraban las tres Marias a ver que el pecho manaba . . .' The three Marias wept to see that He suckled the breast.

Nearing the golden zone, the bus began to empty. Maids and cooks and waiters disembarked before hotels. I strained my neck to see the top of those towers through the low window. Towers.

A young American man hailed the bus. Standing on the bottom step, he asked '¿Los Cerritos?' speaking it slowly and in his nose. Three others stood at the folded doors and waited.

The driver explained that this wasn't the bus for him.

The young man didn't understand Spanish and he was stubborn. '¿Cuanto, Los Cerritos?' he asked.

The driver held up two fingers and began to roll the bus forward. The young man with shaggy hair waved his friends aboard. As the bus started forward, they stood, each on a step, discussing and inspecting coins in their palms before climbing to the fare box.

'Gracias.' The young woman bent to struggle her thank-you into the driver's ear as she dropped her coins into the plastic box.

'Gracias.' The next woman did the same.

The driver stared forward and changed gears, but I could see his eyes in the large rearview mirror follow their hips down the narrow aisle of his bus.

One young man squeezed into a space across from us. He smiled and nodded a greeting at the men on either side of him, then patted his thighs for his girlfriend to sit down. He was shirtless, his chest and shoulders smooth and red-brown, his belly taut. He patted his thighs again, and his girlfriend sat across them, bumping the knees of the elderly man next to her. She leaned and touched the old man's knees lightly with her fingertips. 'I'm sorry. Excuse me,' she said.

The old man cast his eyes to the floor. She was dressed in a pink two-piece bathing suit that shone through a thin cotton cover-up that covered nothing. I had never seen a real two-piece bathing suit before; never seen a woman's belly on a bus. The bulge of her breasts rose above the cover, and clear blisters dotted the crevice. Over her brown tan where she had peeled and burned again, bright fuchsia patched her chest. The boyfriend folded his arms around her, one hand clasping his other wrist at her belly, then released the grasp of a thumb to stroke her belly slowly through the cotton. I thought I could hear the soft whisper and scratch of his thumb and her cloth, but it was my own involuntary imitation of the movement against the collar of my blouse.

'Jesus, María y José.' Mami was distracted from her prayers. 'Is she naked, hija?'

These gringo people were a feast and a curiosity to me. They were not trying to hide. This was no dark alley. The other gabacha couple stood beside their friends, the boy holding a pole in the bend of his elbow. His girlfriend pressed her back against him as if slowly scratching an itch against a post.

Chucha leaned into my shoulder. 'We are near Las Gaviotas,' she said. 'Remember Jesusito.'

The baby Jesus lived three blocks from the Hotel Gaviotas.

Without turning, I reached behind me and felt for the cord strung along the windows.

We stepped down from the blue bus into the bright golden zone, into cleanliness and midday. Mami covered her glasses with her hand to shield her eyes from the stab of sudden light. I dropped my head back to take in the full tower of Las Gaviotas Hotel. It must have been fifteen pisos high and it stood shining white mother-of-pearl against the sky. Gabachos everywhere. They strolled in front of shops holding hands, dressed in new clothes – Bermuda shorts and madras shirts and sundresses – fashions foreign to me. Many were burned red brown from the sun, others just burned.

Mami pressed her palm into the top of my shoulder. 'Almost there.' She pointed me away from the tourists and shops, and the three of us walked in our familiar chain into the Las Gaviotas neighborhood of fancy houses. A few other passengers got off the bus with us. Their destination was the same as ours, but the group

81

moved toward the tennis club on the asphalt street as close as possible to the curb in single and double file without speaking, a timid parade toward Jesus.

Houses were bright and white with clay tile roofs, with gardens of lavender and plumbago and carnal hibiscus. Fuchsia bougainvillea tumbled from balconies and over broken soda bottles mortared to the top of high white plaster walls. Iron fences were topped in pointed spears. We passed the house where I now live, the house that is now as common to me as salt. It seemed magnificent to me then. A castle. So clean. Even the dog that barked through the iron gates was clean, with long combed fur, with legs that were the right length for his body.

A doña near the head of the line dropped to her knees and began to edge along the pavement toward the tennis club. Mami fell to her knees without warning and almost took me down with her. Chucha followed Mami.

This practice, so ordinary on the steps of the church, mortified me in that neighborhood.

'Not here, Mami,' I whispered. 'Please, Chucha, not in the golden zone.'

One by one, other pilgrims descended to their knees. Those standing trailed ashamed behind the low procession at a painful slow pace. The clean combed dog began to race back and forth along the iron gate, barking fiercely, lunging his body against the iron and rattling the hinges. I searched the street surface for smears of blood trailed behind the knees of the visitors. This black asphalt was not so smooth as the worn stones that paved the church grounds.

Mami held the Jesusito prayer card in front of her and pretended to read what she could not see and already knew by heart, 'Little baby Jesus, you are my pillar, my rock, my bastion . . .' Chucha softly joined and they prayed aloud until they reached the part where there was a dotted line to fill in the need or problem. 'Your eyes are always open, and your ears always attentive in . . .' Blank. Mami and Chucha paused there and moved their lips around silent wishes. On the card, there was a dotted line, and above it in parentheses it said, 'Concentrate on your petition.'

I filled the blank with *healing the eyes of my mother*, but the words had no power, no feeling. Even so young, I lacked the faith for Jesus. Mami and Chucha continued aloud, Mami holding the card in one hand like a miniature book. Ashamed to stand and too embarrassed to kneel, I followed behind with my head bowed. I could smell sweet fruit blossoms, and in my peripheral vision, I could see bright color. A child on a bicycle passed us. My curiosity overcame my vergüenza and I raised my head. I had to see the golden zone. A boy younger than me made a turn and headed toward us. His bicycle was speckled cobalt shining like phosphorus in the sea. Colored strips of plastic streamed behind his polished chrome handlebars and snapped in the wind.

A girl called from a window to a young servant girl in the garden. 'Berta, did you iron my dress? My yellow dress, Berta.'

Berta stood still at the iron fence. She spoke without looking toward the window. 'Sí, señorita.' And crossed herself as we passed.

Everywhere flowers, trimmed gardens. Everywhere smooth painted surfaces.

At the gate of the Teatlán Tennis Club, the guard detained us, Jesus' visitors, with only a raised hand. The visitors kneeled or stood quiet and exposed, waiting at the gate for permission to enter while club members, gringos and the Teatlán rich, in short white skirts or shorts with bands of colored terry cloth on their wrists, short white socks and white tennis shoes – a style of dress I had not seen before – bounced by swinging tennis rackets or matching canvas bags. They were buoyant, confident, firm and tan like the people of advertisements in a magazine I had once found.

I pulled Mami to her feet. 'Here, you stand, Mami.' I pulled Chucha to her feet. 'You must stand, Chucha.' It was like pulling sleeping children from their beds. They were sluggish and heavy from prayer. Gracias a Dios, others began to stand.

We were foreigners waiting at customs aduana. Our same group that would have been gossiping and joking loudly in line to buy a kilo of tortillas was stunned and frightened, arms stiff and tight at our sides, silent before tennis skirts and the rich and El Niñito Jesus.

The guard waved us through the gate. María Concepción Fuentes Gamboa waited for us on the steps of a small stone house just inside the tennis club. She wore a white bib apron over a dark dress. Maybe that was her imitation nun's habit; maybe she had been caught in the middle of the preparation of Jesus' comida. She smiled and nodded at all who entered. She held a tray of Niñito Jesus prayer cards and centavos tossed in for exchange. I knew about María Concepción from bits I had heard from my mother, from bits on the street. She dedicated her life to the Jesusito, the porcelain baby Jesus who had arrived to Teatlán's port in the early 1600s. The details of his story – the life and cathedrals and passages of the little porcelain Jesus – I do not know. I only knew that for a long time he had been discarded in a crate, that he was the miracle baby because sometimes real tears trickled from the tiny pink nub of the inside corners of his glass eyes, and that people came from far away to see the little baby cry. María Concepción lived in a small house beside Jesusito.

The old Señor Fuentes, her great-uncle, sold all the land to the tennis club with the agreement that the shrine would always be maintained and opened to the public on Sundays. María Concepción never married. This was her lifework. That's what everyone said: 'It is her life's work.'

My mother paused and touched María Concepción's forearm, uttering, 'Señora,' as if Señorita Fuentes were married, as if she were holy.

A strange hollow thwock echoed against the house. It was a sound that thumped high in my chest, a sound I now understand was that of tennis balls striking the tight gut strings of a racket.

La María Concepción nodded permission to enter. 'Santos y buenos días.'

There were only three rooms and a hallway in the little stone house. Entrance was into the hall with three open doors – one right, one left and one straight ahead. The rooms to the left and to the right were filled with old candy and toys of all kinds – hand-carved wooden horses, trucks, crocheted dolls, orange dump trucks, American plastic dolls with pointing chichis and long legs – all displayed on tierred shelves that began at the ceiling of the back wall and spilled to the floor a few feet from the door. I had never seen such abundance.

Against the doorway leaned a single wooden crutch with dirty frayed rags wound to pad the square that fit into the armpit. From the rubber tip to the rag pad was written in black ink: 'Thank you, baby Jesus. Your tears healed my leg.' The walls were filled with plaques. 'I came here to find peace and I did.' Another: 'Thank you, Santo Mío, Dios Mío, Santísimo Sacramento, for bringing my daughter home.'

'What happened to the daughter?' I leaned over and asked Chucha.

She did not answer. Mami shook her head for me to be quiet.

Chucha's lips moved. She and Mami knelt at the toys, Mami fingering the miracle baby Jesus' picture as if it were a rosary, her knee touching a small green metal tractor with black rubber tires. Three other women knelt beside and behind her and the rest pressed into the doorway from the hall.

In the back room with Jesus, visitors stood and kneeled and pointed and prayed while Jesusito lay inside a glass case on iron legs. I stood over him and his blue hard glass iris stared past me at I don't know what. I could not position myself to interrupt his gaze, though I tried. His poor neck, head always lifted without the support of pillow or mattress, his fingers frozen in benediction. I'd cry tears inside there, too, I thought. My mother and Chucha knelt at either side of me. They cried softly, their foreheads pressed against the side of the glass case among the oval smudges left behind by those who had prayed before them.

I wondered if Jesusito ever escaped into the night to play with the orange dump truck.

My mother cleared the tears that had fallen onto her lenses with one stroke of her pointer finger.

'Just one toy,' I whispered so softly through the glass that no one could understand.

I did not kneel, and through the window I could see the carved green gardens. An old man, slow as the plants, moved through the green in dull and dirty clothes. I heard a high scream and laughter. A girl not much older than me stepped backwards, holding something in both hands behind her back. A young man sprang right and left, trying to take it from her, but each time she pulled one shoulder back or the other and dodged his moves, then turned quickly and ran, holding something – I could not tell what – in one hand above her head. The young man stood and watched her, near the edge of anger, deciding if he would continue the playful chase or walk away.

Inside, more visitors had entered the room. They pressed behind me and kneeled at my waist. The mustard-colored walls mumbled prayers.

I stood over Jesusito and tried to concentrate on pleas for my mother's eyes, but instead I remembered the young woman we had passed on the street, Pedro Infante's lips against the back of a woman's hand, the couples on the bus. Jesusito's two fingers pointed up to me, his vacant eyes angled past me, his chile lay asleep and hidden between his chubby legs. I remembered the young woman's dark hair, how it fell in one heavy and slow motion like a wave. I practiced. I stretched my neck first to the same shoulder and then rotated my chin toward my chest, slowly stretching, exposing the nape of my neck to the Niñito Jesus. I leaned my head back as if caressing the chest of a man behind me, gracefully extended the back of my hand to Jesusito, fingered my own belly and then began again the repetition of my new skills. Again the wave of my hair, again the stretch of my neck.

Lost in my rehearsal, I did not hear or feel my mother and Chucha rise and stand beside me.

Mami popped my cheek with the back of her fingers. 'Ya,' she said. Enough.

She carefully placed the single disc of hard red candy on top of the glass case. 'From me and my sister and my daughter, Magda,' she said.

I looked down again at Jesus, and I knew that he would not heal my mother's eyes. He would not play with the toys or eat the candy. He was nothing to me. If he had responded in some small way – cried a tear for my mother or Chucha or looked into my eyes – if he had done something besides shine white and cold

87

in his clear case. Maybe then he would have captured my attention. But he didn't, and to me, he was only a cold glass baby with a cinnamon candy that I wanted and too many toys.

Mami and Chucha mumbled Santísimo and Mío and Niñito and don't ever leave me, Jesus. That was the last line of the prayer on the back of the baby Jesus' prayer card, 'Nunca solo me dejes,' just above his name and address:

NIÑITO JESÚS   FRACC. GAVIOTAS
CALLE IBIS 32 (PRIVADA)   TEATLÁN, SINALOA,

the address that is now so close to my own.

Their prayers surrounded me, but the candy disc wobbled slightly on the glass, and my attention stretched back to the prisoner friend that I had freed years before. Jesus was silent under the glass. It was my friend I heard.

I felt him touch my chin and I heard him say again, 'You're going to be okay.'

My first years were spent collecting what I thought were unrelated fragments, observations of the world. And then, though I cannot say just when, I understood that they were of the same puzzle. El Oscar, my parent's fighting – Don't go – Please stay. Son of a whore – children chanting nasty names – chiles, huevos, changuito – women teasing, exposing their soft necks – Ay, mamacita – my grandfather's catcalls, the shy touches of novios. All was of the same puzzle. There was a link between the tenderness and the flirting and the teasing that churned low in my belly, and the mero mero sex – the banging bodies of Silvia and el Oscar in the alley. Once I recognized this, I began to piece together all that was related to sex – near

88

everything in the world – at a pace that caused a deep ache like the growing pains of my long legs.

I began to act all the roles that I observed. Sweeping the roof, I took on the posture of a macho and sucked down a pretend oyster. My slitted eyes traveled the full length of the broom handle, slowly taking in all its womanly pretend curves. I bit my lips and growled at invisible women, 'Qué buena estás.' I fingered my clavicle and stretched my neck like a long yawn, practiced a near imperceptible wink, molded my hands over every contour of myself. I rehearsed in the sala of my abuelito, walking alone on the streets. I stopped and studied movie posters and took on the expressions and postures of women in them. I did not know that I was rehearsing. A sexy wisdom encouraged me forward. A deep and inexplicable knowing urged me to gather.

Gather for my future.

*I even thank my cabrón of a father who
walked the boardwalk every Sunday with
his girlfriends instead of our family and my
mother, llora, llora, llora, crying at the
table. Because of them, I made the promise
to myself and the Madrecita de Dios that
no man would make me cry at my table –
that no man would use me – though
occasionally, I have had to use the man . . .*

My father made tejuino in a gray metal bathtub on the
roof, and sold it from a two-wheeled wooden cart
that he pushed along the streets near the port and along
the boardwalk. Tejuino is an old-fashioned corn drink
that some Mexicans like but tourists have never heard
of. My brothers and me, we told Papi that he could
make more money selling something to the tourists,
but he didn't listen.

'The gringos have money,' one of us, all of us told
him. 'They'll buy any little fucker thing – squawking
chicken toys, sun hats, something. Walk the beach and
you will find out what.'

He did not respond. Not with words. There on the
roof in a garden of rebar and drying dull laundry, he sat
on his crate beside the grinding stone and the washtub
of bubbling liquid corn. He lifted his chin to point to

a sack to be opened and poured, and his eyes darkened. No one suggested more.

When I was too young and my father would not allow me to work with him, I watched. To be near Papi and the tejuino, I swept dust over the edges of the flat roof onto the street, clipped laundry onto the line, all the time taking in the recipe of tejuino.

Even so young that I could not lift the bags of piloncillo and corn kernels or hold the broken paddle to stir the tejuino, I longed to work. Not the work of the women and the house. Always I had passion to leave the house to work in the world. I longed to earn coins and feel their weight in my palms, to count them again and again.

I followed the making of tejuino, tracing the pathways in simple shapes back and forth and back and forth through our house with buckets of water, sacks of corn, dark cones of sugar, and armloads of wood through our house in one long, worn straight line. From the front door through the narrow lane room that was sala and eating and cooking and sleeping room, through a cloth curtain to one tiny sleeping room and straight through to the back door that opened to a cement shaft of a room that was open to the sky.

Within that cement room open to the sky, there was a cement sink, circular iron stairs and, behind a curtain, a seatless toilet. When the sink and toilet were not backed thick-black with sewage, I stood under the stairs and watched through the dark diamond mesh. He stepped heavy, weighted by dead sacks balanced on one shoulder, circling slowly to the roof. The metal stairs rattled with each step. They were not designed for the heavy use. Too many winding trips up with sacks of corn and piloncillo and buckets of water, wet clothes. Too many trips down with five-gallon buckets of tejuino and armloads of stiff laundry.

I longed to be directed by the dark eyes and occasional words of my father. I longed to travel the repeated route through our house back and forth and back and forth, spiraling up the stairs with corn and wood, breaking piloncillo into the tub, holding the broken boat paddle and stirring slow roundness in the golden liquid. Even now, I travel the shapes of tejuino. When I find absent scribbles on the back of an old envelope or used paper, it is often filled with the pathways of tejuino – horizontal straight dark lines and vertical curls – as if somewhere in my self, I am still making my route in and out of the narrow house of my mother, up and down the stairs to the roof.

When I had nine years, I wrapped gorditas with manteca in a cloth. 'Don't worry, Mami,' I said. 'I will find him.' I longed to go to the streets, to sell to the world. Instead, I took Papi comida. Mami thought he walked and walked the streets. At night when Papi returned, she rubbed his legs. Squeezing his calf, pressing his sole, she would repeat, 'Ay, mí vida, so much walking, so much walking.'

He was easy to find. When I rounded the corner of Zuñiga y Zaragosa, there was Papi and his cart. The cart had two large spoke wheels and two long handles. It was a cart that a horse would pull behind him but that a person lifted and pushed in front of him. Papi sometimes walked through the neighborhoods, by the port, sometimes on the boardwalk, but mostly he parked on a slow shaded corner and waited.

The man had no sense for sales. Even so young I knew that. He was no Lazario kind of friendly salesman who laughed and called, '¡Tejuino!' No one bought tejuino for the pleasure of his conversation.

Yet women came. Mercedes, Beatriz, Esperanza. They came for free tejuino, for the dangerous dark quiet of his presence. The same quality that kept customers away attracted women.

Women have got no sense about men. Even so young I knew that.

Papi dipped his ladle into the bucket of tejuino. He turned his wrist and poured with the ladle close to the cup, then pulled the ladle high, making the tejuino stream slender from above. I was glad to see him pour fancy. I thought it might help business, and I thought how I might tell him that he should also smile.

The woman smiled and took the cup just as I came to the cart. She asked him how much.

Papi stared into her eyes without speaking, then slowly flipped one hand next to his face. 'Next time,' he said.

'Ten centavos,' I said.

Papi silenced me with dark eyes. 'Esperanza,' he called after the woman. 'Don't go.'

She smiled over her shoulder and raised her cup of tejuino.

Papi sat on the curb and unfolded the triangle of cloth. He frowned at the dark brown flecks of fat that soaked the gorditas, then bit into them and chewed with a too-full mouth while staring after Esperanza.

I sat beside him and asked, 'How many cups of tejuino this morning?'

Esperanza's roundness bounced beneath the blue flowers of her skirt, and Papi stared after her nalgas long after I could see them.

With ten years, I was permitted to soak the costal sack in water, lay it flat on the roof and spread the corn kernels evenly inside. Daily I checked to see if the tiny plants had pushed through the seeds to light so that my brothers and mother and aunt could grind the seeds and infant plants against stone.

With eleven years, I was allowed to blend the tejuino.

After measuring the water, ground corn and piloncillo into the metal tub, Papi stood opposite me, the tejuino bubbling between us, and spoke only to instruct. 'Now is time to blend all to smoothness.' He pointed with his cigarette in a moving circle that followed the edges of the vat.

I stood on the ends of my toes and pressed the paddle's side along the edges the way Mami scraped every drop of batter from the sides of a bowl.

'No. No. Nunca así.' He threw his cigarette to the roof and grabbed the paddle from my hands. 'You've waited too long. You've pressed too hard.'

Papi stirred a silent figure eight at the center of the liquid. I brought my open hand close to my face. A thick gray splinter of wood lay blurred deep inside my palm.

'Give me attention, hija.'

He stirred without effort and his voice became soft. Secretive. 'The paddle must never touch the vat once a crust has formed. Once the corn and sugar have hardened on the sides, they are lost to the rest.' His shoulder circled in a slow dance with himself. 'Hard crust will float separate in the liquid. Ruin its texture. Never blend.'

On the surface of the tejuino floated lumps of dark sugar, some crusted corn. I hoped he wouldn't notice. I hoped he would speak more words.

It was not long before I learned well to make the tejuino. I nurtured the corn kernels until they sprouted, then ground them fine. I stirred the gold liquid alone on the roof, sorting and blending my observations of the world – water, corn, piloncillo. I traced the washtub rim, looped three eights in the center without touching the sides or bottom. My father's rules were inside me. His dark eyes watched even when he was absent. *Blend to smoothness. Scrape. Too late. Crust has formed. Lost to the rest. Never blend. Ruin.*

When I had fourteen years, when my father, el macho, was strolling the boardwalk with a girlfriend and had not worked or returned home for days, I prepared the tejuino alone, and alone I took his cart to the streets. 1964. Women never did anything like that then.

I carried the full plastic tubs toward the pushcart chained in front of our house. Leaning away from the heavy bucket to balance its weight and to keep it from scraping the stairs, I paused every few steps in the route down from the roof and through the house to allow waves of liquid to calm so that they would not crest over the sides. I stood still, my head tilted as if listening for something, my neck and shoulder stretched and burning against the weight, fist clenched around the arced metal handle.

At the cart, I set the buckets down and squatted beside them. With elbows bent and an open hand on each bucket side, I pressed my palms into the plastic and straightened my legs to stand, holding the bucket before my chest. *You can do this*, I repeated to myself. *You're going to be okay.*

Abuelito saw me with the cart and yelled from his window, 'Ay, thief! Stop the hija! Stop the puta! Stop the escandalosa!'

Only Tía Chucha heard him, or only Chucha listened.

She came quickly to my side. 'Don't, Magda. This will change everything, Magdalena.' She spoke before regaining her breath. 'This may hurt you.'

95

Her scent was strong of bleach and lye soap. I carefully centered the last bucket over one of the holes cut to size in the bed of the cart, lowered the cylinder down into it, then set a wooden lid atop. Two buckets of tejuino – thirty liters filled but rarely sold.

Abuelito yelled, 'Face of an angel, guts of a demon. ¡Pocha! ¡Puta! Stop her!'

I kept both cart handles in tight fists and stared ahead. Already the muscles of my arms burned and I had just begun. 'I'm going, Tía.'

'Don't go, Chucha!' Abuelito had begun to cry for his daughter. 'Don't go. She had no bones,' he wailed.

He was speaking of Chucha. Telling himself her story. The story of her ruin.

'Chucha,' he muttered. 'I found her in the barn, and she had no bones.'

I pushed the cart forward into the street of the barrio.

Behind me, I could hear Chucha trying to calm Abuelito. 'Quiet, 'Apá. Calm yourself, 'Apá. I'll fix you something to eat.'

La Magda, the scandalous, walked the streets, the docks, the boardwalk, in short shorts and a sleeveless shirt tied under her breasts, long firm legs shining cinnamon in the sun, chichis quivering a lying promise beneath her blouse. I walked wherever there were men with ten centavos, yelling 'Tejuino!' tossing my black curls back to arch and expose my smooth neck, flashing my white teeth to laugh and mock, to flirt with fools. Each movement was an experiment, mimicry of women I had watched, the dress rehearsal after years of little rehearsals on the roof. With each tejuino sold, as I pinched the lime back and forth between my thumb and forefinger to squeeze the last drop over the drink, I took note of my methods – a sway of hip, a wink, a mock-harsh word – to know which had brought success.

It was a long golpe de calcetines. I beat my socks and earned more money in one day than the pendejitos, my father and brothers brought home in a total week.

When I rolled the cart to our house at the end of that day, Abuelito whispered to me in the dark. '¿Chucha?'

I walked past his window and did not answer.

He ripped the curtains from the windows, calling, '¡Puta! ¿Hija? ¡Puta!' not able to decide which I was.

Inside my house, I spilled the pesos into the lap of my mother. The heavy coins pooled in her skirt and sagged between her legs. I could hear Abuelito yelling himself ronca, his voice dying, growling every bad name there was for a woman. 'Ladrona. Malinchista. Llorona. Diablita y puta. Puta. Puta.' Thief. Traitor. Devil. Whore.

'Thank you, hija.' My mother spoke quietly under the noise of Abuelito. I kneeled beside her chair, and she scooped and held coins in her double palms.

Abuelito's insults filled the streets. We listened together.

'She will corrupt the angels with the naked flesh of her thighs!' His words were becoming forced and slow. 'Call the League of Decency.' Abuelito was near exhaustion. His words had lost their heart. 'Let them bind her breasts.'

I rested my cheek on Mami's soft thigh. Abuelito probably lay his cheek on the windowsill.

'Someone save her,' he said.

The street was quiet as if all the barrio were listening for Abuelito's next words.

My mother released the coins into her lap so close to my face that I could taste their scent of dirt and sweat and metal. She began to finger the cloth of my blouse, as if checking the quality. 'You must,' she said. 'You must, hija, apologize to your grandfather. And to your father. And to your brothers.'

Apologize. I pressed my cheek harder into her thighs, trying not to speak. *Apologize?* I wanted to pierce her dough thigh with one fingernail, to sink my teeth deep through flowered cotton through her flesh to the bone.

Once I allowed words to come from my lips, they would not stop. '*I* should apologize, Mami?' I pinched the cloth of her skirt between my fingers and began to flip it so that the coins bounced upward and jangled against each other. '*I* should?' I turned my head and spit on her floor.

Mami grabbed my wrist in hers and pushed her fingernails into me. 'You are not too old to beat, hija.' She shook my hand. 'But you are old enough to know respect. Old enough to know the way life is. Así es.'

'The way life is, Mami . . .' With all my strength I pressed against her grip to push my hand to her lap and rustle the coins. Her nails broke my skin, and pain gave me the acid for my words. 'We feel hunger while the lazy putos we call father and brothers and sons, huevones with balls so big they can't move, stand on corners waiting for customers to come to them, for the coins to jump into their pockets. We feel hunger while those cabrones give free tejuino to cualquier fulana with chichis?' I circled a finger in the coins and felt my cruelty rise. 'Where is Papi now?'

Mami released my wrist, and with her bloodied hand she slapped at my face, missed, slapped again to catch my cheek and eye.

I did not cry. 'Why is his cart free for me to take, Mami? Tell me where he is.'

She slapped at me twice hard again and stood. Coins spilled from her lap onto the floor, onto me. 'You will apologize,' she said. She hit my back again and again

98

with her open hand, repeating, 'You will apologize.' Then she sat down. A few coins still spun on their sides. 'That is the way life is.' Mami wrapped one open palm around her other fist, and I could see the pale smear of my blood between her fingers.

I left her seated, and slowly circled up the iron spiral to the roof. The metal stairs rattled with each step, and with each step, fury against the words of Mami pulsed through me. *Así es. Así es. Apologize.*

My family waited for my apology. I saw no reason to apologize for earning money. From his window, Abuelito cursed me, he cursed all women, and again and again, he told himself Chucha's story. Papi was a stiff threat of danger. When I descended the stairs or swept the roof, I was certain that I felt his desire to push me from behind. Mami averted her eyes when I entered the room as did my sisters and brothers and cousins.

Chucha spoke to me. She said, 'You have stirred a deep wound in your grandfather.' Then she too left me alone.

My family knew that I would apologize. They depended on it just as they depended on the ordinary – that night would turn to day – with indifference, without appreciation. But until I apologized, while I disturbed the workings of the ordinary world, they wanted nothing to do with me.

On the third night, I sat in the chair on the rooftop. Noisy barrio life continued below. I could let all the noise wash together like the static between the radio stations, or I could turn my head and tune to particular sounds and scents and from them, know the scene, the characters, the time of day.

'Ay, Conchita Lorena, huevona.' The nasal scolding of Señora León. The scent of guava. It must have been eight o'clock, Conchita León arriving with her

99

basket and her belly each half full of unsold guavas.

'No, Mami, No.' I heard Señora León slap her open palm on the calves of her daughter.

Jesus Trujillos sang off-key with Cuco Sánchez on the radio: 'Este corazón . . . This heart . . . is now dying.' I knew that he was leaning back on two legs of a chair against the front of his house, three Pacificos into his evening. 'Afternoon by afternoon . . .' he sang.

Flaco Afilado Bustillos returned from his day with the click and squeak of his mobile scissors/knife sharpener, a single bicycle tire he connected to a sharpening strap. He pushed and balanced it before him through the neighborhoods where women could pay, yelling, 'Scissors! Knives! Everything sharpened!' I had passed him on my day in the world with the tejuino cart.

Little Rito pulled the string on the toy he sold to tourists, making the awful chicken-squawk noise. After all day walking up and down the beach making that noise, the mendigo still pulled the string.

'Calla, ése, Rito,' Señora Hernández shouted from inside her house. She yelled for him to shut up that thing every evening.

Jesus began a different song: 'No vale la pena . . .'

Chucha's open hands rested on my shoulders. Without turning, I knew it was her. She wasn't there and then she was. The warmth of her palms against my skin. It brought all my sadness to the surface. Still, I sat without moving, in hope that she would not take her hands away.

'It is unfair,' I said.

'It is.'

Tears fell steady with the understanding. Deep and quiet.

Chucha kneeled at my knees and took my hands in hers.

Sitting in the chair, understanding weighted me. I had unsettled the nature of my family – its stinking unjust nature – and it was for me to restore the normal workings. The apology was not about tejuino or coins or rights, but about the order of our lives. My family needed my earnings and they demanded my apology. I would apologize, yet I knew they would quietly let me continue to sell tejuino. The only way to change anything was to appear to change nothing. I was the only one capable of putting things back in place. No one else would. Only I could.

Tía lay her head on my lap.

Then she lifted her head and pinched the mocos from my nose between her thumb and first knuckle and wiped it on her blouse. 'There is only one thing to do, Chupita.' And she said aloud what I knew I would do.

'I am sorry,' I said.

Five males sat in the dark front room around the table of Uncle Pelón and at the bedside of Grandfather. Five times I said, 'I am sorry.' Each time looking at the mouth of the relative.

'I am sorry, Abuelito.'

'Perdóname, Papi.'

'Lo siento, Tío.'

'I am sorry, Hermano . . .' down the line.

I was not sorry.

Each male nodded and accepted the expected – my apology – satisfied, casual, as if I had set an ordinary plate of beans and rice on the table before them – their tiresome daily due.

There was power in the apology, and the power increased each time I repeated 'I am sorry.' I was completely aware of all the rules and roles of my family and my community, of the full picture of my world.

101

The order of my family depended on my apology. I was in charge. *I* was.

I stood quiet beside the table after the apologies were complete, perhaps for too long, because my father dismissed me with a cutting glance.

'Yes, Papi,' I said, and walked to the back door and up the stairs to check the tejuino.

Father build a second cart soon after from money that Mami passed to him without mention of its source. I took the cart out most days after that, careful never to mention my earnings, careful to leave quietly in the early hours and quietly return with the dusk, careful so that no one had to weigh his need for my earnings against his own pride.

As he had always, Abuelito still invited me to sit on his bed when I visited. 'Siéntate, mi vida. Soy un hombre decente.'

Sit down, my life. I am a decent man.

He told me about the spirits that visited at his window in the night: his wife, young and güera, a fair-skinned beauty complaining that her eyelashes never grew back after the fever, that heaven's food lacked salt, that her neighbors smoked; his drowned son, Filiberto, who dripped ocean water on his bed and sang out of tune; and he spoke over my shoulder to the angel of death, sending her to the fucker place.

I knew our visit was over when he began to sing the song that became our ending song. He sang low and to himself, rocking from the waist and squeezing his three fat rolls together, staring at the end of his legs, and I would leave without his noticing.

> *¿Dónde estás, corazón?*
> *Ya no te oigo tu palpitar.*
> *Es tan grande el dolor y no puedo llorar.*

Quisiera llorar y no tengo más llanto
La quería tanto y se fue,
Para nunca volver.

Where are you, heart?
I cannot hear you beating.
The pain is so great, and I am unable to cry.
I would like to cry, but I have no more tears.
I loved her so and she left,
Never to return.

Inside his home, Abuelito knew me as his grand-daughter, but when he watched me from his window lift the two wooden bars of the cart, my triceps and nalgas tightening with the load, I was another to him.

'Ay, where are you going, mamacita?' he called through his window. My old grandfather bit down over his bottom lip and sucked through his teeth like a young pendejo on the prowl.

As I pushed the cart away from the house, he called after me just as the lusting construction laborers on the street did, '¡Qué buena estás, chiquitita!'

'Así es,' I mumbled to myself as I pushed the cart toward richer ground. 'Como la Santa Elena, cada día más buena.'

I am. Every day better.

*I light a candle to the puras tonterías of
sex . . .*

A boy scrubbed the marble alcove of El Cine Maravillo
with a handbrush, his bucket set to hold the front door
to the theater open.

Every day for more than a year I had passed the
theater with my tejuino cart. Pedro Infante was long
dead and I'd never even stepped inside the cine.

This was my chance.

'Oye, chico,' I called his attention above the
rhythmic whoosh of his brush. 'Do me the favor of
throwing an eye on my cart?' I held out to him a cup
of tejuino, and he sat where he had kneeled, set down
his brush and accepted my offering, the only male that
morning uninterested in my long bare legs.

I was swollen brava with my success selling tejuino
and took the chance, sliding sideways, sucking myself
small to pass through the opening to Cine Maravillo
without touching the quilted leather door. Inside,
marble, jeweled lights hanging from the high ceiling.
Dark-burgundy-carpeted stairs on each side of the
theater led to the balcony that I didn't know existed.
Stone wild animals set at each banister's head forbade
passage. I felt naked in my shorts with my blouse
tied to show my panzita, just as I might feel in the
cathedral. The air was cool and still, but smelled of

the rancid oils of popcorn and coconut candies and pork tortas.

I no longer felt so brava as I had before entering. I wished for a rebozo to cover myself, for a place to hide.

Straight before me was a glass case. Red jamaica and horchata bubbled in clear vats set atop it. Popcorn balls as big as grapefruits, cocadas set on oil-stained squares of brown paper. These sweets common to the streets and homes seemed more special inside the glass case among the boxed store candies.

'¿Señor Beltrán?' I called softly, sensing someone near. I had never used Gordo Chuy's apellido that way, had never spoken to his face. On the streets, the adults just called him Gordo Chuy.

'He's in the theater,' someone said.

A hand reached into the case to stack popcorn balls. A young man in a white shirt and stiff bow tie squatted behind the case, filling it for the day.

'Through those doors.' The young man pointed with his head.

I stood for a moment before a circle of glass in one of the double doors where the pimpled bato had pointed. A giant Pedro Infante in tones of brown lit a giant screen in an empty theater. Hundreds of seats scalloped before me. I pushed through the double doors and inched my way down the aisle, hypnotized between the dotted lines of tiny lights on either side of the walkway.

From a small square in the wall above and behind me, a bright beam shot straight toward the screen. The beam grew larger as it distanced from its source, like the beam from el farol at the docks.

On the screen, giant Infante was at a party. A pigeon-breasted old woman with round black-rimmed glasses and white braids wound on her head smoked a cigar. Señor Infante danced with one angry young woman

105

and another, and then walked alone through the people and sang, pinching cheeks and chins, pleasing some and annoying others. Women wore long old-fashioned dresses. Pedro Infante wore the clothes of vaqueros and mariachis, pants with silver buttons along the sides of each leg, a short jacket with buttons and braid at the borders, a white shirt, a loose cloth bow at the collar, a pistol in his holster. I stood mesmerized before the party.

Señor Infante sang, 'Dicen que Soy Mujeriego,' and I swayed to his song.

When Infante began the chorus, someone stood up from a seat just a little ahead of me in the center front of the theater. The man extended one arm just as Pedro Infante did, and sang the same words so loud that I could no longer hear the giant Infante. 'They say that I am a womanizer . . .' The silhouette darkened the screen and Gordo Chuy Beltrán stood amber and brown from the movie rays, singing the words of Infante, reflecting his every movement.

Everyone said that Gordo Chuy was crazy for Pedro Infante, but only now did I know what that meant. I sat and slumped in a seat so that Gordo Chuy would not see me.

Gordo sat down when the song was finished, but he continued to speak the words along with Infante. I felt afraid to leave and afraid to stay, but built my courage and stood to leave.

'We're closed,' Gordo yelled behind me.

'Si, señor.' I turned to face him. 'Excuse me.'

'What are you doing here?'

'Tejuino,' I said in a voice too weak. 'I came to see if you wanted to buy my tejuino.'

'The tejuino girl?' He laughed. 'The tejuino girl. Come watch the movie with me.'

'No, thank you.' I no longer wanted to see the giant Infante. 'My tejuino . . .'

'I'll buy all your tejuino.' His voice echoed in the empty theater.

Though my good sense did not trust this, I walked down the aisle.

'Come.' He waved his hand to call me forward.

I descended to his row and sidestepped my way toward Gordo Chuy, relieved that the seat beside him was filled with food. Popcorn balls, half-eaten tortas on stained brown papers, cocadas, boxes of chocolate nuez, tins of cajeta sat between us.

'I have seen you on the street,' he said. A large cloth napkin was tucked into the tight collar of his shirt like a baby's bib. The light of the movie pulsed on his shiny face. Gordo looked at me longer than I wanted and then turned his attention to the screen, pointing for me to watch also.

Gordo Chuy Beltrán moved his lips silently with the words of Infante. Then he forgot about me and began to speak aloud. '¿Lo ve, Abuelito? Solito se baja el agua.' Pedro Infante bragged to his grandmother of an easy conquest. The water will fall by itself. Chuy spoke with a mouth full of sticky popcorn, and crumbs spewed from his lips.

The sassy woman showed no interest in Pedro Infante – Pedro Infante who was also called Pedro in the movie: Pedro Dos Amantes. Leaning against the fireplace, the taffeta ruffle of her evening dress tracing her bosom, she mocked Pedro Dos Amantes, tossing words over one bare shoulder. 'A fast talker falls harder than a coconut,' she said. She teased him, laughed at him, refused to dance with him. Her name was Flor. La Señorita Flor. She was the one he wanted.

Gordo pulled the cloth napkin from his collar and

spread it on his lap. He stopped speaking with Pedro. I stared at the screen and counted the potential pesos of a full cart of tejuino. If I sold my whole cart – thirty liters – in the morning and filled it again for the afternoon – double the money. I felt Gordo Chuy touch my arm, but kept watching the screen, kept counting my money.

'Pssst,' he hissed, and when I turned to him, he pointed to the napkin in his lap. It was dark until a bright scene lit us and Gordo, as if waiting for the light, pulled the cloth from his lap and waved it above his head as if he were performing a magic trick. The cloth was one from any household – white, large enough to rap around tortillas, with some woman's colorful stitched flowers at its edges. The trick stood erect through the opening in Gordo Chuy's pants under his fat belly.

Cochino.

Gordo released the cloth in the air, grinned so big that his eyes squeezed almost shut and turned again to the screen. He closed his fist around his chile and squeezed himself, rotating like he was opening a jar.

Holding my breath high in my chest, I waited for Gordo Chuy Beltrán to do something dangerous. *Men are dangerous.* In the streets and alleys people talked about what men wanted girls to do. Touch it. Watch it. I had seen real sex in the alley years before. I waited for Chuy to demand something of me, but he did not. He watched Señor Infante, speaking Pedro's words aloud. He seemed to have forgotten me.

When I knew that he was not going to make me do anything, my curiosity dominated me. The only chile I'd seen close was Abuelito's, and Gordo's hard chile was entirely different from Abuelito's. While Abuelito was sleeping and his boxer shorts gaped open, I had stood over his cot and tilted my head just the right way to see inside. His limp chile lay on a thinning bed of dry gray moss. Unsatisifed with my view, I had taken my pencil and pushed apart the cloth of Abuelito's calzones to open the gap. There it lay. Very ugly, de veras, but harmless there sleeping between his legs. I thought I saw it move, but it was movement so subtle I could not be sure. The movement came from a slow swelling – like a baby slowly waking, still in a dream. It grew more and then rolled over in slow motion to lean against his other leg. It had a life of its own. It was not a full erection, but what I know now to be the half erection of a man already satisfied, or in the case of my abuelito, a man never to be satisfied again. I stepped back from the lolling movement of the chile and saw then the sneaking half-open eyes of Abuelito.

Señorita Flor on the movie screen sat at the public fountain with Pedro Dos Amantes and pulled the tassels of her sash through her fist again and again, caressing them like a pet. She teased Pedro Dos Amantes, told him in her way that he was not man enough for her.

I wanted to stay for my money, for the movie, to see what Chuy did with his chile. On the street, I'd heard talk of mocos – what spurts from men's chiles. The thought of seeing the mocos come out of Gordo's chile tightened my heart and turned my panza. I wanted to stay, to leave. *Men are dangerous.* I watched Pedro. He was after Flor with the bare shoulders.

Gordo was absorbed in the movie, the sassy Señorita Flor. His chile. He did not look at me. His closed fist moved up over the end of his chile, then down, stretching its outer casing back toward his legs. Pedro sat at the fountain with his sombrero tilted back on his head, describing the woman he would marry – rubia, güera, full-figured – unlike la Señorita Flor. Gordo

109

moved his fist slowly, as if he'd forgotten about his chile, as if he were absently scratching his belly.

He did not seem dangerous. Gordo Chuy was too content to be dangerous.

With my index finger, careful that only my finger-nail touched it, I moved half-eaten food aside to see if something fresh lay under it. Gordo showed no interest in me. Under the mess and waste left behind by Gordo Chuy Beltrán, I found a layer that he had not reached. A torta untouched, a popcorn ball still in its cellophane, a full box of peanuts. Watching Chuy, watching the movie, I covered the empty seat beside me with the cleanest papers and arranged food neatly over them, a picnic feast. I lifted the torta to my mouth and bit through the hollowed crust and into the thick pork al pastor. Dios mío. What flavor. I chewed slowly, meat and fat and chile savored in my mouth, and on the giant screen, while Señor Infante sat and watched, while Gordo Chuy watched, Señorita Flor danced.

Peanuts. Sweet popcorn. Dios mío.

In the hacienda of Doña Rosa, viuda de Dos Amantes, the pigeon-breasted, cigar-smoking, cowgirl grandmother of Pedro Dos Amantes, Señorita Flor admitted her love for Pedro. 'Birds trilled when he kissed me,' she told the abuelita.

Abuelita Doña Rosa advised Señorita Flor to be care-ful, not to be easy, to make Pedro work and wait, to make him suffer. 'Do not kiss him again,' she said. 'If you kiss him, you will fall.' She told Flor of her own Señor Dos Amantes, of their first kiss. 'También me hizo oir pajaritos.'

With my hunger satisfied, I ate slowly, sucking one by one the peanuts until they were soft, melting sweet popcorn kernels against the roof of my mouth. Making flavors last. I watched Chuy's chile in hand

110

and wondered if the mocos would come. Without looking at me, he pointed to the screen with his other hand and said, 'Careful not to miss this. He will win her.'

Flor sat at the teats of her milk cow and sang, 'Tengo una vaca lechera.' With the chorus, she pulled the long pink nipples, squeezing milk into the metal bucket and singing, 'Ti lín, ti lín. To lón, to lón.'

I cut my eyes to Chuy's lap. His movements were even and slow. Pedro swung off his white horse and strolled into the barn. 'How happy we'll be when we marry,' Chuy and Pedro sang.

Señorita Flor sang that Pedro was making illusions. She insulted him. He insulted her. 'Malcriada,' he sang. 'Grosero, borachín,' she sang, and then bent the long nipples upward toward Pedro Dos Amantes and squirted his face with milk – 'To lón, to lón.'

Scenes later, a bull chased Señorita Flor up a tree, and from the saddle of his white horse, Pedro lassoed the thick black neck of the animal, and Gordo Chuy spoke to me without turning his head. 'Say her words,' he said. 'Please.'

On the screen, Señorita Flor stood in the crook of a tree, 'Help me down,' she whimpered. 'But close your eyes.'

I did not speak her words.

I swallowed the soft popcorn and faced the screen.

'Mangos,' Pedro and Chuy said. 'Válgame Dios.' Pedro looked up Flor's dress.

'I hate you. I hate you. I hate you.' Señorita Flor squealed and threw apples from the tree.

I thought again to leave the food and money and movie behind to run up the aisle and out the leather doors, but Señorita Flor fell from the tree and Señor Infante held her unconscious in his arms and told her that he loved her and kissed her long on the mouth,

111

and when she opened her eyes, he and Chuy said, 'Forgive me, Flor, but you know that it was only to wake you.' And he kissed her again.

The movie continued. Bien padre. There was venganza from a lover scorned, and Pedro Infante who was Pedro Dos Amantes in the movie was accused of abandoning his daughter born out of marriage. And Señorita Flor left him. And Chuy beside me whispered again, 'Please. Say her part. The abuelita's this time. Just after she does. Just until you learn the words.'

I did not.

Chuy pulled the napkin from the back of the seat where it had landed before, covered his lap with it and closed his eyes, all the time speaking the words of Señor Infante.

Pedro's spurs jangled as he paced around Abuelita Rosa sitting on a velvet love seat.

'This is how you will learn to be a man. Responsible for your actions.' She sat on the edge of the little couch, holding the top of her cane in both fists and banged the cane's tip against the floor. 'I don't want a título de figurín. To be a man is to face the consequences of your dirty canalladas and not to hide them.'

Gordo Chuy spoke with Pedro. 'Abuelita, I have known all kinds of women, but none have hurt me like you.' The napkin bounced on Chuy's lap. His breath whistled in his nose, and he choked Pedro's words. 'You are the woman that I love more than any other. You, Abuelita. You have hurt me where most I hurt.' Gordo Chuy's chin dropped to his chest. He had deflated. Maybe he was dead. From disappointment. From Pedro's pain. From whatever went on beneath the napkin. Perhaps from mocos.

'Shut up, Pedro, so that I can dominate you,' I spoke softly the words that Abuelita Rose had yelled.

The screen lit Chuy's face, and I saw that his lips

112

moved with Pedro Infante's words. 'No, Abuelita. A man is dominated by affection, by passion.' Chuy lifted and tilted his head to better hear me. He opened his eyes to the screen.

'Lárgate, demonio,' I said in a stronger voice, though still it did not match the strength of Abuelita Rosa viuda de Dos Amantes.

Chuy answered with Señor Infante, his attention beaming toward Doña Rosa on the screen. 'It's okay, Abuelita. I'm leaving.'

Seeing Chuy revived, I faced the screen, and a beat after Abuelita spoke, I spoke. Pushing my words up and forward to join with Abuelita's and Pedro's and Gordo Chuy's on the giant screen, I said, 'No te vayas, Pedro. No te vayas.' And my voice cracked just as Abuelita Rosa's did.

Gordo Chuy held the top of the seat in front of him in both hands, leaned forward and turned to me. 'Don't worry,' he said. 'In the end, they will be happy again.'

We watched to the mero mero end, until Señorita Flor in her long wedding dress and Abuelita Rosa and Pedro Dos Amantes stood at the doors of the cathedral, until large letters and nonsense symbols and numbers filled the screen and it finally went dark. I was queasy and elated from the thought of mocos, from so much food, from seeing so many new things, from being in the movies.

After the last symbol had flashed and the screen was blank, Gordo Chuy turned to me in the darkness and said, 'How much for the tejuino?'

My mouth made more spit than it had for the sandwich. During the movie, I had calculated the numbers – servings of tejuino per liter ten times centavos – so that even though I didn't expect it, I was prepared for the impossible.

*   *   *

113

Gordo Chuy stood beside me in the cool alcove in front of his theater as the boy who had scrubbed the marble unloaded the tejuino. I fingered the bills in my pocket. Bills, not coins.

'Come back in two weeks,' Señor All-Business-Chuy said. 'Perhaps we'll watch a movie.' He twisted his pants with a hand on either side of his belt buckle and pulled them up over his big panza. 'Perhaps I'll buy your tejuino.'

The boy struggled past us with the tejuino bucket hugged to his chest. Gordo Chuy Beltrán stopped the boy, touching him lightly on the shoulder, then lifted the wooden lid, bent over the tejuino, closed his eyes, and inhaled deeply over the fermented liquid as if checking a simmering caldo.

I thank the generosity of the guilty,
the meanness of the moral . . .

Through the small arch in the glass above the counter
of the ticket booth, la gorda wife of Gordo Chuy
inspected the free passes given to me by her husband.
Her fingers, puffed above red nails, tore three joined
tickets from a faded green roll and pushed them part-
way through the small window. I pressed my own
fingers on the tail of tickets to slide them the rest of the
way through the opening, but the wife of Gordo Chuy
pressed them firmly, and before releasing them, her
eyes narrowed in concentration as if divining who
touched the other end. It stirred in my panza, the
nervous power of my secret: that I had shared food and
Infante with her husband, that I knew just how crazy
Gordo Chuy Beltrán was for Pedro Infante.

Chucha stood behind me at the Infante photographs,
Mami attached just behind her, one hand resting on
Chucha's shoulder.

'Gracias,' I said in a voice that was too high, a voice
that was not mine or the strict Abuelita Rosa's or the
sassy Flor's or the dignified Niña María's; it was not
the voice of any character whose role I had played.

'Señor Infante is very handsome?' Mami asked.

'He is güero and smooth-skinned with a dark, well-
groomed mustache,' Chucha answered. 'I have heard

his voice on a radio. They say he was a gentleman.'

'He looks very elegant?' Mami asked questions, though the answers she already knew.

'Very,' Chucha answered as if they'd never discussed this before.

'He holds her hand?' Mami evoked the picture.

'He does.'

Three green paper tickets I held in front of me between my thumb and fingers in full view so that no one could deny our entry. We were wearing our best dresses and rebozos, but through the eyes of la gorda wife of Gordo Chuy, they were not good enough. She watched with suspicion. Disdain. Pobres with tickets gratis. I pushed through the quilted leather door and stepped into the theater. Chucha and Mami followed close behind.

Chucha described everything. 'What high ceilings, hermana. Golden light fixtures hang from the ceiling. People I don't recognize.'

'Ay, sí.' Mami said at each observation as if her sister's details brought everything into focus.

This was my first visit to the theater during regular hours. I led Mami and Chucha through the close crowd toward the case of candy and tortas.

'Jamaica juice bubbling and horchata and a box with palomitas pressing against the glass. Smell the popcorn, hermana?'

'Ay, sí.'

With money from Gordo Chuy himself, I bought popcorn and horchata and jamaica and coconut macaroons, sweet popcorn balls.

I pushed through the double doors to the theater, my aunt and mother attached behind.

Inside the theater, heads were silhouetted above the hundreds of seats that I had only seen empty. The lights were dim, but brighter than during Gordo's

116

viewings, and I felt exposed in the light, anxious to find a seat and disappear into the crowd, anxious for the movie to begin.

'So many soft chairs,' Chucha said.

I led them to seats in the theater's center.

'Up on the platform, look at the curtain, hermana. Hundred of yards of burgundy velvet like at the confessional box in the cathedral.'

'I see it.'

The darkness increased and Tía and Mami were silent. Mothers shushed and threatened children. Someone whistled.

Gordo Chuy walked onto the stage and stood in front of the rich fabric. 'Damas y caballeros . . .' He raised both short arms out to the audience. The standing microphone squealed.

'¡Cácaro!' someone yelled.

Gordo Chuy continued, 'As part of the Teatlán's talent month, before presenting our feature film, I introduce Señorita Teatlán.' One stiff arm extended to his side as if directing traffic.

Gloria Guerrero Trujillo appeared from the side of the stage, walking straight-back stiff smiling to the standing microphone and kissed the cheek of her mother's cousin, Gordo Chuy. She wore a sequined strapless gown and a rhinestone crown.

'Who is that young woman?' Mami asked.

'La reina de Teatlán,' Chucha whispered.

'What will you sing for us, hija?' Gordo Chuy asked.

'"La Paloma,"' she answered.

Each bent forward from the waist when they spoke to place their lips inches from the microphone.

Gordo backed away from the queen, and a recording of the introduction to her song scratched through the speakers before she began to sing.

*   *   *

117

For almost two years I had come twice a month to the Cine Maravillo, but never had I seen any movie without Pedro Infante, and always I had been one of two in the audience.

The Wednesday-morning ritual that had become Gordo Chuy's and mine developed without explanation. Only repetition. Casually, Gordo Chuy and I had reached agreement and formed a partnership with unspoken rules of ritual. Two Wednesdays each month, I entered the dark theater and found the same seat with popcorn balls, chocolates, peanuts, pork tortas and cocadas piled high. 'Buenos días,' Chuy said into a microphone in the projection room, and I raised one arm and waved before sitting beside the food.

Gordo would speak the title of that morning's movie – *Cuando Habla el Corazón* or *La Oveja Negra* or cualquiera – and then introduce the film from press releases he had memorized. 'Much action, a beautiful girl, many songs and a hero more valiant and loyal than any, a hero who knows how to defend his love but also knows the value of true friendship.' Gordo Chuy turned on the projector and hurried down the aisle to his seat on the other side of the food.

That is how we began.

Each Wednesday was much like our first movie together. Gordo Chuy spoke the lines with Pedro Infante. Sometimes he mumbled them from his seat, other times he stood, inspired to sing or to recite in full emotion and voice. Gordo was Pedro Infante who was Pedro Dos Amantes, the scoundrel, or Pedro Infante who was Tizoc the simple, wise Indian, he was the good son of the abusive father, the outlaw. And when Gordo Chuy wanted me to speak the special lines, he always whispered, 'Psst, these lines, Magdalenita. These.'

I learned to be a close echo behind the voice of

118

an actress, and I became the strict abuelita, the self-sacrificing mother, the scornful beauty, the spirited artist, helpless. I had seen twenty-seven Pedro Infante films. Six times I had seen *Dicen que Soy Mujeriego*; four times, *La Oveja Negra*; five times, *Tizoc: Amor Indio*. Ours was a fair exchange: money for thirty liters of tejuino. Food and movies for a leading lady who asked no questions.

Gordo Chuy did not always touch his chile, but when he did, he was delighted by it. He never asked me to touch it, though he enjoyed my audience. When his chile first erected – the only time he showed it to me – he whipped the cloth from his lap and waved it in celebration, smiling to reveal his pride and trick just as he had done that first day. So pleased. I never saw his chile squirt mocos, though when I scolded him or begged him to stay, when I sent him to the devil or wept at his death, Chuy Pedro Infante sometimes quieted and choked his lines.

Halfway through each film, Gordo Chuy went to the projector room to change the reel of film, and that is when I gathered food from the center seat in a large tortilla towel brought from Mami's kitchen and tied the top in a safe knot. Food for my family.

Men are not always dangerous; ritual is sometimes simple.

The queen of Teatlán's voice was strong. '*Coooca roooo cacooo*, paloma . . .' She sang the chorus just enough off-key to make my shoulders rise. Chuy stood at the stage edge with his hands clasped behind his suit jacket – the proud cousin, the good citizen.

Señorita Teatlán finished her song. Gordo Chuy joined her, and the two walked off stage, la reina clutching Chuy's arm, Gordo Chuy clutching the microphone stand.

119

The velvet curtains parted. Trumpets sounded. 'Cima Films Presenta' in cursive on the big screen. Church bells.

María Felix stood at the top steps of the cathedral with her new husband, bien bonita in her wedding gown, bien brava with one hand on her hip. 'Viva la Revolución!' she yelled to the crowds in the church-yard. 'Que mueren Los Pelones!'

'She's not very feminine,' Chucha said.

'No. Mal hablada,' Mami agreed.

'But very pretty. Who is she?' Chucha asked.

Chucha and Mami had never seen posters or photos of this movie outside.

'María Felix,' I answered. 'She's called Valentina in this movie.'

This was the first time I had entered the theater with a ticket, Mami and Chucha's first movie.

The screen filled with a smuggler pendejo with a parrot called Don Perfidio on his shoulder selling guns to the Pelones, then returned to the wedding night of Valentina. Her husband was shot right off the balcony by the same soldiers. At the funeral, the preacher called her a 'victima de inoportunidad,' she dressed in black and veil.

'Dead before they even kissed,' Chucha said.

'Sí,' Mami answered, 'widow and virgin.'

'Who knows, hermana.'

María Felix/Valentina spoke in a deep voice. She walked the streets of her pueblo with her head high and her back straight, both fists set just above her hips at her small waist. A man called, 'Ay, yah, yay, mamacita' to her in the streets, and TRAZ, chingazos, she struck him down.

'La más macha,' a man in the audience yelled out.

'Knocked him right to the ground, sister,' Chucha said.

'Dios mío,' Mami answered.

Two little boys ran into the aisle and acted out the scene, one striking the other to the sticky floor.

'Where is Señor Infante? The señorita behind the bars?' Chucha asked.

'They are not in this movie, Tía.' I was selfish not to bring them to see their friends from Gordo Chuy's photos. 'Eat your palomitas,' I said.

Valentina on the screen sent her suitors away. None was man enough. None was revolutionary enough. 'I want a real man, head to toe,' she said. 'De los pelos a los patos.'

'Here I am,' a man behind us yelled.

'She has more huevos than you,' a voice answered from the front rows.

The smuggler with the parrot kidnapped Valentina to pay the debt to a man who had saved his life. He made her ride backwards on her horse. She made that look easy. Like dancing, always the woman backwards. Valentina fought the smuggler all across the countryside, her brothers and father in pursuit.

'He has robbed her, sister,' Chucha said as if informing Mami of a death.

'Mi pésame.' Mami took Chucha's hand in hers.

When the smuggler left Valentina chained to a tree, he returned to find her rotating his parrot on a stick over a small fire. She watched him suck the leg bone clean, her eyes pulsing wider, just the way they had when the her lips had come close to the lips of her husband on her wedding night. The smuggler complimented Valentina – what a good hunter, what a good cook – before realizing who he was eating. '¿Don Perfidio?' He held the bird leg before him and looked over his shoulder to the branch of the small tree where he had left his pet.

Valentina smiled.

121

'Don Perfidio.' The smuggler blinked at the small drumstick in his hand. 'Ay, Don Perfidio.' So sad the smuggler. 'That bird was like a father to me,' he said.

Valentina laughed a man's HA HA HA, slapped her knee and tore a bird leg off the roasted corpse for herself. She held it by its bony end, pointing it at the smuggler.

'Then you are without a father and a mother,' she said, 'because you've never had a mother.'

Just after she said that, just when she brought Don Perfidio to her lips, the film jumped and started, voices garbled and then froze with the giant face of María Felix tearing the flesh with her teeth from the roasted bird.

'¡Cácaro! ¡Cácaro!' The audience yelled to fix the film.

Mami and Chucha had become quiet.

The movie jolted back into action and María Felix chewed the flesh of Don Perfidio and smiled meanness. Everything on the screen happened just as it did in the Pedro Infante movies, nothing like life in mí barrio. The smuggler and Valentina fell in love, he became a revolutionary too, and in the end, after she was safe again in her father's home, the smuggler/revolutionary robbed Valentina for himself.

Again her family pursued, but in the last scene, María Felix, this time chained to the smuggler turned revolutionary, called down from the soft leaf bedding in their cave, 'Ya no nos sigan.' The words stretched long from the cave down the rocky trails. Don't follow us anymore. 'Ya no.' And ya no echoed down the valley to her brothers and her smiling father.

The audience applauded and stood to leave.

The movie had ended. Names rolled over the screen. Music. I stood to leave, but then decided to do what was not part of the Wednesday ritual: alone I went to study the bright beam that shot straight toward the screen.

'I'll be back in a little moment,' I said.

I squeezed toward the screen and stage of the theater, moving against a strong tide of children and parents and novios pushing up the aisle toward the lobby without sympathy for a body moving in the opposite direction. I made myself small and sidestepped slowly toward the stage.

'Con permiso. Con per. Con per,' I said down the aisle.

The beam was even more beautiful from below. Flecks of dust squirmed in the light, and I could see that it was not one solid blast that fired out from the projection room, but so many thin beams, all that burst and drove forward from the small square at the back of the theater, all focused to create some part of the same picture.

'Psst,' someone called to me from the curtain's edge. 'Magdalenita.' Gordo Chuy looked over one shoulder and then back down at me.

'Abuelita,' he said. 'I have known all kinds of women, but none have hurt me like you.'

I stared up at Chuy's panza for a moment before I knew that it was his favorite movie, *Dicen que Soy Mujeriego*, that inspired his words.

Pendejo.

'You are the woman that I love more than any other. You, Abuelita. You have hurt me where most I hurt,' he continued.

Our ritual was out of place and time. I felt that just beneath my skin. I looked over my shoulder and whispered Abuelita Rosa's response, 'Shut up, Pedro, so that I can dominate you.'

Behind Gordo Chuy, large letters and nonsense symbols and numbers filled the screen.

Light pulsed on Chuy's face. He was lost in Pedro Dos Amantes. 'No, Abuelita. A man is dominated by affection, by passion.'

'Lárgate, demonio,' I said without ganas, turned and walked up the aisle and away from Chuy.

'It's okay, Abuelita. I'm leaving.' Gordo Chuy increased his volume.

I did not say Abuelita Rosa's words, 'No te vayas, Pedro. No te vayas.' But I heard them inside me, and they swelled in my throat to be spoken aloud, not because of their meaning, but because they were the lines that came next.

As I neared Mami and Chucha, alone in the theater, I could hear their words, sparse with long pauses between responses. They thoughtfully discussed Valentina, the same way they would talk about something that had happened to a neighbor in our barrio.

'He robbed her for love?' Mami asked.

'Sí, in the end he did.'

Mami sat quiet still holding Chucha's hand. 'That's not the way it is,' she said.

'No, hermana,' Chucha answered. 'That's not the way.'

We walked in a silent chain – me, Mami, Chucha. At the end of the aisle, I turned to see the empty seats, scalloped again. Gordo Chuy was still standing on the stage, but he was not alone. Beside him stood his fat wife. Only the lights at the stage floor shone, illuminating both panzas from underneath the same way children lit and shadowed their faces holding bright candles under chins to frighten themselves.

I led Mami and Chucha through the quilted leather doors into the lobby past the candy torta counter and into the familiar marble alcove and the soft evening.

Mami broke the silence. '¿Eres tú, hermana?'

'Soy yo,' her sister answered.

124

The next Wednesday, Gordo Chuy and I watched *Tizoc: Amor Indio* for the sixth time. I was a fiery and dignified María Felix/Niña María, and Gordo Chuy was an honest and passionate Pedro Infante/Indio Tizoc.

Tizoc, dressed in the simple white muslin pants and shirt of the Indians of Oaxaca, stood in the small chapel at the feet of the statue of La Virgin María. He trotted on his toes from one statue to another, robbing flowers from saints, from Jesus, placing them at Her feet. Holding his wide-brimmed hat over his huevos, his face lifted to Her, he sang, 'Madrecita, dame tu amor, Y pedir a nuestro Señor, Perdonarme por favor, Que mire tus ojos. Ave María.'

Tizoc had come to look into Her eyes. She stood high above him. Fair and benevolent.

El Indio Tizoc brought hides to trade at the tienda and saw for the first time the güera daughter of the wealthy estancia owner from Mexico City. So much she resembled the fair statue of La Virgin in the chapel that Tizoc thought La Virgincita had come to him in the flesh.

He ran away.

He called her Niña María.

He fell in love with her.

Niña María met Tizoc in the mountain meadows. She knelt beside the dark Indian and took his hand, told him that he was a philosopher, that he was a poet who saw and knew things that others could not know.

'You are a good man, Tizoc,' I said with María Felix.

'No, Niña,' Gordo and Pedro answered. 'Good is the earth and the sun and the water of the river, like Tata Dios.'

A fiesta.

A fight.

Much longing.

Because la Niña María did not know the traditions of El Indio Tizoc, she gave him her handkerchief to wipe his bleeding wound and told him that she cared about him. Without knowing, she had promised to marry herself with him. She had given Tizoc her pañuelo.

While the priest on the screen explained Niña María's error, I sipped horchata and watched Chuy from the corner of my eye.

Niña María attempted to explain her mistake to Tizoc, but he interrupted her with a simple song he had written: 'I love you more than my eyes, more than my eyes I love you.' Chuy and Pedro Infante sang the song of Tizoc. Chuy and Pedro Infante proclaimed their love for the Niña María. 'Te quiero más que mis ojos, Más que mis ojos te quiero.'

Niña María cried.

Tizoc grabbed a stone and struck his own face with it.

'¡Tizoc! What are you doing?' I said with María Felix, and there was another voice that blended with the Niña María's and mine. I turned to see a large woman standing in the aisle behind us.

'I am hitting the man who made you cry,' Chuy said. Blood on the face of Tizoc.

'Por Dios Santo, Tizoc, don't be bárbaro!' the woman answered with María Felix in perfect sync. 'It is not you who made me cry, but the affection I feel for you . . .'

I was silent.

María Felix leaned to touch the bleeding mouth of Tizoc. 'Lend me the handkerchief that I gave you,' the gorda and María Felix said.

Chuy still was too deep into the movie to notice. 'No, Niña,' he said. 'This handkerchief is not for my blood.'

Chuy gripped the edge of the cloth napkin that covered his lap in his fist.

'Understand things, Tizoc,' the gorda answered in a hard and angry voice that cut against María Felix's tenderness.

'Magdalenita?' Gordo Chuy turned his face to me. '¿Qué pasó?'

With a small motion of my head, I signaled for him to look behind us. 'What?' he asked. 'We were doing so well.'

The gorda wife of Gordo Chuy stepped down the aisle into shadowed view.

'Do not give so much importance to the pañuelo,' she said long after María had spoken those lines.

'Virtudes,' Gordo Chuy said as if naming a ghost.

'Jesus,' she answered.

I had never heard anyone call Gordo Chuy by his birth name.

On the screen, Niña María spoke gently to Tizoc.

'Tizoc.' Chuy's wife nodded her head to her husband as if greeting someone she has not seen for much time. 'Niña María.' She nodded to me.

'Señora Beltrán,' I nodded.

The voices of the movie, of Niña María and Tizoc, tore my nerves.

'Adulterer,' the señora said to Chuy in the same even tone of introduction.

'No, Virtudes. No, mí amor.'

'Puta,' she said to me.

Chuy stood and his napkin with stray popcorn and chocolates spilled to the floor.

'Sit down,' his wife said.

Chuy sidestepped in front of the food seat.

'Sit down, Jesus!' Her voice was loud and wild.

Chuy sat and zipped his pants.

'How long have you been having filthy relations

with this corriente?' Señora de Beltrán spoke from the darkness.

'No, it's not like that, Virtudes,' he said. 'I buy her tejuino.'

'I know what you do.'

I stood and stepped to the aisle. 'Con permiso, Señor Beltrán,' I said. Señora de Beltrán did not step out of my way. 'Con permiso, señora,' I said, but she did not move, and though I squeezed myself small, I still brushed against her soft bosom and belly as I tried to escape.

She took both my shoulders in her hands as if I were a relative she did not recognize. Her eyes wandered without vergüenza over my face and breasts and long legs, and as she registered all my attributes, all she had lost or never had, Señora de Beltrán's face contorted and I braced myself for her to spit in my face, but she did not. She released me and backed a step away to collapse on the arm of the aisle seat.

The señora's arms hung limp aside her enorme bosom and she spoke to the floor, to herself. 'And if I asked you to forget me?' she said just behind María Felix.

I turned from her and walked up the aisle toward the lobby.

'Without you, Tizoc dies,' only Pedro Infante said.

As I pushed against the leather doors, I realized that Gordo Chuy had not yet paid me for the tejuino.

An owl called from a tree above Tizoc and Niña María, and Tizoc/Pedro Infante said, 'A técolote. Do you want to know what his song means?'

With my back to the leather, I could still hear the movie. Niña María said, 'Keep the handkerchief.'

And Tizoc asked, 'La Niña repents her love of the Indian Tizoc?'

'No, Tizoc,' she answered, and I knew that Niña María rose from the log and walked away.

Days later, on my father's favorite corner, Zuñiga y Zaragosa, I squeezed a lime between my thumb and foreknuckle over the cup of tejuino that Don Gilberto had purchased.

Old Don Gilberto's spine curved to a painful C, a malady that naturally placed his feet a meter away while his head nearly rested on my chichis.

'Just one more lime, chula.' His head bobbed as he spoke.

He asked for more lime, for a straw, for a piece of brown paper – anything to keep his eyes over my breast.

'Ya, viejito,' I said, lifted the handles of my cart, and rolled away from the disgusting Don Gilberto.

'Wait,' someone said behind me. 'One more, please.'

Señora Virtudes de Beltrán walked calmly to the side of my cart. She was dressed the way wealthy women dressed for society luncheon. Her best. Her lips, pressed together and pouted forward slightly in a pose that women use to look in mirrors, shone a red that matched perfectly her nails. Her hair was fresh-from-the-parlor-stiff.

She was a different Virtudes than the wounded one I had faced in the cine. Señora Virtudes de Beltrán was composed, society ready, rehearsed.

'One tejuino, please,' she said as if she did not recognize me.

I ladled a full paper cup. When I reached for a lime wedge with my fingers, the gorda wife of Gordo Chuy creased her brow. 'No, No,' she said quickly. 'No lime. Please.'

I handed her the cup as she handed me coins. Señora

de Beltrán stood looking at me without speaking, the tejuino still raised in front of her, a green shiny purse hanging from the wrist of the hand that held the paper cup. Her skin was fairest güera and the plumpness of her face pushed wrinkles smooth. She had the fine fair skin that Mexicans think so beautiful, and an attractive woman may have survived beneath fifty kilos.

'Anything else?' I asked.

Señora de Beltrán smiled. 'Oh, yes,' she said. And she opened the shining green purse that matched her shining green pumps and the foliage on the fabric of her dress.

'Yes, there is this.' She handed me an envelope. 'Magdalenita.' Señora de Beltrán pressured each syllable of my name with a sneer, then turned and walked away with the cup of tejuino poised at her side. As she passed an open gutter, she relaxed her grip to let the paper cup and tejuino drop.

The envelope contained one sheet of stationery from the League of Decency.

Señorita Guadalupe Magdalena Molina Vásquez:
It has been brought to the attention of La Liga de Decencia that Guadalupe Magdalena Molina Vásquez of Calle Viva Villa Street 67 in Barrio Rincón has consistently behaved in a manner that threatens the moral standard of Teatlán. While selling her wares in the streets of our city, Señorita Molina has been witnessed in indecent attire and heard using profanity and sexual innuendo.

The League of Decency will not condone or tolerate such public displays.

The League of Decency will not tolerate moral offenses to our community.

We officially charge Guadalupe Magdalena Molina Vásquez with public indecency: indecent dress, public profanity and lewd public behavior. She is a threat to the moral characters of our children and our community.

> *Signed,*
> *Concerned citizens and members of the League of Decency*
> *Ma. Teresa Trujillo de Sandía, presidente*
> *Gabriela Montebella de Hernández, vice presidente*
> *Virtudes Hernández de Beltrán, secretaria*

I looked up from the notice to see who might be watching. La gorda was no where in my sight. But someone watched.

I could feel it.

I had seen members of the league. Learned to recognize the gold pin worn on a collar or over the bosom. I had heard stories of them. Still, I had never thought them real – the League of Decency – not real to my life. Once on my way to the mercado I had stopped in front of the glass window of Donné's, a favorite luncheon place on the zócolo, and watched the heavy-breasted, rich women who sat at a long table. Their plates were mounded with food, their hands weighted with gold, their faces thick with makeup.

Abuelito often threatened to call them, the League of Decency. My brother, Rigoberto, told a story of when the League had tried to stop Carnaval, how señoras had come to the malecón in the night with banners against debauchery and drunkenness and adultery, and how the crowds had pushed and swarmed around the women, as Carnaval crowds will, taking special care to rub close against the righteous. Men in the swarm reached between the legs of the decent señoras and squeezed their cositas; they fondled the breasts or

131

licked the necks and pinched the nipples of league members. There is no way to know where the hands come from in such a crowd.

I wondered which woman in that group had lost her husband to the madness of Carnaval. What personal story was behind that pendejada demonstration. Chucha had told me. Philosophy and politics, she said, are always personal. So that even then, even so young, I knew. That what people called issues – those mad causes of the religious and the political – were about something else, something private. No one, not virgin or even saint, was motivated to act unless something large – hunger, loss – touched and threatened their own bien estar.

The sadness of Señora de Beltrán had converted to an angry cause.

I did not retire my cart. I did not change my dress. And I could feel the eyes watching.

Watching.

Over the next weeks, PUTA was painted in red on the side of my tejuino cart. PUTA on the front of my parents' house. PUTA with an arrow pointing toward my house was on the house of Tía Chucha and Tío Pelón. It is what Abuelito screamed from his window as I pushed the repainted cart away from the house: '¡Puta!'

'What is this about?' Chucha asked.

'What have you done?' Mami asked.

They called me whore. The word was said, the word was painted, and that was all the proof needed. Neighbors whispered. 'Ésa es más puta que las gallenas.' More whore than the chicken hens. Abuelito ranted, '¡Puta! ¡Diabla! ¡Vieja hedionda!' Papi would not look at me or speak to me and his rage was just beneath his skin, threatening to burst through the pores.

132

*   *   *

There was no place safe, and each day, early in the
morning, I painted over PUTA on our house and on
the cart, and imagined the ladies coming in the night
with their matching purses and pumps, their gold Liga
pins and nalgonas gleaming in the moonlight, but I
knew that they hired others to perform their tasks. A
league member would not come to a barrio so poor and
dangerous.

Each day I lifted the handles of my cart and rolled it
along the streets, I called 'Tejuino' like always, but
men smelled the difference in me. The smelled my
weak spirit, they sensed there was no fire in my play,
and for the first time, at the end of each day, I did what
was before unthinkable: I spilled unsold tejuino into
the trash heap at the beginning of our barrio just three
blocks from my house.

I parked my cart on Papi's favorite corner of Zuñiga
y Zaragosa and waited for customers to come.

Leaning against the stone wall, I watched a loud
three-wheeled motorcycle cart with a wood-plank
bed over its back two wheels pull to the curb. I had
thought to one day buy a similar motor cart for my
father when he could no longer push the tejuino. The
quiet boy who cleaned Chuy's alcove, the one who
unloaded tejuino from my cart each week, who performed all the low tasks of Cine Maravillo, left the
loud motor running, walked to the cart bed, and
untied a bucket.

I had never known his name. '¿Qué tal?' I greeted
him.

He paused at his cart and said, 'It is my job. I do
what I am told,' then walked to my tejuino, lifted his
bucket and tipped it. As if alive, bloody intestines slid
into my vats and onto the ground below, spattering
my legs.

'I apologize.' The quiet boy climbed back on his motor cart and engaged its gears. 'Nothing personal.'

I returned to Zuñiga y Zaragosa three days later with a clean cart, stubborn to reclaim my father's corner. Midday, during the hours of comida, I sat on the curb eating beans and tortilla. As soon as the motor cart turned the corner, I ran to my cart where I kept the broken handle of a boat paddle. The quiet boy would suffer for his job.

He stopped meters from my cart and held his hands in the air. 'No. No,' he said. 'Believe me, I have nothing destructive.'

He slowly dismounted and walked toward me.

'Don't you come any closer, hijo de la chingada, or los Beltranes y la pinche Liga will find your intestines fried on that motor.'

He held a white envelope above his head. 'No. This is from the señor. *Señor* Beltrán.'

I pounded the wood against the curb, and the quiet boy dropped the envelope on the sidewalk and ran to his cart.

The envelope contained a short note: 'I am three blocks away at Calle Mariposa 100. Meet me now.'

Pinche Chuy.

Since the League had threatened me, three times I had been to the back door of Cine Maravillo, three times I had knocked on Gordo Chuy's office door, and three times he had pretended not to be there.

Coward.

I parked my cart in front of a dirty window with peeling letters that had once said LOCKSMITH, CALLE MARIPOSA 100, and pushed the door open.

Chuy stood from behind a metal desk. Boxes of keys were neatly stacked to one side, and dark rectangles of metal shone up from the dust in a scattered pattern on the desktop. 'Magda,' he said, 'I cleaned a seat for you.' He extended an open palm to the chair on the other side of the desk.

Seeing Chuy stand there, clean and round in his suit, sad in his eyes, I hoped. Perhaps he had come to my defense.

'You wanted to see me?' I said.

'Magda,' he began. Gordo Chuy sat, leaning forward, pressing his palms together, and the springs of the office chair squeaked slowly. His white shirt cuffs grayed from the desktop dirt. 'Magdalenita,' he began again.

'Magdalena,' I corrected him.

He watched the thumbs of his interlaced fingers, placing one on top and then the other. 'A man of my position . . .' He cleared his throat. 'A man with so much to lose . . . the theater . . . my reputation . . .' He ducked each thumb inside its fist and looked up.

'Magda, have you told anyone about our time together?'

I had not. Even so young I knew not to endanger what we had, and I knew that our private ritual could never be explained.

'Tell what, Señor Beltrán?' I drew a circle in the dust. He was silent.

'That you touch your chile beneath a towel while pretending to be the mujeriego or the abused good son? That you needed me to be your grandmother or a sassy woman who scorns you or . . . ?'

Our ritual was safe and normal only when we were alone in the cine on Wednesday mornings. Sex cannot bear public eye.

'Have I told anyone that you are a coward who allows his wife to torment me and my family?'

'Have you?' Chuy stared at his fists.

'No. I have not told anyone.' I drew a slow careful bolt of lightning in the dust. 'But I may.'

I would not. Even so young, I knew that I would be blamed. Puta, diabla. That women were at fault. And even so young, I knew to keep Chuy unsure.

'I am sorry for your trouble,' he said. 'I have missed you. I have missed your talent.' Gordo Chuy pulled a thick envelope from a drawer. 'Now that the league is involved, there is nothing that will stop them.'

We had never spoken so many words that were our own.

'There are things, Magda, that I cannot risk, things that you cannot understand – reputation, property . . .' He pressed the envelope under his fingertips. 'Responsibilities you cannot understand – family, civic duty.' His voice had no power.

'Civic duty to spill animal entrails over my livelihood? Responsibility to paint PUTA on the home of my mother?'

'Magda, I am not responsible for . . .'

'Not responsible for your wife? Have you once spoken with her or her Liga of their actions? Have you asked her to cease?'

Gordo Chuy pushed the envelope across the desk. 'Inside there is money to help you. I cannot protect you. There is too much for me to lose. You should leave Teatlán for while.'

In the moment when my fingers touched the paper, something expanded inside me, a pressure that paralyzed every organ. For one full moment, I hoped the Gordo Chuy might rise in character to become the proud macho, el Indio Tizoc. But the Chuy before me was an ordinary man. Weak and civilized. He would not strike himself in the face with a rock to punish himself for hurting me; he would not raise a hand to anyone; he would not even speak words to help me.

I tucked the envelope inside my shorts, stood, pushing the chair back with my bare knees, and turned to the door. A key of gold can open any door, they say.

'You are the woman that I love more than any other. You, Abuelita. You have hurt me where most I hurt.' Gordo Chuy spoke those favorite lines from *Dicen que Soy Mujeriego* to my back, and in that moment, I felt as old as Abuelita Rosa, but not as wise.

I skipped to the words that came at the end of that scene. 'Lárgate, demonio,' I said as I had six times before. Get out of here, devil. But it was I who stepped through the doorway into the hot, damp air of midday.

*I thank these long legs and even my small
breasts, because even if the Mexican men
say they don't like the thin flaquitas, they
do, and the American men do. I thank the
instinct that guides me, that tells me los
pasos a seguir . . .*

I tell Isabel stories I should not tell. Stories she should
hear. The story of the señora who thought she was
moral, the story of a rich rancher man who thought he
loved me, of a rich widow woman who thought
she didn't, of a generous marijuanero: the stories of
stepping-stones in my path.

With almost eighteen years, and money set aside from
tejuino, money from the envelope of Gordo Chuy, I left
Teatlán for the first time on an Estrella Roja bus for
Tijuana. No one knew.

The tejuino cart no longer served me. The sassy
Magdalena in short shorts who worked the streets
selling tejuino when she had fourteen years and fifteen
years became a threat to society with her sixteen years.
And a larger threat with every year.

On the bus I wore the sweet flower dress of my sister,
Rosa. Her best one. I borrowed it and told myself that
I would send it back along with a better one.

I'm sorry, Rosa.

138

I left the quiet of Chucha's rooftop.

Dream with the angels, Tía Chucha.

On our table under a bowl of moist salt, I left a note to my mother that was addressed to all. I could sense the moment when my mother rubbed the paper between her fingers, pressed it against the lens of her glasses and then handed it to the closest eyes so that someone might read the note aloud to her.

Forgive me, Mami.

All my bills and coins sat heavy in a pouch pinned inside my bra. The prisoner's pesos were marked each with a red dot of fingernail polish so that I would not spend my good luck unless I had to. Not every tejuino coin was shared with my family. I'm no saint. Papi had once stood behind me as I stirred the tejuino. 'Are you long of nails, hija?' he had asked.

You cannot steal what is yours.

'No, 'Apa.' I had answered without facing him, the bolsa of damp bills pressed to my heart.

Daily I worked the tejuino cart, daily I hid a few coins in different places – under stones in the alley, behind loose bricks of old walls – monthly I converted coins to bills and tucked them inside a bolsa in my bra. And with the envelope of Chuy . . .

In the waiting place of the bus station, I recognized no one. Travelers sat on wooden benches that groaned as bodies rose or settled. Boxes tied with brown twine, cracked vinyl suitcases secured with rope or belts, nylon shopping bags were at the feet of those who waited. Under my arm, I pressed a bundle: my tejuino short shorts and short blouse, a skirt, a cloth to clean myself, a pen to write – all wrapped in the cloth of a masa sack.

Adiós, Papi.

Abuelito.

To my sisters and brothers, I silently spoke my

wishes and good-byes. Besos to Kikita. Strength to Rosa, already married to her pendejo. A la chingada with hermano Rigoberto. A tree born crooked can never be straightened.

I sat so that I could watch a wall clock, a yellowed face in a black circle with Saint Valentine arrows pointing to black numbers. 8:05.

The travelers seemed tired. A man slept on the floor curled on his side with a nylon jacket pulled over his shoulders. His socks had fallen down inside the heels of his shoes, and his tight heel tendons were dried pale.

An announcer called bus numbers in nasal static over a speaker. My attention held tight the two spending pesos in my sister's dress pocket, my bundle pressed against my side, the ticket in my fist, the clock. My street-smart mouth was closed. Silent.

After each announcement, people pulled their boxes, their children, their own bodies from the bench and moved weighted toward the door. Each time the door opened, the noise and stench of straining revved engines and burning oil blasted through.

At 8:20, I walked through the door and into the loud stink. Eight buses were parked parallel to each other with engines running. I showed my ticket to a man in a brown uniform. He pointed. Under the engine roar, I thought I could hear the smooth leather soles of my red flats pull away from the adhesive asphalt. Down the line of buses, I showed my ticket again, and another man tapped the radiator grate of a bus to motion for me to get on.

Two nights and two days later, the bus pulled into the Tijuana station. With my bundle clutched to my chest like a schoolgirl's books, I stood from my seat, bumping the child who slept sweaty against my shoulder, squeezed through the aisle of passengers unloading their boxes and stepped down from the bus. Without stopping to use the toilet or to ask a question, I walked. Everything in my young body urged me to move forward, to focus through and past the station chaos to a better place, to my new life.

Some streets later, my pace slowed, my focus softened and my belly spoke the truth of its emptiness. A handwritten sign advertised comida corrida, and I stepped into the small alcove, sat at a table and secured the bundle between my feet.

'Buenas,' a woman said as she bent to relight the burners beneath large metal pots.

It was late for comida and the tables, all but mine, were empty.

The woman soon stood over me with a plate in one hand and a tortilla basket in the other.

'¿Comida?' She set the plate on the sticky oilcloth before I had answered, and returned to the open corner that was the kitchen.

The last serving of the day was mounded lukewarm and over-cooked on the plate before me – sopa seca, carne asada, frijoles, a basket of tortillas – and though the sopa seca was sticky and the meat tough, it was cheap and the first real meal I had eaten since leaving Teatlán.

'From where do you come, hija?' The woman reached her arm deep inside a stained and dented pot to scrape the remains of the food with her hand.

'Teatlán, Sinaloa, señora.' It gave me pleasure to do something so ordinary as push a fork full of beans creamy with manteca against a rolled tortilla; to hear the detached and easy voice of a woman working; to hear my own lies affirmed in my own voice. I told her that I was going to be a dancer, that I would send money to my family, maybe buy them a car, have a nice place of my own.

141

'Already you have a job, hija?' she asked.

A man holding a sack of sugar on one shoulder stepped into the niche and the cook raised her chin to him in greeting. She pointed to me with her head. 'A friend from Teatlán,' she introduced me. 'My husband.' She nodded from me to him.

'Eugenio de Dios, para servirle.' He set the heavy sack on the floor by his wife.

I nodded and spoke with a mouth too full. 'Magdalena Molina Vásquez.'

The young me thought it decent that this couple would be kind to me, that they would offer to rent me a room, I thought it nice that Eugenio de Dios would insist that he accompany me to find a relatively safe job dancing at Club Leona. Remembering Tijuana with all I know now, I understand what a verdadero milagro it is that I survived. A true miracle. Thank La Lupa. Thank cheap bad food. Thank los angeles Carmen and Eugenio de Dios.

Tijuana was filled with dancing jobs. Dancing meant many things that I had not imagined. There was dancing without clothes, dancing over the faces of drunk men who inserted cash and coins into the cosita. Dancing I would not perform. I learned this all after I was go-go dancing in Club Leona. Listening to the gossip of dancers and bartenders and busboys, I heard the stories: of private curtained lap-dance rooms, of a woman from Club Tigre who inserted a shot glass full of tequila into her cosita, danced her hip circles, then took the glass out still full and drank it; of men who squeezed limón halves over the cositas of putas to check for sores that would burn from the acid; of a woman who danced around the giant chile of a donkey; of a dancer violated by a customer on the stage while the audience applauded. Some of the dancers at

Club Leona carried a potent powder to dissolve into the drinks of aggressive customers.

Pure luck, pure ignorance and grace – pure something – protected me.

Then I did not know just how grateful to be. I did not know enough to have fear.

But I knew shame. Sometimes, dancing and sweating in color and tassels through blinking lights safe in the go-go cage above the crowd at Club Leona, I would imagine my mother fingering the good-bye note slowly, pretending she could read it, moving her lips the way she did, crying, crying at her table. Chucha standing behind Mami's chair. I imagined the warm weight of Chucha's open palms pressing on the top of Mami's shoulders. I had left Teatlán knowing that I must escape, hoping I could earn more if I went to Tijuana, telling myself it was for my family too, that maybe I would earn enough to heal Mami, to buy them a house, more food. Good doctors. Lies to help me flee. I danced through the shame.

Every night I celebrated and grieved. I safely burned my soul on that platform. Dancing.

I had learned to dance on rooftops. The dance grounds were not far from our house, and with my mother and my brothers and my sisters, I would stand on our flat roof and listen to the distant music. My sister, Rosa, taught me los pasos a seguir. She held me in her arms and we danced, damp faces together cheek to cheek, circling the rebar, the tejuino pot, ducking the clothesline, until she tired from holding me and set me on my feet so that we continued to shuffle circles cheek to belly.

When I had nine years, my sister, Rosa, took me to her friend's rooftop that overlooked the dance grounds.

From surrounding ranchitos and barrios, people came by bus and car and foot. To dance. Each man was given a strip of white cloth to tie on his upper arm after he paid the five centavos. Only men paid. On the rooftop, men who couldn't afford a white band, women and girls too young or shy to attend, danced, and from that roof's edge, my sister and I watched the dancers below, an ocean of cowboy hats and dark heads rocking, bobbing, spinning beneath us, couples curved and tangled, to the tuba and clarinets, the churning of the Sinaloense. So many people pressed together so tightly. They danced to the song 'No Volveré,' and looking down on the people, I wanted to dive from the roof like the beach boys from the cliffs over the ocean, just like them to arch my back and then point myself like an arrow into the dancers, to swim in the middle of elbows and knees, to disappear into the music.

When I was old enough, I attended every Saturday dance, and people commented on my dancing. Some said I was without shame. Some said I could be professional.

For a time in Tijuana, I was every man's dream. Dancing beyond reach on a platform. Eighteen years old. 1968. Working in the Club Leona, dancing in color and tassels through blinking lights, safe in the go-go cage above the crowd. Not just Saturday, but all the nights, I danced. Some people think I was a prostitute when I tell them I worked there. Menos mal, I was a virgin.

I noticed a boy in the audience every night for a week. He was timid but guapo, such a pretty güero, and he always removed his hat. From his dress I knew that he was from the North of Mexico; from his manners, that he was bien educado. I knew he had fallen for me, knew he had money.

After one week, roses. Every night, roses. Not the wilting cheap ones sold by the pobrecitos in the streets, but the big long-stem roses like I had never seen before – roses delivered in long white boxes tied with crimson bows from the fancy flower shops like in the United States of America.

Miguel Angel was crazy for my dance and my coastal spirit, but when he learned that I was a virgin, he became obsessed. Lost. The virgin wild woman: every pendejito's dream. Week after week, he sat in the audience at a table at my feet. During the day he took me across the border and bought me clothes, to Disneylandia; at night he watched me dance until he fatigued, and then he left behind his driver, Armando, to keep me safe until closing, to walk me to my room in the house of Carmen and Eugenio de Dios.

He was a man. Like any other man, my Miguel Angel Aguilar Llosa. I thank him for showing me the United States of America, for my fancy table manners.

The first time Miguel Angel took me across the border into the United States of America, I spent three hours in Sears and Roebuck.

'Sears and Roebuck! Stop!' I pressed my face to the car window glass. I had once pulled a Sears and Roebuck catalogue from a trash pile, and for years after that, I had wandered through America in its pages.

Once inside the store, I opened the lid of washing machines and polished the chrome of tools with my skirt. Department by department, I caressed goods. Lingerie, bicycles, women's clothing.

'This is a cheap store,' Miguel Angel insisted. 'This is nothing, Magda.'

I pressed my fingertips on the glass case of costume jewelry.

'She would like to see that one,' Miguel translated.

He pulled me away from jewelry, but I escaped into women's clothing. I had never seen so many new things. I was mute. I cried.

Miguel Angel took me by the hand out of the store. I was drunk, obsessed. I wanted everything for myself, for Mami, for Tía, for my family.

In the car he said, 'That is a department store, Magda. And the goods are not quality.' He smiled as he turned and backed away from Sears and Roebuck. A private joke with himself.

He wanted me then. My ignorance, my bravura, my weakness, my cheap taste. Everything. In the courting time, all is charmed. He wanted to teach me, to save me, to have me.

Miguel Angel drove to a small shop where the women of his family bought their clothes. A tall, thin woman in pale hose and what I know now to be a linen shift greeted Miguel Angel, walking toward him with open arms. 'Miguel Angel,' she said and took his hand in both of hers. That is all I understood. She made pleasant sounds of lilt and coo.

Miguel Angel turned and touched my shoulder. 'Señora Gates is the owner of this store,' he said in Spanish. 'She has very good taste.'

I was not so brava in that store. There were no men to charm but Miguel Angel, I did not understand English, and the owner's tight smile did not match the judgment and disdain in her eyes. Against her, my new best flowered dress clung to my body and cheapened, my skin darkened.

Inside the dressing room, I fingered the material. Brought it close to my face. Each piece was perfumed with the store's special scent. I imagined the woman misting the racks after closing, her neck stretched tall, her chin at a slight haughty tilt. Step, pause, mist; step, pause, mist – hers would be the pace of a bride walking

146

the cathedral aisle. Thick beige carpet pushed beneath my toes and filled my arch. Naked on a satin brocade chair surrounded by mirrors, I examined the price tags. Dios mio. Each piece of clothing was ten times more than it had been in Sears. It took my breath away. The cost of one pair of silk panties would have fed my family for a month.

The owner knocked twice and opened the door, and I pulled the loose clothes to cover my bare self. 'Momentito,' I said.

She stood and spoke gibberish, raising her eyebrows and a dark blue linen shift much like the one she wore, then hung it on the back of the door. She held a string of pearls at the neck of the dress, set stockings atop shoes gently on the carpet.

'Magda,' Miguel Angel called through the door. 'You have already clothes muy sexy. Maybe you might try some things a little more conservative. For church, Magda. To meet my family.'

I was trying to think how to sell these clothes and buy the others at Sears. To save the difference.

When dressed in the navy linen, the pearls, the pale hose, the suede pumps, I walked out and smoothed the material against my thighs before standing tall. I stood before my pale counterpart, dressed just the same. Touching my shoulders, she turned me to face the large mirror.

'Muy elegante,' the woman attempted Spanish.

'Así es.' Miguel Angel sat in a satin chair with his legs crossed. 'Una verdadera lady.'

In the reflection, I saw myself, the shop owner, Miguel Angel on his throne. I matched my stance to the Señora Gates', stretching my neck long and filling my chest high so that the pearls rose against my dark collarbones.

*   *   *

147

Of the night I gave my virginity to Miguel Angel Aguilar Llosa, I remember only pieces. Alone in the family house in Tijuana, except for servants sent to their quarters, except for the veladores in the night, I remember bougainvillea born fuchsia from the balconies, the first meeting of crystal glasses, the shadow of the watchman each time he crossed the terrace, circling the house. This house was limpiacita, so clean it made me suck my breath with happiness. In the shining saltillo floor tiles, I could see the marbled reflection of my own brown legs.

The act itself, after all the tenderness and generosity of courtship, was a quick and uncontrolled pounding that crashed my bones.

'¿Católica? ¿Católica?' he panted.

Miguel Angel, lost to me, hard thrusting, kept saying, 'Are you Catholic?' as if he could not climax until I said yes.

I wondered if the diaphragm his American doctor had given me would tear, if I would tear as he drove himself into me.

I remembered a very pregnant woman I had seen standing in front of a wedding shop, holding the hand of a dirty barefoot child in each of hers so that the children's arms stretched taut above their heads.

'¿Católica?'

That woman's hair had hung limp and oily; her children were smeared with dirt, their feet callused thick. But she had stood quiet for a long moment, staring into the window where a pale mannequin wore yards, yards of white wedding lace.

'Are you Catholic?' Miguel Angel thrust. '¿Católica?'

He already knew, the pendejo.

'Yes,' I screamed.

He thought I screamed from pleasure and passion. He climaxed.

I screamed from impatience. From pain. For the pregnant woman. 'Yes.'

They shook their heads and waited for me to fall – dancers, bartenders, dishwashers, the manager of Club Leona. The story was an old one for them: a girl gives herself to a rich man before marriage; he disappears. El conquistador.

Soy tonta, pero no pendeja.

Like Guadalupe, except for the sex, I was la conquistadora.

I gave Miguel Angel Aguilar Llosa my virginity, but I would not be conquered. One taste, and his appetite exploded. For one night he was el conquistador, but for every day after, I made him question his victory. With every day, Miguel Angel became more possessive, more protective and proud for his newly deflowered wild woman. He called it love.

Never question the power of desire.

Soon after, I married with Miguel Angel Aguilar Llosa in the judge's office in Tijuana and left my go-go platform to live with my new husband and his family on their ranch in Northern Mexico. Monterrey.

There is not a bigger place in this world. We flew in a small plane to the airstrip on the ranch. The pilot circled the boundaries of the land.

'Chingada' was all I said, looking down on the miles of wild nothing.

'Don't say that so much here, Magda,' Miguel Angel instructed.

Twenty barrio houses would fit into the ranch house. Ten inside the barn. Inside the home, the furniture was for giants. Thick slab wood tables and chairs. Fruit bowls big enough to sit in. Most of the furniture would not have fit through the door of any house I had seen before. Before, when to me a cornfield was a ranch and gruel was a chocolate drink. Before, when rich to me meant to own any house, to own anything, to eat meat and vegetables and dessert every day. To be clean.

Los Aguilares owned land that took four days to ride horseback one end to the other. They owned cows they could not find, people they did not know.

La viuda Socorro Llosa de Aguilar descended the stairs to meet me without hurry. Her hand floated smoothly just above the curved wood rail. She was the age of my mother, but their similarities stopped there. Rich can afford youth.

'Mami.' Miguel's head lifted to her. He held his hat in one hand and my elbow in the other.

'Hijo.' The señora smiled down at him. Her voice was low and calm, her pace even. She paused on the bottom stair so that when he stepped to her, their height was the same. Miguel Angel's mother held his face in both her hands for a moment before kissing the air on either side of his cheeks and then resting her lips on his forehead. Long enough to ignore me. Not long enough to be rude.

'Mami,' he said, gently taking her hands from his face, holding them inside his. 'I introduce you . . .' Miguel Angel said, stepping aside to reveal me, '. . . to my wife.'

She smiled, but did not step down toward me. I stepped to her and extended my hand, and after a pause unnoticed by her son, she brought her hand to mine.

'Encantada, señora,' I said. 'Your home is so beautiful and I am happy to be here and to know you and I hope that . . .'

'Yes,' she interrupted. 'Igualmente.' She removed

150

her hand from mine and hooked her arm into Miguel Angel's.

Later I would learn. La señora would teach me. By example and in our daily lessons. *A lady does not babble.* 'Know this, Magdalena. If you notice too many words coming from your mouth, recognize that either you are mistakenly too weak or too aggressive.' And she imitated my strained voice in our first meeting.

When I remember my first marriage, it is not Miguel Angel that comes to my thoughts, but the widow Socorro Llosa de Aguilar. Miguel Angel was a man. Like any other man. But la señora. From her, I learned so much. The cool dignity of Monterrey. Quiet power.

The mother of Miguel Angel left us alone in the early heat of our marriage, when Miguel Angel wanted only to stay with me, to show me his world. His ranch. His life. His sex. I don't need to say that his mother was not so pleased with me, but she knew that a pair of tits pulls harder than two horse carts. She knew that with her son, at least in the beginning, I had the power.

She waited.

But even as la señora waited, she began her slow reclamation of her son. In our private moments together, I learned the cold power of manners. She never raised her voice, never said any words that if repeated would sound mean. She spoke to me in gesture and tone. When she addressed me formally, it was a mockery; when she used the familiar form, it was as if she spoke to a servant; and when my husband began to settle into the contentment and dull routine of married life, she made her first strike.

One night, as Miguel Angel buttoned his pajamas, he said, 'Magdalena, I've been thinking about the money we send to your family. I think it is best not to continue to shame your family with charity.'

I knew that these words were not his. They were the precise and formal style of his mother.

'Gifts are less embarrassing than money,' he continued.

Have you no mind of your own? No huevos? I screamed in my head, but even then, even so young, I knew not to demean my man aloud.

'Mami says that she will be happy to make up appropriate packages to send.'

I had seen her packages. La señora would send Swiss chocolate, silk scarves, soaps three to the flowered box to my family who had no meat, no chayote, no fruit. It mortified me to imagine Chucha with an expensive scarf draped around her worn dress and Mami lifting perfumed soap to her nose when I knew that their bellies were empty.

La viuda Socorro Llosa de Aguilar was a religious woman. On the ranch near the house, there was a private stone chapel built by the bisabuelo of Miguel Angel. Padre Alejo came every two weeks on horseback to give private mass and receive confession. He stayed for dinner and the night.

La señora went every morning to chapel to pray.

She took me there one morning.

At the steps of the chapel, she pulled a fine black lace from her coat pocket and draped my head and shoulders silently. I followed her down the short, narrow aisle, touching the end of each pew, counting them – one, two, three – to find my way in the darkness. At the altar, la señora struck a long match and touched it to the wicks of votive candles; light pulsed on the bloody wounds of Jesus. She kneeled before Him, before Mary, before porcelain saints. And I kneeled beside her. From her prayers, familiar words escaped to my ears – humildemente . . . nuestro Señor

. . . la merced . . . los pecados. A leather pad cushioned our knees. The floors were worn stone.

'My blessed son,' I thought I heard her say. Then 'Guide him to the light of truth.' I kept my head bowed. La señora prayed for me to hear. 'Open his eyes to the deceit of the woman he calls wife . . .' she said. 'A matrimony outside the church . . . not married in your eyes. Forgive him. Forgive her. Forgive me . . .' La señora returned to her quiet private prayers.

I bit my lower lip and tried to silence my rapid breath, mumbled pretend prayers, leaking words of my mother – Niñito Jesus . . . Santísimo mío . . . la niña de tus ojos – gathering my thoughts.

The prayer spoken aloud for Señora de Aguilar was the most sinful of my life. I prayed with hate and fury, I prayed lies. 'Viuda . . . Generous . . . Charity . . .' I said for her ears. I breathed deeply to slow my voice and began again. 'Bless this kind woman who from the very pureness of her heart shares her wealth,' I said. 'La señora de Aguilar . . . Generosity . . . my family . . . only the best chocolate . . . my undeserving self . . . forgive me.'

We returned to the house in silence. 'Thank you for accompanying me.' La señora removed her veil and handed it to the servant waiting just inside her house.

Inside the confines of our suite, I paced, cried and cursed, bit my fist. I wanted to tear into the cushions of our sofa and chairs, overturn the antique desk, break the banisters of our bed and burn them in the fireplace, flood the bathtub. Living in a suite that was fancier than any place I had known, fancy as that hotel suite on the Coronado Island where we spent the honeymoon, I felt no triumph. No gain.

But the war had begun.

Though I did not return to pray with Miguel Angel's mother, daily I returned to the chapel alone. Cara de beato uñas de gato. For two weeks, I kneeled every afternoon at the altar in the dark cool chapel before candles and saints and blood of Christ.

Face of the pious, claws of a cat.

Padre Alejo arrived one morning. I waited for him at the stable.

'Will you take my confession, Padre?' I cast my eyes to the hooves of his horse.

From his saddle, Padre Alejo leaned over and touched the top of my head. 'Of course.'

That afternoon in the darkness of the confessional, kneeling on hard wood with my elbows pressed against the shelf, I spoke through the cane to his shadow. 'Forgive me, Father, for I have sinned. It has been four years since my last confession.' My voice caught in my throat. 'I have succumbed to the sexual advances of a woman,' I said. 'And I am ashamed.'

'Go on, hija,' he said.

'For the food in my belly and the luxury of his house that I do not deserve, I am grateful.'

'Speak your sin, hija.'

'She comes to my room when the men are away.' I covered my eyes with both hands.

'Go on, hija.' Padre Alejo's lips moved closer to the screen that separated us.

'When she takes my face in her long, elegant fingers . . .' The story took me. The story knew no fear. 'The musk of her perfume. The smoothness of her voice. Her skin against mine.' I closed my eyes. Sucked slow breath through my open mouth and filled my lungs.

'Yes, hija.'

I leaned forward so that my lips almost touched the cane screen. 'Every nerve of my skin waits for the slow click of my door latch. She enters my room and moves like a cat toward me. She speaks no words, Padre. There is no need for words.'

'Why do you not deny her, hija?' He sat back against the close wall of the confessional.

I whispered to draw him close again. 'She unbuttons my blouse, padre, while her eyes burn love and hate pure into mine, and with the soft tips of her fingers, she traces every contour – neck, clavicle, belly – as if she has found something lost long ago, as if she has found something all new, and my soul rises to meet her touch. I cannot deny her.'

I told Padre Alejo of the hungry tongue, the gentle tongue, a gentle palm. Inside my thighs, circling my cosita. Nibbling fire and fear and shame.

'And I am afraid, Padre.'

'For your sins, hija?' he asked. His face was shadowed and checkered through the screen and I could not read his reactions.

'Claro, I fear God, padre, but more I fear my husband. La señora . . .' I corrected myself. '. . . the woman is not always gentle in her passion.' Again I brought both hands to cover my face, but it was to cool my own rising sex.

'Continue, Magdalena.'

I spoke to my open hands on my lap. 'Yesterday, in a moment so heated, she dug her fingernails deep into the meat of my back. I have eight scratches long and scabbed. And one fingernail is broken, lodged close to my spine in a place I cannot reach. What if my Miguel Angel sees this?'

Padre Alejo sighed long and far. He turned from me so that I could see his silhouette and prescribed ten Ave Marías and Our Fathers. 'Things left to God are well avenged,' he said as the shutter of his window closed, muffling *avenged*.

Perhaps the padre did not believe me, but I had convinced myself. I had lost truth and self in the story and detail. The telling had aroused in my young body a yearning that threatened to eat me from the inside out. With the telling, I remembered all I longed for. That tenderness. That passion.

And it stirred me crazy in my heart.

For two weeks, I had planned revenge on the mother of Miguel Angel. It had been a rumbling in my tripe, a need to make her pay – for her wealth and arrogance, for the hunger of my family. But I felt no satisfaction.

At comida that day, Padre Alejo sat to the right of la señora seated at the head of the table; I, much further down the long plank table, past brothers and cousins, beside my husband.

'You are kind to travel so far to see us.' La señora Aguilar nodded as she spoke and poured cantaloupe water into Padre Alejo's glass, her eyes on the liquid.

'It is my duty and my pleasure,' he said.

Their casual words were stiff with meaning and secrecy, and my thighs clenched under the table at the thought that Padre Alejo might have betrayed my confession.

'And it is good to find that all is well in a pious household,' he continued.

La señora poured herself a pastel drink and raised her glass slightly before sipping. 'This family will always strive to make that true.' And though she spoke to Padre Alejo, her gaze was to me.

Padre Alejo kept his eyes cast to his carne asada y arroz.

La señora raised her glass and her chin to all. 'To our dear padre,' she said.

We raised our glasses and repeated her words,' To our dear padre.'

156

Padre Alejo looked up from his plate, smiled and nodded humbly, and then, bless him, lost his grace for only a small moment when he recognized one short broken fingernail on the expensive manicured hand wrapped around la señora's glass.

La señora de Aguilar knocked three times on the door of my suite, and when I opened, she stood with two books, silverware and china stacked on a tray. 'Will you invite me in?' she asked.

I always called her Señora de Aguilar, and she did not encourage a name more intimate.

La señora placed the tray on the table of our sitting area and stood beside the small couch. 'Will you ask me to sit?'

'Please,' I said, still holding the doorknob.

She corrected me. 'Please, señora, won't you sit down? Make yourself comfortable.'

I understood that she instructed me, and I repeated her words, 'Yes, please, señora, won't you sit down.' But I feared that she had come to punish me, and maybe in her manner, she had.

Señora de Aguilar sat at the edge of the couch with her knees pressed together and her ankles crossed and tucked slightly to one side, and I mirrored her position on the couch opposite her.

'You,' she said, 'are a clever young woman.'

Even now, her mean compliment is one I value.

La señora leaned forward, arranging plates, bowls, forks, spoons, knives, glasses. 'If you are to advance, as I know you desire,' she said, 'and if you are to represent this family for even the briefest time . . .' She pulled a handkerchief from her bosom. '. . . you must learn the art of appearances and attain a certain grace.' Holding the wineglass to light, she pressed soft linen to lint. 'At the art of deception, you are quite gifted.'

She held the stem of the wine goblet before her and lightly thumped the glass before setting it in its place. 'But you cannot imitate what you have never viewed.'

I sat opposite la señora while she pretended to serve and eat a full meal. She spoke only to explain what was unclear in her acting. 'Do not begin to eat until your hostess has finished her first bite.' She gracefully unfolded her napkin and spread it across her lap.

After pretend port and fruit, she silently stacked her table setting. At the door, she said, 'I will leave the items on the tray so that you can practice. Sessions will be daily at four o'clock. Read this book.' She pointed to the worn cover of *Doña Perfecta* that she had left on the table. 'Tomorrow you will read aloud, and I will correct your diction. You will not embarrass this family.'

In our daily sessions, I learned from her the manners and mannerisms of the rich. Manners are manners, one might say. But rich etiquette holds its head high. Rich etiquette demands the belief that you expect and deserve all that you have, all you will have.

La señora taught me about books. *Doña Perfecta* was a book for tontas, but she brought me others. On the ranch of wild nothing, I read Sor Juana Inés de la Cruz. '. . . Which is more to blame? . . . la que peca por la paga o él que paga por pecar? – she who sins for pay, or he who pays for sin?' And Pablo Neruda. '. . . it would be delicious . . . to kill a nun with a blow to the ear . . . it would be beautiful . . . to go through streets with a green knife giving yells until I die of cold.' La poesía was less sensible than dichos, but sometimes more beautiful. And sometimes more potent. Words that rumbled beneath my reason.

She taught me which words in Spanish would reveal my background. My favorites – *chingada, cabrón, pendejo* – I already knew not to use. Of others, I was unaware. 'Do not fill silence with *este*,' she told me. 'Silence is to gather thoughts. In silence there is power.'

I have taught my daughter, Martina. No *ums* or *estes* in her speech. I will teach Isabel the same.

'No sentence begins with *pues*.' Señora de Aguilar was composed and fierce.

'In public, hands have no reason to be near one's face or hair.'

'In the United States of America, flush your toilet paper.'

La señora did not converse with me, she lectured, and I learned early that the price of interrupting her was a look that deflated me to childhood.

After two weeks of lessons, la señora entered my suite without greeting and sat in her usual place on the couch. She wore a low-cut leotard and nylon wrap skirt – not her usual style – clothes that I now know she must have worn to exercise in the privacy of her own suite. Her body was taut, slender, much like my own.

When I took my seat before her, she allowed her eyes to inspect me from head slowly to toe, and then she spoke. 'Consider, Magda, what you want to evoke.' She fingered folded cloths brought for that day's lesson. 'Lust or longing?'

La señora paused to allow her question its proper consideration.

I sat on the edge of the love seat with my ankles tucked together to one side, my spine erect, my hands relaxed in my lap as she had taught me in the posture and grace lessons.

'El hombre es fuego, la mujer, estopa. Llega el diablo y sopla.' La señora leaned forward from the waist and blew into my face.

159

Man is fire, woman, kindling. The devil arrives and blows.

'A smart woman controls the fire,' she said. 'You, Magda, let the fire blaze so that the fuel is used quickly. Smarter is the slow burn. The slow smolder.'

I smiled pleasantly and nodded as she had taught me in the art-of-conversation lesson.

'The short, tight skirts you like to wear . . . they stir men, no doubt, but they stir a lust that is too immediate, sometimes dangerous. And short lived.' She unfolded cloth and snapped it like laundry, open full between us. 'But a well-draped breast . . . contours shadowed behind Irish linen . . .' La señora draped a whisper of white cloth from one shoulder to the opposite side of her waist and her contours became secrets almost revealed.

I removed my shoes, pulled my ankles tight to one side of my hips, pushed back against the love seat's soft pillows and nestled my toes between the seat cushions. This lesson was not to be in posture, not to be in public grace. I hugged a small silk cushion to my lap.

After smoothing the linen over the couch back, she pulled a silk free, draping it loosely between her shoulders like the curtains above our bedroom windows. 'The quiver of a breast beneath silk,' she said, 'or the smooth skin high on one's chest. When carefully presented, these are things that will stir a man deeply, things that can permeate his soul and create a longing.'

As she spoke, the señora rested curved fingertips in the well of her own beautiful clavicle. I mirrored her movements without intention.

'Yes,' she said. 'Much longer lasting, that yearning.'

La señora was lost in her thoughts for a moment.

'Or the back of the neck, Magda.' She bent her head forward to stretch the back of her own neck long and sweep light hair that had escaped from her bun. 'In Japan, I have read, this is a part of a woman most highly regarded. Women called geishas who are educated in the art of womanhood paint two white Vs down each neck cord.' She traced the path of the imagined white makeup pausing at the tip of each V. La señora slowly rolled her neck to one side, still caressing her nape with a gentle hand, and the return of her dark gaze melted my marrow. 'Let me see your hair pulled up away from your neck.'

I gathered my hair from my shoulders to the top of my head, turned my back to the señora, and dropped my head forward as she had.

'Yes,' she said. 'Yes, that would do.'

I thought I felt her fingertips waiting just above my nape's skin. I felt the gnawing, a knot that would not relax, weeping threatened just beneath my control.

Again, I remembered what I longed for.

And again, it stirred me crazy in my heart.

We never became friends, la señora and I. Light a candle to a good enemy. She was the mother of Miguel Angel and she was determined to save him from me. I would be the same if a man deceived my Martina. But during my daily lessons, la viuda Socorro Llosa de Aguilar looked into my eyes and recognized me. It is something too rare in this world, to be recognized. She looked into my eyes and knew what drove me – pride and fury and determination.

La señora fired my cosita as no man ever had. Not because I am a lover of women. No. But near her power and her finesse pulsed something so familiar, something that was at once within me and unattainable. A

161

sigh so long and far. Beside la señora, I felt all that I would and would not have, I felt the price of my choices. I saw a woman I could become.

The taxi rolled slowly over the holes in the dirt road before my mother's house. Small hands and faces pressed to the car windows while Miguel Angel handed bills over the seat to the taxista. Señoras stood in their doorways with arms crossed over their bellies. Conchita León, who sold guavas, polished the front bumper of the car with her skirt and lowered her face to smile into the distorted reflection. 'Who is it?' her mother called. 'Take yourself away from that taxi.'

I stepped into the powder dust and hot sun of Teatlán. Across the roof of the car, Miguel Angel lowered his head and pretended to scratch under his nose with one finger, and I knew that he was trying to block the stink.

'Like Jackie Kennedy,' someone said, only she pronounced it Jockey.

'Sí, like Jockey,' echoed through the crowd that was forming.

'Magdalena,' someone else whispered.

There were whispers I almost heard. I knew their little summaries of me. 'Puta, pero siempre trucha.' A whore, but always a smart whore. 'Always with luck in life, la Magda.'

'La Magda,' echoed through. 'La Magda. La Magda.'

'Married rich.'

'Mira the clothes they wear.'

'Jockey.'

'Pinche Magda.'

This is when Abuelito would have yelled from his window, called for Pocha. 'Qué mujer tan guapa,' he would have said. He would have broken the stiff moment. He would have invited me to sit on his bed

162

at the window. 'Ven. Siéntate,' he would have said, 'Soy un hombre decente.' But he did not. Abuelito was dead, and I had brought Miguel Angel to his novena; I brought him for the first time to know my barrio. Abuelito died of a heart attack. That's what everyone said: 'He was mal del corazón.' It was what they said about most deaths, since always at death, the heart stops.

Abuelito's window was empty, closed by curtains. The front door was shut and a black cloth draped over the frame. I stood in the calle and no one ran to me. No one hugged me welcome. Neighbors stood entranced as if by a movie. As if I were a stranger.

Chucha stepped from the doorway and stood between Miguel Angel and me, cupping an elbow in each of her palms.

'It is only Magda,' she said to no one, everyone, as she guided us to the house. 'The same Magda.'

'Thank you for coming, hijo,' Chucha said.

'Mi pésame, doña,' Miguel Angel muttered.

Chucha nodded acceptance, leading us into the sala. My eyes blinked luz, adjusting to the darkness, and I heard my name whispered, muttered in low tones that ricocheted off the walls of the small room: 'Magdalena,' 'Magda,' 'Magda with her husband,' 'Magda rica.'

Women sat in chairs crowded like too many teeth in rows before the short lime-powder cross where Abuelito had lain dead before burial. I imagined the imprint of Abuelito's shoulders and pompis in the powder. The outline of the cross was distorted where feet had pushed into its boundaries. Men stood behind the chairs with their backs to the cross.

At novena, women mourn; men tell stories and get drunk.

Mami sat beside the wall at the end of the first row,

at the top of the cross where her father's head had been. Wilted gladiolas and a brick pillow at her feet. With Miguel Angel at my hip, I sidestepped down the row, knees rubbing against neighbors', careful not to step in the lime.

'Mi pésame,' Doña Beatriz de la Cruz took my hand in both of hers.

'Gracias, doña.' I introduced my husband to her with a twist of my waist and an open palm. 'Mi esposo,' then bumped to the next person, repeating the same: 'Mi pésame,' they said. 'Mi esposo,' I said. There was no room for the seated to stand without pushing me into the cross, and I bent over each one, took each person's hand in mine while the silent vacuum of Mami sucked me toward her and dead Abuelito demanded that I turn to his window, to his cross.

'Pinche Magda,' my brother, Rigoberto, called from the group of men in the back of the sala and raised his bottle of cerveza to me in salute.

'Respect.' Chucha's quiet spit and hiss cut through the burro's drunken volume.

Mami's absent gaze was fixed above the lime cross. She gave no notice of her daughter's name repeated.

When my knees touched Mami's, I bent from the waist, rested my hands on her soft thighs and pressed my cheek to hers. 'Mami?' I whispered as if to wake her.

'Hija,' she said. The thick eyeglasses she had worn all the years I had called her Mami were absent and her eyes were weak and small, sunk into gray sockets.

I stood. 'My husband, Mami. Miguel Angel.'

She did not pretend sight, she did not lift her chin to us. 'Your mother sends presents,' Mami said. 'Chocolates.' Her voice faded, then returned. 'Thank her.'

'Where are your glasses, Mami?' I asked.

She lifted her chin to point to the lime powder.

There were only candles spilling wax on the floor and hot flowers. 'Where, Mami?'

Doña Ramos seated next to Mami tugged my skirt, a child tattling. She leaned forward at the waist and spoke as if Mami were not present. 'Her eyeglasses, she put them on Don José. The pesos were in his sockets, but your mother insisted. La doña put her eyeglasses right on his face so that he would be sure to see the white dog, she said. So that Don José could see the path to heaven. I told her to take off the pesos, but . . .'

I turned to Mami and my panza churned, my breath grew short. *You give the little sight you have to the dead? Qué te pasa? Why not give him your legs?* I said nothing.

In seven days, the lime would be swept up and buried above Abuelito's coffin, and for a little moment, I considered that an opportunity to open the lid and reclaim Mami's eyeglasses.

Abuelito had told me about death. About the rough roads and troublesome animals, about the river to cross, the white dog who swims with you, about the man at the other side of the river with the outstretched arm pointing the direction to take, his hand burned black from the sun because he never lowers it. I knew the stories, but I felt fierce impatience for Mami's gesture. That, and fear.

Her indifference scared me skin to bone.

I knelt at the lap of my mother. My stockings popped at one knee and crawled up my thigh. Mami's hands were limp, fingers curled and palms up in her lap. I wanted to slap her awake. I wanted her to choose to live. I wanted to fill her. With courage, with voluntad, will and vida. My own strength drained down heavy arms and fingertips. Her weakness sucked me near dead, but to no purpose. My life did not escape me to

165

enter and fill Mami's emptiness. I lay one cheek against her thigh, and my strength vaporized. It rose and lifted out Abuelito's window. Useless to anyone.

In the hotel room, Miguel Angel lay against the white sheets. He had been quiet for the ride home from the barrio. Quiet through novena.

I removed the ridiculous pillbox hat from my head and thought of Mami still sitting where I'd left her, paralyzed in the chair against the wall, staring vacant above the head of Abuelito's cross.

'The stink, Magda. How could you live there?' He rolled to his side and looked out the balcony doors to the ocean.

I slipped the dusty suede pumps off my feet, clipped the ruined pale stockings from the garter, wondered if anyone in my barrio knew that Jackie Kennedy had married again. Jackie O., they called her in the USA. I should have never listened to my suegra, never worn a dress so rich and different from the barrio. The pride I first felt when I had stepped from the taxi had quickly melted away. The linen, the hat, the whole outfit had made me so different. Sisters and neighbors had sneaked a feel of the material of my dress, looked for excuses to touch my hat and my stocking, but few had come to me as they would have if I had not been draped in richness, if Miguel Angel had not been beside me, the two of us dressed to make their poverty shine.

Everyone had been very polite, but the wall of what they really wanted to ask and say – How much did that cost? What do you eat at comida? Is your house grand? May I please have a little money? – kept them from me.

I washed my teeth, pressed bristles of a brush hard into my scalp, pulled them down my hair, and Mami sat in a chair with her shoes in Abuelito's lime.

The weak make the capable guilty.

166

I brushed harder so that my chin lifted against my own force.

'Don't go back,' Miguel Angel said, still facing the ocean.

The fierce brush through my hair. 'Only five days more,' I said. Crazy to fill my mother. Crazy because her emptiness threatened my will, threatened my strength, threatened all I'd fought to be.

After completing the novena, after burying the lime with Abuelito and taking Mami to the doctor for new eyeglasses, we returned to Monterrey, but I felt an inexplicable yearning for Teatlán, for the warm sun and ocean, for the ruido noise, for dancing, for the heart of my mother. From the window of my suite in Monterrey, I could see over corrals and barns to silent forever. The air there so arid. It sucked the sweat off my body before it was my own. Un calor tan feo, that dry heat, heat that wouldn't even allow me to sweat bien bonito. In the expanses of Monterrey, without the familiar glue of humidity, I felt my células begin to dehydrate and distance from one another. I felt that soon I would not be whole, that my cells would dry and separate and blow to the winds.

I began to invent reasons to return. My mother was weak. My father injured. My mother's eyes, my father's leg. I wrote the letters for my sister to copy in her own hand so that I had evidence of the misfortune of my family, letters calling the strongest child home. Each tragedy invented called me to the house of my parents, to the hot shores of Teatlán.

When visiting Teatlán, I wandered the Central Market, drinking the crowds and noise I had so missed while living with the silent rich on the ranch: the surge of buses and cars without mufflers, the constant *beeop* whistle of the traffic policeman, the fast talk of the tonic salesman. Some merchants had purchased microphones and talked nonstop about their wares like radio announcers, or called out to friends on the street, to pretty women; others blasted their favorite music – Vicente Hernández, Lola Beltrán, Vicki Carr – one blended into the next.

I strolled to the fruit and vegetable stands. Papayas were stacked, nipples up, like large breasts. Onions, peeled shiny naked, shone in the sun. I ate: tunas, pale green cactus fruit nestled in ice on carts, thorns peeled away and ready to bite; spears of crisp jícama and tender papaya in a plastic cup; pitayas with sweet florescence roped and wound inside, ready to burst; mango on a stick carved like a golden flower. I squeezed small limes and sprinkled salt and red chile on everything except the pitaya. I bought papaya, plátano, manzanito, marlin and meat. Vegetables. Filled pink and green plaid nylon bags and sent them bulging, lumpy as old women, to my mother in a taxi with my cousin Enrique.

Walking home from the market, I passed the Cine Maravillo and forced myself to rest under the awning. It was a dare. It was my right. I made myself stand there in the shade long enough to demonstrate my ease. I studied the same old photograph. Pedro Infante wore a cowboy hat and a leather coat zipped up, and I leaned closer to see that just above the curled bottom edge of the picture, at his hip, there was the butt of a pistol. Ay, pendeja. It was all the time the serene woman who was in the jail. I wondered if Gordo Chuy had studied the photographs as I had. Pedro Infante forever kissing the hand of the serene woman behind bars. Then I noticed that she was slightly taller than he; she looked down at his mouth on her hand, and there was a gas light attached to the wall on Pedro's side of the bars. The serene one was not standing behind jail bars, but sitting behind the proteciones bars on the window of her own home.

Julio, the son of the whore, I met on one of my trips to Teatlán. He came from poor but had the ambition. He spoke English, managed a restaurant with loud music and lots of tequila for the tourists. He was ugly and dark. Wore white starched shirts. A good dancer. A marijuanero.

I thought him a safe diversion for my soul while in Teatlán. When the devil is bored, she plays with her tail. Julio was no catch, no man to marry. The cabrón would walk his lovers on the boardwalk in front of his wife just as my father had, but there was something to gain from him: he knew how to feed the Teatleca in me like the cool norteño husband never could. I'm not speaking of sex, but of the fire and dance and noise and wildness – all that was sacrificed to sophistication by the rich Aguilar of Monterrey. I told myself that for just brief diversion, I wanted a man who could drop his head back and yell high in his throat when the mariachis played.

I came to Teatlán and stayed the first time for a month and the second for six weeks, and after the third, I never returned to el rancho Aguilar de Monterrey.

There is no explaining the pendejados of youth.

One afternoon at the house of Julio, I answered a knock at the door. Without speaking, Armando, the driver for the familia Aguilar, handed me a letter and turned to leave. A taxi waited for him in front of the house, and I knew a small plane waited for him at the airport. The letter was from Miguel Angel's mother, and written in black ink on thin paper in her educated hand, it said in a cold list, just the way she taught me manners: that an investigator had been following me in Teatlán; that our marriage would be annulled so that Miguel might, in the future, marry in the church a proper girl; that my belongings would be sent to my new address; that attempts to contact her family would be futile; that alimony was out of the question. She had instructed me during our afternoons that a lady must correspond only in black ink. Beneath her practiced signature, she had added a line: 'Be careful, Magda.' Enclosed was a small check.

I never saw Miguel Angel again.

'Pendeja yo.' I cursed myself for being the idiot who would leave a marriage to the richest man with only a small check and some American clothes. I had used my most valuable tool to lure Miguel Angel, and it was a tool that could only be used once.

Del plato a la boca, a veces se cae la sopa. From the plate to the mouth, the soup sometimes spills.

Teresita, the servant who loved me most on the ranch, had packed my belongings. Each sock and panty was ironed, folded and tied with a blue ribbon. I inhaled their fresh scent before placing them in the small dresser.

I was home, near my family in Teatlán, and for a while, for convenience, I lived in the house of Julio.

Recovering my coastal soul, I forgot my direction. Forgot los pasos a seguir. Went crazy for a little. Was a hostess in the tourist restaurant. My English bettered. I danced to the disco music with Americans who bit their lower lips like beavers to concentrate on their movements.

Puras pendejadas.

The money of Julio flowed. Each morning I shopped the market for food and sent it in a taxi to my family. Julio paid. He gave me much money. Always the same way, turning my hand up, opening my palm and then folding my fingers over the thick roll of bills. The restaurant made good money, but the drugs made better. There is something about drug money that begs to be spent, and Julio was drunk to spend it, drunk with the power of it. He tipped waiters and busboys, taxistas and flower girls 100 percent. More. Julio was known in all the clubs and restaurants. Hosts and waiters gave us sticky sweet service. It was powerful and common.

Who can explain the ironía: that surrounded by unimaginable wealth in Monterrey, there was not one centavo I could touch, yet with the common Julio, I was bathed in cash efectivo. It was good to help feed my family, good to be at home, but I knew that it was not an arrangement that I could sustain. Not even I was not willing to pay a price so high as a life with Julio to feed my family, them a deep pit of need. Food sent, there was no money for gas to cook it. Gas tanks filled, the stove broke. Never enough. Never. Money poured into their daily maintenance and minor tragedies: Rosa's baby born with a crooked foot, Rigoberto in trouble with the police, Mami's eyes, Chucha's worthless son, Papi's sickness, a tejuino cart stolen . . .

Sundays we sometimes rested. Más o menos. Julio and I went to the playa norte, the beach at the bridge north of the tourists, to the thatched palapa where Don Cipriano fried the best red snapper in Teatlán. We settled our towels on the sand between the water and the palapa, let the tide wash through us, the sun bake down to bone.

'Go tell Don Cipriano to fix us two big campechanas,' Julio told me. He spoke with his eyes closed.

I sat in the shade of the palapa at the counter and watched the preparation. With the loving patience of a santo, Don Cipriano selected the best pieces of conch, oysters, shrimp, turtle, pulpo, and layered them into a large cocktail glass. He poured the seafood broth over the mixture while, on a gray scarred plank, his wife carefully chopped the onion, cucumber and tomato into the tiniest cubes to be spooned over the top.

'I will teach my daughters to chop so finely, doña,' I said.

When I returned to the towels, there were two men from Culiacán. One sat beside Julio, his leather street shoes digging in the sand, a wide belt cutting under his belly, his face sweating grasa; the other stood wiry guard behind them, his gaze sweeping the beach and my breasts for trouble. An earthworm scar inched across his nose and down one cheek.

Julio threw hot sand at my feet. 'Tell Don Cipriano to fry his biggest snapper. We'll eat it under the palapa.'

I handed each man a campechana.

'And bring us some beers while we're waiting.' He reached up and pinched my thigh. 'Stay out of the sun, vieja, you're getting too dark.'

I turned, watching my near-black toes grab and push off the sand.

Business. I left the men to gorge on their fish and seafood, to bark orders to the old couple, to drink too much, to fill their noses with cocaine. A long walk on the beach. Planning. Business of my own.

There I was with three corrientes on the beach. I saw myself with the eyes of Señora de Aguilar and felt tight disdain and disappointment. I had longed to return to my coastal beginnings, had longed for money that I could hold in my hand, but these men . . . This life . . .

When I returned, Julio and the Culiacano mirrored each other, pushed away from the table of empty

Pacífico bottles and fish skeletons, each balanced on the back two legs of their chairs dug in the sand.

Julio turned his head and said, 'Where have you been?'

The turn unbalanced his chair and he fell backward into the sand, beer bottle tumbling in the air.

The Culiacano brought the front legs of his chair down, slamming his fists on the table, laughing.

'For a walk,' I said as I helped him up. I did not laugh, but I could not help but smile.

Back in his seat, he said, 'Did I tell you not to stay in the sun?' He narrowed his eyes. 'You are black as a negra.'

'Así es,' I said.

In one deviled motion, Julio grabbed my wrist and banged my knuckles against the table. 'Así es?' he said, tightening his grip around my wrist.

I did not pull away or look down at my hand. *I should murder you in your sleep*, I thought, but I only nodded.

He threw my hand into my lap and turned his attention to the man across the table. 'Another beer?' he asked.

Under the table, I tried to squeeze my wrist as hard as he had. To duplicate the pain. And to remember.

Mami sat at her table, her hands palms down on its sticky oilcloth.

'Let me wipe this clean for you,' I stood and tapped her hands lightly for them to move.

I poured vinegar into a cloth and traveled over the surface, but it grew stickier.

'I'll bring you a new cloth from market.' I gave up cleaning and sat with her again.

Mami replaced her hands on the table. She no longer squinted and blinked in attempt to see me, but sat frog-eyed behind the glass. Yellow manteca had splattered and smeared over one lens.

'Oye, Mami. You don't want me to clean your eyeglasses?'

'No, hija,' she said. 'I am fine.'

'Soon, Mami, we'll go to the doctor in Guadalajara. Julio says that he'll have the money soon.'

Julio had promised to send Mami to the special eye doctor in Guadalajara. With the next bonus, he said. That's what he called his drug money: bonuses.

'Sí, hija.'

When I visited again, the smear was still on her lens.

I sat at her table and leaned close to the face of my mother and pulled the arms of her glasses to remove them.

She did not resist.

'I'll have the money, and Tuesday we will leave in the early morning,' I told her.

Mami sat still and waited for me to clean her glasses.

'I will come tomorrow to pack a few things, Mami, you can tell no one.'

Mami did not respond – as if she'd gone deaf when I removed her glasses.

'Listen, Mami.' My voice rose. 'This is important. Did you understand me? You must tell no one. Not Papi or Rosa or even Chucha. No one.'

As I spoke, I worried the smear in circles over the lens. 'Do you have more vinegar, Mami?'

'No, hija,' she said.

I went to the bowl of soapy water that stood on the counter, always ready for cleaning, and dipped her glasses in, then circled them between a clean dry place on the hem of my blouse. 'I'll come to get you very early in the morning. You say that we are going to market.'

'No, hija,' she said again. She sat with her back

straight and did not bother to turn her face toward me. 'You go.'

I pulled her chair away from the table, kneeled before her and wedged myself between her knees as far as her skirt would allow. 'Mami. This is your hope. Maybe your last hope to see.'

Mami slowly took the glasses from my hand and replaced them before her eyes. She looked toward my face, and her breath rose high in her chest to lift the small-flowered fabric at her collarbone.

I knew that she would not change her mind.

With her hands on each of my shoulders and my face inches from hers, Mami moved her head to see what she could of the room. She looked up toward the ceiling, over my head to the square of light in the window, toward the dark shapes at the counter and toward the cots.

'Mami?'

She dropped her eyes toward my face, traveled her hands up the back of my neck to cup my head. 'You go,' she said. 'Make your mistakes. You must. But hija, keep yourself safe. Please. Tell no one.'

At midnight, on the sixteenth of September, I left the restaurant. 'I am too tired, Chiquitito,' I told Julio. 'I will wait for you at home.'

My cousin, Enrique, the taxista, drove me to the house of Julio. 'Wait here,' I instructed.

Inside, I packed my suitcases – the crewel-cloth fancy ones bought in Houston under the guidance of my mother-in-law. My hands trembled as I folded my American clothes around gold: my wedding band, chains from Julio, his own jewelry, a broken Rolex watch. Too much gold looks common, la señora had told me.

As Enrique loaded four suitcases into his taxi, I

175

instructed him, 'You must help me, cousin.' I pressed twenty American dollars into his palm. 'At five-thirty this morning, not one minute later, at five-thirty you must be parked just out of sight behind the wild bougainvillea. Lie down in the taxi so it looks empty, and wait.' He nodded. 'Do not speak of this to anyone.'

I paced the floor, trying to calm myself, to breathe. I knew that Julio wouldn't return until early in the madrugada with the first light. Cocaine. Perhaps another woman. My flight to Guadalajara left at seven o'clock.

The key did not turn in the lock until five-fifteen. I was waiting in my shorts and sandals. Market clothes.

He lay down on top of the bedcovers, 'Come back to bed with me,' he said. Him stinking with alcohol, his chile limp with cocaine.

Still, I felt some bad for this generous man – the one who had given my family food and money. I sat beside him and took his hand in mine. 'Better you sleep,' I told him.

'I'll sleep after.' He reached to unbutton my shorts.

I slipped over just out of his reach. 'For you, Julio, I am planning a feast.'

He cared not so much for the food as for the idea of me inside the cocina cooking, cooking, just for him.

'You can go after.'

'Later, mi vida. I am fixing the special mole from Amalia's in Puebla. Her sister brings only a few kilos early on Tuesdays. It will be gone by six o'clock. I have to go to market to get the best and first of everything to make the special meal. I invited your compadre Rogelio.'

'A la chingada with Rogelio,' he said.

I stood. 'Don't be like that, Julio.' I could sense Enrique, impatient just down the road, Julio before me on the edge of anger. Calofrios pushed through the skin of my legs, I could feel my heart pressure my veins.

Julio rolled to his side and closed his eyes. 'Chingada madre,' he mumbled.

'I will bring you something special from the market.' I spoke to his back. What I had waited for, four zippered vinyl pouches, the accumulated deposits from the long holiday weekend, sat bulging on the dresser top. I slipped them into my nylon shopping bag, and the fortune lay quietly in the bottom.

Julio continued to mumble, but he had calmed. 'Go on, then, but only if you buy me some of those little manzanito bananas.'

I turned to the door. 'Ahorita vengo, Julio.'

If I could choose an end to my life, though I would not have chosen it then, it would be in a moment like that, steps from escape, pasos from returning to myself, my face to the door, those last words at my back, '. . . but only if you buy me some of those little manzanito bananas,' when I felt one hand on the door-knob, the other grasped firmly around the handle of the mesh bag, and all the possibilities on the other side of the door.

I thank my own clever mind,
  my own rare suerte . . .

Guadalajara was a sweet descanso. A dulce rest. And
though I had only twenty-four years in 1974 when I
arrived at the home of Doña Mercedes Ortega in a
hand-painted black taxi, a rest was needed.

The taxista took me straight to Doña Mercedes from the
Guadalajara airport. Maybe the doña was a cousin or
an aunt, a friend of the family. Maybe she paid him.
  'Take me to el centro,' I told the taxista. Every town
must have a center.
  'Para servirle, señorita,' he said.
  I did not correct him. In Guadalajara, I would again
be a señorita.
  And as the taxista drove slowly away from the
airport, I turned hard to see out the back window, to
check that Julio was not in an automobile behind us.
  'What place in el centro, señorita?' the taxista asked.
  I pushed my fingers into the hard cracks in the vinyl
seat and invented the where that I did not know. So
busy I had been with the intricate plans of my escape
that I had not considered exactly where I would arrive.
  'To a boardinghouse,' I said. 'Some place economi-
cal. And clean.' I created my list of requirements as I
spoke to his dark eyes in the rearview mirror. 'Walking

distance from the center. Someplace with meals.' I squeezed the large leather purse that held the restaurant's receipts between my knees. 'Someplace secure.'

'There are few residences in el mero centro, señorita, but I can think of a possibility.'

Behind the old taxista, I stepped into the dim entry of la doña's home.

He spoke formally. With polish and flowers. 'This señorita, my esteemed Doña Mercedes, is in need of shelter and comida, and I thought that by some milagrito that you might have available quarters and that you might consider her as a renter.'

Doña Mercedes Ortega stood with her hands folded gently in front of her pastel skirt, her low dark pumps pressed together. 'How kind of you to remember this home, Don Luis.' Only her head moved.

'¿Señorita?' she asked my name.

I too stood like a lady as best I could with the clumsy leather bolsa clutched in both fists over my private place. 'Guadalupe Magdalena Molina Vásquez, Doña, para servirle usted.'

The doña stood quietly, nodding as if she recognized my name.

'¿Estudiante?' she asked. And in that moment, she gave me the role that I had never performed, a papel that was new and inviting. She told me who I would be in Guadalajara.

'Sí, doña,' I answered. I liked the sound of the role. 'Estudiante,' I said again, and my chin lifted with confidence.

Doña Mercedes became quiet again. Again nodding. She had no hurry to fill the silence. Then she told me where. 'The University of Guadalajara,' she said.

'The University of Guadalajara,' I repeated.

After a moment, she spoke to the taxista. 'Don Luis, would you be so kind to do us the favor of bringing in the señorita's belongings? We would be happy to have the company of a stimulating young mind.'

I stood in silence with Doña Mercedes, tasting the idea of my new role. I would invent a course to examine, buy a mochila and fill it with books, sit on a bench near the university and read about life.

It is easier to read about life than to live it. Even so young I knew that. Even so young I needed a rest from living.

Don Luis struggled into the entry with the elegant luggage that Señora de Aguilar had chosen for me, and I sucked breath and waited for Doña Mercedes to recognize the inconsistency. It was not the luggage of a student who lived in a boardinghouse. The cost of one bag could have fed my family for a year, bought three tejuino carts.

La doña raised her eyebrows slightly and tilted her head as if greeting an acquaintance in passing. 'Lovely,' she said to no one, and then turned to study my eyes.

Each morning I stood from the breakfast table, lifted my notebook as if it were a Bible and folded it in the bend of one arm, then raised my mochila to the other shoulder and left the safe home of Doña Mercedes to go to the University of Guadalajara.

'Que te vaya bien y que aprendas mucho.' The doña each day lifted her coffee cup to me and spoke the same words with the same odd smile. That you may go well, that you may learn much.

In my mochila were two books purchased from a secondhand bookstore, a history of Mexico because it was worn and thick with pages, two thin volumes of poetry – Sor Juana Inés de la Cruz and Señor Neruda

– for the sentimental reason. These books were not beautiful like the books in the library of la Señora de Aguilar. The covers were made from paper and plastic, the print inside surged dark and light, in and out of focus.

The university, I found, was not in one big campus as I had imagined, but spread across the city. Many centers, many schools, each with a long name. El Centro Universitario de Ciencias Sociales y Humanidades, El Centro Universitario de Cicenias Exactas e Ingenierías, El Centro Universitario de Biológicas y Agropecuarias . . . Ay. Poco a poco, I learned the buses and found the schools, and I watched. In each center, I studied students, noted gesture and dress, ate cheap student food – mushroom and potato tacos, refried beans on toast – and I squeezed late through the doors of large lecture halls to write in my notebook facts or observations that I might share with Doña Mercedes at cena.

All the time watching for the dark quick form that might be Julio.

After weeks at the university, after weeks with no sight of Julio, I walked one morning from Doña Mercedes east and south to the Plaza de Armas. So dry in Guadalajara. Tan seco like Monterrey, the same dry blue sky.

At the entrance of the Palacio de Gobierno, the ticket taker asked, '¿Estudiante?'

I adjusted the mochila strap on my shoulder and smiled that I looked my part. 'Sí.'

There is where my serious study began. There in the cool stone of the Palacio de Gobierno, I walked the history of Mexico in the murals of José Clemente Orozco.

At the base of a wide and elegant stairway, one that rose and parted gracefully like the fallopian tubes the

181

professor had drawn on the chalk board in a morning lecture, I stopped. With one fist raised above his head, the other clenched around a flaming rod that came toward me, his eyes to heaven, the giant in the mural forbade me to ascend the stairs. His torso rose from a field of dull gray corpses to war in blood storm skies. The giant face filled the wall and he appeared fierce and sad, God or the devil, the savior. As mad as my abuelito. Bald with wild gray fringes.

A man stopped a few steps above me, raised an open palm to the mural, and said to the group that trailed behind him, 'Miguel Hidalgo y Costilla. Born, 1753; Mexican revolutionist, national hero, priest; famous for "El Grito de Dolores," his call to arms that began the Mexican Revolution for Independence in 1810: "Long live the Virgin of Guadalupe! Down with bad government!" – the same cry inscribed on the banner Hidalgo carried always with him in battle.'

The man moved up a few more steps the way Pedro Infante maneuvered stairs while singing, his face always to the audience. The group moved as one behind him. He lowered his voice as if telling them a secret. 'Notice, ladies and gentlemen, how Orozco has depicted the priest. In a style typical of the artist during this period . . .' His English was as polished as la Señora de Aguilar's.

When the steps of the man and his followers faded on the stone floors above me, I climbed each step slowly to approach the giant padre. Miguel Hidalgo y Costilla. What pact did he have with Guadalupe? He drew me like a God. Confused me like abuelito. *Sit down, mí vida. I am a decent man.* I closed my eyes to Hidalgo because he knew my thoughts.

It took only one week to find the huevas to follow behind the tour groups, to listen and learn without paying. Then every day I listened, every day I took notes. Every day I walked the walls of murals in the Palacio de Gobierno, in the Hospicios Cabañas. In books, I walked with the Mayans and the Toltecs. I visited Cortés, Moctezuma, Malinche, Hidalgo. Benito Juárez. I walked the history of Mexico that I had never known. I walked the history of man, of woman, of the world. Following the tours, I memorized the tour talk: 'José Clemente Orozco (1883–1949), born in this state of Jalisco. One of the grand masters of mural painting that surged after the Mexican Revolution.' The conversation at the cena table of Doña Mercedes became full of Orozco, the palace, painting. 'Orozco, a man of intense expressionistic temperament . . .' At her table, I rehearsed: 'a bloody but entertaining caricature of the carnival of ideologies . . . a general sense of human brutality . . .' I mimicked the tour guides whether or not I understood them.

One day strolling along the periphery of el Mercado Libertad, hoping to find the señora who brought pitayas from the desert, I passed the blind man with a maraca in each hand. All the day he sat on the cement, shaking one maraca and then the other, waiting for kind or guilty humans to toss coins in his bowl. I passed a vendor who sold green and pink plastic buckets, and my favorite sandía stand with cross sections of watermelon, pink wheels standing in line.

New color called my attention. On a blanket that lay on the cement slab, a small woman that I had not seen before sat among her clay creations. I paused to study her bright figures – Jesus and disciples around the table of the last supper eating tortillas and watermelon, a bus driven by a devil, Saint Francis with a tiger and a bird at his feet. All from Michoacán. Each was coarse, formed by hand with clay.

La Virgin de Guadalupe stood in an open gazebo that

was supported by the tails of two iguanas and four dark-skinned mermaids with pink nipples. Guadalupe was glazed brightly, and She stood, as She still stands, in a cobalt shelter, pink spears emanating from her body, her face and hands cinnamon shining, Juan Diego with wings at her feet, existing only from the waist up.

I kneeled next to the blanket to touch the small bright Virgin.

'Doña,' I asked, 'Why is it that Juan Diego never has legs? In all the pictures and statues, always he comes up from the clouds or from the earth, beginning at the waist, as if he has been only partially born.'

The old woman touched her fingertips to the face of little Juan. 'Así es,' she said. 'Perhaps he traded his lower half for wings.' She brought her hand to cover her laugh.

The clay felt cool.

Nuestra Señora. La Virgin.

'Wrap her for me carefully, doña.' That is all I said.

The Michoacana lifted her chin to me and contemplated my eyes. 'Yes,' she said. 'This Virgin is yours, señorita.'

It was in my small room in the house of Doña Mercedes that Guadalupe and I became friends. I set Her on the table beside my bed to face me, so that it was Guadalupe that I last saw before sleep and when I opened my eyes in the morning.

Sitting in bed at night, I sometimes read la poesía aloud to Her. *'Who has more blame en una pasión errada . . . she who falls from prayer or he who prays after falling?'* I practiced the English tours. 'Notice, Madre Mía, below Padre Hidalgo is an image of cataclysmic rebellion, a horde of dead figures in a sea of flags and flames. The conflict is of total confusion and desperation.'

184

I first called Her Madre Mía, Nuestra Señora, Madrecita de Dios. And with more time together, I began to call Her Guadalupe. Then Lady Lupita. It was one night after I had told the Virgin about the prisoner I helped escape from the school jail when I felt her friendship swell my heart. I rolled to my side and watched Her closely, waiting. For warmth. For something. 'Lupa.' I whispered my own special name for her for the first time. 'Más que mis ojos, Lupa.' Then slowly, I pushed myself up on one elbow, stretched my neck long, and touched my lips to Her.

After much practice, after I knew the tours by memory, I went to the Palacio de Gobierno to the office of Señor Federico Aragón.

'You are?' He looked up from his desk.

'Magdalena Molina Vásquez.' I released my mochila on the floor beside me. 'Para servirle usted.' And I walked to his desk.

'¿Estudiante?' Señor Aragón half stood from his chair. I clasped my hands behind my dark blue skirt just as I had seen the tour guides do. I wore the white blouse and dark skirt that they wore.

'Sí.'

'Universidad de Guadalajara?'

I nodded.

'In which school?'

'De Ciencias Sociales y Humanidades.'

'Course of study?'

This was farther than the question had before gone.

'La historia,' I answered.

'I know well the dean of the department,' he said. 'You're studying the history of . . .'

I blinked. Remembered the murals. 'Of México,' I said, but it did not seem enough. 'Of man.' Nor did that. 'And woman. Of the world.'

185

'That's quite a course of study.' He smiled.

'I know all the tours,' I said. 'By memory. And I would like to be a guide.'

'Señorita,' he leaned forward on his elbow, 'our guides are credentialed. Experienced.' Señor Aragón removed the cover from his pen and pointed it toward me. 'I am a busy man, señorita.'

'If you would just stand beside me for a moment, Señor Aragón.'

I stood and walked to the outside wall of his office, and to evoke my imaginary mural, I lifted one open palm to large gray stones. 'In the mural that adorns the entire staircase, José Clemente Orozco, in a style . . .'

Señor Aragón sighed long and came to me slowly. 'Señorita . . .' he tried to interrupt.

But I would not be interrupted. I quoted word for word the tour guides. When Spanish did not win him, I spoke the guide's words in English as I had practiced in my small rented room.

Señor Aragón seemed as bored as the tourists who fidgeted in the rear of a crowd.

I walked slowly, tracing the walls of his office, pointing to the murals, returning to the imaginary base of the stairs under the gaze of Miguel Hidalgo. Aragón was a blur in my peripheral vision, a heaviness at my left shoulder. I switched to Spanish. 'Don't you ever wonder what Orozco knew about Hidalgo to paint those eyes? What exactly he did to rise to power, that Hidalgo priest? What women he may have known?'

I dropped my head back and broke the quiet of the Palace: 'Long live the Virgin of Guadalupe! Down with bad government!' Boredom was something I could not tolerate on a man's face.

'Señorita, please,' he said. 'I remind you where you are. A serious place.'

'In all seriousness, Señor Aragón.' I smiled, nodded

186

at him and turned my attention to the mural. 'We talk of Miguel Hidalgo, Padre de la Patria, liberator of all slaves in Mexico. Without question or thought, we say the same words about him again and again. "Padre de la Patria, liberator of slaves, padre, liberator." But look closely at this painting.' I raised my upturned palm higher and stepped closer to the imaginary mural. Señor Aragón also stepped closer. 'Have you wondered what lies behind the old myth? The first time I saw this mural, Señor Aragón, I thought that Hidalgo was a dangerous god or devil and I wanted to turn and run down the stairs to escape his madness.'

'It is fierce,' he agreed. He leaned toward the wall.

'But I have studied this painting as I have listened to the tours, this Padre de la Patria who sometimes haunts my sleep. He is not always fierce. There are days I think him half tonto, his eyes focused upward on nothing and his mouth open to catch flies. I think him insane, I think Orozco saw Hidalgo driven mad by all that he fought against, that or mad from the beginning, but now, he is trapped here on the walls of the most elegant stairway forever, with charred corpses at his feet.'

'Extreme.' There was evidence of a smile contained on the lips of the administrator.

My hand was still lifted to the invisible Hidalgo.

'A little melodramatic, señorita, and unsophisticated,' he said.

He commented on my tour as I had heard the art critic's comment while standing before the murals.

'Common, even. But passionate. And enthusiastic.'

Passionate, he said, and it wasn't about sex. Passionate. About a mural. About being a student.

We both stood looking at the imaginary mural of José Clemente Orozco who criticized the ideologies of his

187

time. That is what the tour guide said. That he criticized the ideologies of his time.

'Señorita.' Señor Aragón pulled from the spell. 'Though your enthusiasm if admirable, I cannot hire you.' His words were spoken to the wall.

I stood staring at the bland wall that had been filled with murals moments before, then stepped away from the administrator to catch the strap of my mochila and leave Señor Aragón in his empty office. 'Thank you for your time,' I said.

'There are, señorita,' Señor Aragón said as I stepped through his doorway, '. . . you may have noticed, certain independents who solicit individual clients outside the palace though they are not employed or promoted by the museum.'

I did not turn around, but stood and listened to his words.

'Your audience would be considerably smaller, but I have heard that the independent guides are sometimes well compensated. That, of course, would be for you to negotiate.'

In the small plaza across the street from the main entrance of the palace, I stood so that guards could not send me away, waving brochures stolen from the palacio over my head. 'Tours. Tours of the Palace of the Government,' I called. In English.

When I had first begun, I was reluctant to yell so loud, reluctant to lift my hand and wave. I looked always deep into the crowd for Julio, but I had not seen him or sensed him near. I felt in my panza that he had a new woman. I hoped.

Sometimes a woman can save you from a man.

'Palacio de Gobierno,' I called in Spanish.

It was different and the same, this sale of tours and the sale of tejuino. In both, it was not the product – not

188

the tour nor the tejuino – that was sold, but myself. The self, though, was somewhat different.

With a schoolgirl conservative blue skirt and white blouse, I mostly remained in my papel de estudiante – a young woman studying to better herself, passionate about education and art. I was not the sullen, intellectual leftist student in fringed poncho and giant cheap earrings that still mourned the student massacre of '68 in 1975. I was Magdalena, the good girl trying to better herself, Magda who came from a poor family and who believed that with an education she could earn an honest sueldo and help her own.

A young foreigner, most likely Americano, sat on a bench near the gazebo and read. He shook his head without looking up when I asked if he'd like to tour the palace or the Hospicio Cabañas. He was tidier than many young Americans who visited el centro. Not so tidy as the too-good-too-clean missionaries in dark suits who came to waste their time converting Catholics to Protestants, and not so unkempt as the American hippies who took pride in their dirt and smell and chosen poverty – filthy pendejos who would lounge barefoot all day on the benches of the plaza. What good is a tourist that spends no money? Some of those mocosos even begged. Once a dirty American girl asked me for money, and when I refused, she tapped her bent elbow and called me the caló for cheap. I turned to her, and my calm was lost. '¿Codo?' I asked, and took steps toward her, slapping my own pointing elbow. 'I am codo?' I repeated. 'No soy yo. But you, chiquitita apestosa, you are una pendeja bien hecha.' No one called me cheap. Menos, a rich girl pretending to be poor, menos, one that I knew could any time run home to hot running water and the clean house of her parents.

But this American was distinct, and I stood still

beside him to call his attention. He did not look up and I said, 'There are things you cannot know without a guide.'

His hair was medio long. But clean. Shining in curls. And his T-shirt was white. Pressed. Lean forearms with pale hairs smoothed all in the same direction. He read a book called *One Hundred Years of Solitude*. On the bench beside him lay a guidebook to Mexico. He was a plain and serious man.

'Thank you. No,' he said.

A young mother set her güero toddler on the concrete and tossed palomitas around him so that the pigeons would flock near.

'Manuelito? Mira, Manuelito.' The father called the baby's attention to the camera.

A chaparito with a gray mustache stopped before us holding a tray of ten small felt dogs. Some dogs gazed at the moreno's panza, others gazed at the American reading or out into the plaza, all approving with the slowest motion bob of their heads.

'No, gracias,' I said with small sadness to see the calming dogs move away.

I sat on the bench next to the shining *Solo Travel*. I was bored of my role as student, fatigued with reading. 'There is much loneliness in your books,' I said. 'A hundred years is a long time.'

The Americano looked up from his book at his own thoughts with a half smile and a focus that was too private to enter. It was the look of Chucha. I missed my tía, Mami, abuelito, my self.

When Chucha had sat in her chair on the roof with thoughts too far to hear me, I had played a game.

'Too bad the ghosts pissed on the laundry.' I'd kneel behind her chair with one cheek resting on her back. 'The kitchen knife is missing and there is blood everywhere.'

190

Chucha would stare toward the distant ocean she could not see.

'Pues, as long as you're not interested in the virgin birth of your own nephew, I'll leave you.' That was the last thing I would say before standing. Sometimes she would pat permission to leave on my forearm. Sometimes she would come to me from her dreams of day and scold my irreverence and vulgarity. Once she turned her head slowly and said, 'Yes, Magda. Bring me a miracle. I leave it to you.'

Boredom and this distant plain stranger inspired the same game I had played with Chucha. He read. I talked.

'Thank you,' I said. 'Muy amable. I'm happy to sit after standing so long.'

The stranger blinked out his thoughts over the plaza.

'Yes, after beating my socks all day. Golpeando los calcetines. That's what we say in the barrio.'

He looked up, nodded, smiled, and returned to his pages.

'José Clemente Orozco's wife was cross-eyed.' I began to say some things I wanted to say but couldn't during my tours.

The stranger did not look up.

'Diego Rivera was a bug-eyed toad married to a beautiful artist.'

No response.

'Frida Kahlo was impaled right through her vagina in a bus accident.' I said that in Spanish so he wouldn't understand.

'And what of that Malinche? There is a painting of her and Cortés sitting nude as newborns next to each other in straight-back chairs. In Mexico City. I've read about it. Seen photos in an artbook.' Malinche's square features, two thick braids, big black peso-sized aréola. Cortés with a beard, squat, muscular, fair.

The American turned a page with his index finger.

His disinterest gave me freedom. 'The woman everyone loves to hate: Malinche,' I began my own lecture. At the university, I had listened to a conference called 'Malinche and Mexico' given by a woman dressed like a hippie, but smart as a trout. It is a lecture that still hums in my brain 'Malinche's real name was Malinalli,' I informed the gringo. 'Then Malintzin when she was older. Try to say that. It means, in English, to twist, to contort. Then her name changed again to Marina, when she was baptized.'

The man was deaf to me.

I composed aloud a lecture I would never give in the palacio. 'Malinche was actually the name the Aztecs called the couple, Malintzin and Cortés. Now, the name is only for her. "Malinchista," people say. They mean whore or traitor. Betrayer. People blame Malinche for the fall of los Indios. Malinche, the slave who bore Cortés' child, and was then passed along to his lieutenant. Why not blame the pendejo Moctezuma for the fall? Macho pendejo who believed that Cortés was the reincarnation of the god king and gave the Spaniard the kingdom with hardly a fight. I have never heard his name spoken in hate. But the enslaved princess, Malintzin, translates language for Cortés . . . And she is responsible for the conquest. "Malinchista," people spit. "Betrayer. Whore," they say. Why don't they spit Moctezumista? Betrayer. Pendejo. Or Cortesista? Conqueror. Cannibal.'

The poor American missed my first original lecture.

I said to that man who would not listen, 'Each law broken in Aztec times was punished by a specified number of cactus thorns straight through the tongue.'

Nada.

'My grandfather had no legs and no teeth. Diabetes. And he sat always in the front window of my tía's

192

house and called to women passing. He called to the
saints. Sometimes he called me a Malinchista. My
mother is near blind, but she buried her eyeglasses
with my abuelito. Stretched the arms wide to fit on his
big face. My tía mortared her favorite chair to the roof.
She lives still.'

Tampoco. The American sat still.

'I have seen twenty-seven Pedro Infante movies and
memorized some of the parts. You've probably never
seen *Tizoc: Amor Indio*.'

It had been so long since I talked other than to spill
out Mexican history – architects, artists, soldiers,
whores, the kings and conquerors. I had spoken to no
one any truth of myself. It was good that he did not
listen.

I hard tugged at the material of the mendigo's shirt.

'Why are you reading?' I asked.

'I enjoy it,' he said.

'Are you very tired?' I asked.

A middle-aged American couple passed and I rose
to claim them. 'Okay, chiquitito,' I said to the silent
stranger. 'Like José Clemente said to his assistant the
day before he died, "Maybe I'll see you tomorrow."'

'Thank you for the history lesson,' the American
called after me. 'And your family sounds very
interesting.'

Qué cabrón.

I walked toward the couple and away from embarrass-
ment, my hands clasped behind my back. 'My name is
Magdalena and I am a student at the University of
Guadalajara and a tour guide for the Plaza.'

The couple kept walking and I walked beside them.
'Where are you from?' I asked.

'Washington state.' The man cupped his wife's
elbow in his hand and walked faster.

I also increased my pace. Opportunity pushed high in my chest. If the tourists accepted, I would leave the hot sun to stand inside the cool stone walls of the palacio. With a graceful open palm raised to the murals, I would stand before Indios massacred, before the flaring nostrils of horses and the glint of swords, before kings and conquerors. The tourists would pay me and I would stand before art and explain in the accepted way all the changes of the world – how princesses became slaves and slaves became courtesans, how kings were murdered and how soldiers became kings.

I thank las promesas . . .

The promise of rest, of security, of love . . . the promise of a sweet story . . .

El cuento de los principios, the beginnings of Robert and Magda, I tell in the same words always, simplified to sweetness and yearning like a Pedro Infante movie.

'The first time I saw the man who would become the father of my hija, he was reading on a bench in the beautiful plaza before the Palacio de Gobierno in the city of Guadalajara.' That is the way I always begin the story of meeting Robert.

Even young, my Martina grew tired of my lesson stories – my strategies, the stuff of survival, the power of legs, the necessary strength of heart – the stories Robert said terrorized her, but she begged for the too-simple story.

From the roof in the golden zone, I sometimes tell this story to myself and Cortés with the same words my hija loved. I tell it, and promise whispers to me de nuevo, then lloro, lloro, I cry for myself and for the world just like at the movies. It's the promise of happy forever, of rest, of salvation. That is what makes us sob in el cine.

Ours was no Pedro Infante/María Felix kind of love, but still, there existed el sabor de esperanza y el olor

195

de oportunidad. The flavor of hope, the scent of opportunity. Without it, I could not have let my fear and contraceptive pills and creams and shields fall away long enough to allow seed and egg to join in my panza. Without the simple story I told myself, there would be no hija, no Martina with the conqueror's blue eyes and tousled honey brown curls of her father, no Martina with the dark skin of her mother, the woman, and of Guadalupe, the saint.

I last told the story to my hija the night before I left Idaho, the night before I left the nine-year-old her. On a blanket in the backyard grass of our Idaho home, I lay on my back and Martina wiggled beside me. I can still smell her innocent child sweat. There is no scent of wrong in a child.

'Tell it,' she insisted. 'Tell how you married Papi and made me.'

'Bueno pues.' I yielded to my hija for this last telling. '. . . The air was dry and the sun, hot, but the man who would become your father sat fresh and bien planchado alone on the fancy iron bench. I was a tour guide teaching people about the art and the buildings of Guadalajara – the Hospicio Cabañas, the Palacio de Gobierno . . .'

Martina squirmed for the action of the story.

'Your papi, who was not yet anyone to me or to you, gave me no attention. Imagínate. I told him my name. Nada. Asked if he wanted a tour. Tampoco. His mind was so far away, and I began to talk nonsense to win his attention. I told him good chisme about the artists and I told him the interesting details of history: how José Clemente Orozco had a cross-eyed wife and about Frida Kahlo's broken vagina and poor choice of husbands, how Moctezuma was a pendejo. I even talked about my abuelito at the window and my tía on

196

the roof, because I thought he gave me no attention, but clever man, he listened.

'The next day, inside the Hospicio Cabañas, I spoke for a small group of pale and plump people from Nebraska. "José Clemente Orozco never explained his works," I said as we entered the capilla. Always the same memorized tour words. The timid group nodding, half listening. "But like the great symphonies, his murals have some fundamental themes." I had never heard a great symphony. I led them under Hernán Cortés and Felipe II kissing his difficult cross, past missionaries and soldiers. "Please, put your embarrassment aside," I said to them. "Lie on the benches and appreciate the murals in comfort." There were wide, flat wooden benches under each ceiling mural just for that purpose. Some lay on their backs, but they usually kept one foot anchored on the floor like drunks. I remember soft knees doubled over the edge of the benches.

'"The two faces of the conquest," I said, lifting a hand, and then continued to the cupola. The tourists settled under the dome. I stood with my neck aching from arching upward, pointing to arms, feet, head ablaze, to the naked man that twisted and rose in the flames of the dome as if ascending to hell. You know the picture taped to the mirror above Guadalupe's altar, the man in the fire? That is the one. I admire the mural for none of the stiff words that I repeated daily. I admire it because I know it in my panza how it is to twist through the flames, but that is not what I said to the tourists. I said, "This represents the maxiumum point of the Mexican mural – free of political and historical obsessions, reaching the infinite space of meditation and philosophy." Do you know what that means, hija?'

Martina nestled into my side and lay one plump

child hand on my panza. She shook her head against my shoulder.

'Neither do I, but I read it in a book, and I said it aloud, and then brought my gaze to the group, and sighed a private prayer that they would ask no questions that I could not answer, and at the south end of the chapel, lying under Hernán Cortés with his sword impaling the groin of an Indio, I thought I saw the American man from the plaza. He lay flat on his back, alone in the center of the bench.'

'Papi,' Martina whispered.

'Don't get ahead, hija.'

The stars are more brilliant in Moscow, Idaho than ever they are behind the ceiling of moisture in Teatlán. I remember noting that while I told Martina the story, I existed at the same time in Guadalajara and on the blanket in Idaho. At once there was cool air of the Hospicio Cabañas, echo of my own voice against stone walls, young Robert lying on the distant bench with ankles crossed and hands folded over his chest, and there was moist warmth of my hija beside me, bang of Robert pulling down my tapestry suitcases from storage, scent of lighting fluid burning in the barbecue next door. Like a woman in fever, I noticed.

'Then your father invited me to dinner,' I continued.

'No, Mami. You don't get ahead. At the end of the day . . .' She pushed my ribs with her fingers. 'Go on. At the end of the day . . . without any warm-up words . . .'

'Bueno pues. At the end of the day, when I was shaking hands and saying good-byes to my tourists in the hot sun outside the palacio, the man from the bench appeared again and shook my hand as if he were the last member of the group. This man who would become your papi, this Robert, whose name I did not know, said to me without any warm-up words,

"Would you like to have dinner with me?" Just like that, he said it. No woo or flirt eyes or court or how pretty I am or flowers of any of the flirting that is so delicious and Latino. A Mexican man can woo. But that day, I thought your father and his no flirting were so tierno – formal, without soft edges, like a child without manners – and I called him mi profesor, him with tousled brown curls, his fair skin, his conqueror's blue eyes.'

The story twisted inside my throat.

Martina inched down and lay her head high on my panza near my heart so that she could listen to my voice through my body.

'You loved Papi,' she said.

'Love does not arrive so quickly.'

'You did,' she insisted.

'There are things that you should know about love, hija.'

Even in the middle of this sweet and simple telling, I was tempted to insert the hard lessons. I did not want to lose an opportunity to teach Martina again: that love and lust are as common as hair. That happiness can make you weak. About the surprising charm of tenderness, the lazy seduction of security. That more cabrón than hunger is the person who has suffered it.

'I want you to know well, hija . . .' I began.

Martina pinched the meat of my thumb. She wanted none of my lessons, and no wandering details from other stories of my life, no dichos, only the promise – the happy story of her family and herself.

'No, Mami.' She pushed her head into my diaphragm. 'Tell about the church. Tell what happened in the church.'

I swallowed down my lessons, memories, filosofía. 'Bueno pues. Only weeks later, inside a big cathedral in the zócolo in Mexico City, the man who would become your father and I stood together looking over Santa Felícitas. It was not really her, but a porcelain body that looked like her. There she lay in a glass case, muy chaparita, de veras, only a meter and a half long. Her eyebrows were painted dark, her lips and cheeks colored pink, her skin was porcelain gray. Recessed in her chest, atop her dusty taffeta dress, there was a delicate bowl, and inside the bowl, there were a few dry bird-like bones leaning against each other like starter chips for a tiny fire. Those bones were really of her – the real and dead Felícitas.' I pulled strands of Martina's hair between my thumb and dedo indice. 'Santa Felícitas is the santa that guards all of the women in childbirth. I thank her for that.

'The man who would become your papi stood beside me and looked down at the santa. The light was dim. A small mass was being held at the front of the cathedral, which was almost as far as to Grandma's house, yet it was still inside.

'While we were standing over the santa, looking at her little bowl of bones, your future papi set a turquoise velvet box on top of the glass, just over the santa's own heart. "I can't wait longer to ask," he said. "Guadalupe Magdalena Molina Vásquez, would you marry me?"' I imitated the funny way he pronounced my name. 'Right there, right there in a dark cathedral. Not over candlelight at a dinner in a fancy restaurant or at a romantic picnic. He did not hide the ring in a surprise box of chocolates. No. Right over the dead santa's bones, that Robert asked me to marry with him.'

'And you said yes.'

'And something more that I have not told you before.'

Martina raised on one elbow, suspicious that I might spoil her story.

'Robert took my hand and we sat on the last bench farthest away from mass, and he spoke with his lips close to my ear. He told me that he loved me and that he would always love me. "It is you, Maggie," he said. "It will always be you." And he said that I could tell him anything, that he knew that trust did not come easy to me, that his big hope was that one day I would trust him. And I spoke into his ear. In rapid Spanish that he could not understand, I told him that I had married for the money of a man from Monterrey, that I had stolen from another in Teatlán, that I had used many and loved none, that if ever there were a man to trust, it might be mi profesor. Tears rolled over my cheeks and mouth and under my chin to wet my collar. I wept for happiness. Sitting so close to a man that some day I might trust, I wept for fear.

'And then I told Robert that I would marry myself with him.'

I extended my arm and held my hand up against the stars to see if light would catch in that ring and spark my daughter.

'A year later, after all the papers were legal, I moved to Moscow, Idaho, in the United States of America with my husband who would become your father.'

'You love Papi.' Martina lay back on her back.

'More cabrón than hunger is the person who has suffered it,' I said to the night. 'But I do.'

Martina reached toward the sky, toward my hand. She thought and I hoped that I was going away to Teatlán to see my mother. She thought and I hoped that I would return to her father, to her, to our life in Idaho. She wanted to touch the shining stone on my finger, to hear the story again.

I light a candle to my own pendejados . . .

I tell few stories about my life married with Robert in Moscow, Idaho. Martina wants only the sweet belonging. I will give Isabel only the end. The stories about ease and comfort have no value except when they tell of comfort attained or comfort lost.

Soon, I will tell her. First, I will compress our life together into a sentence, 'I was married to Robert, the father of Martina, for eleven years,' and then I will tell Isabel the story of a marriage ending, the much longer story of leaving behind husband and home.

Robert gave me signs that he was leaving, but pendeja yo, I didn't know the reasons an American husband could leave you – for cultural differences, for communication problems, for irreconcilable differences, for what every chingado matrimonio has. I could understand being left for a woman, perhaps. Perhaps because I didn't care for my looks, grew ugly, forgot what the job of wife is.

For eleven years I was the wife of Robert. I never forgot my job. Simple. My job was to keep my man happy and interested. I kept him satisfied but not too satisfied, kept him a little off balance, a little confused, and in return, he kept me. That's how that job works. And there was always a test to show if I was doing my job. If my viejo looked for me in bed, I was doing a good job; if he didn't, I was not. That is how I first knew that something was wrong.

Now, with the clear vision of distance and time, I can see that there were signs long before the bedroom.

Even so far back as when Martina was still little enough to hold above my face, I would fill up with that love that made me want to squeeze the guts right out of her, but instead, I would hold her with my two hands under her belly, her flying just above my face, clench my teeth, and say, 'Ay, chiquitita, hijita de la chingada, como te quiero. Ay, putita mía, como eres.' And Robert, though his Spanish was poor, understood the curses – little daughter of the fucked, oh my little whore, how I love you. It sounds bad in English. The real meaning is all in the coochy baby love talk, in the emotion held back and then squeezed through the teeth.

Once when Robert heard me, he said, 'You shouldn't talk like that, Maggie.' And I put Martina down in her crib and went to my husband and kissed his neck, massaged his nalgas and gave him the same love talk. 'Ay, hijito de la chingada, como te quiero a ti también.' Even then, so early in our marriage when he was easier to manage, Robert pressed his shoulder and head together to avoid my kisses, he resisted my cursing love talk.

And there was a time that I stood behind little Martina before the vanity mirror and we applied face cream.

'Like this,' I said, and with my chin lifted, I lightly strummed up, hand over hand, fingers relaxed and separate as if playing up my throat like a harp. The sound of that motion could be felt more than heard. Distant horses running on dirt, a heartbeat.

'Always up.' I pressed gently with four fingers on each cheek so that my eyes closed some.

Martina imitated me, but dragged her cheeks down.

'Gravity needs no assistance.' The words of la Señora de Aguilar from my lips.

Combing her just-washed hair, I continued the lesson. 'Use what you have, hija. You have good hair, honey curls with wildness that will make men crazy, so don't go yearning for straight, dark hair.'

Martina had five, almost six years. 'Braid it like Susan's,' she said.

'Bueno pues, hija, but listen. Take what you have and use it all.' I held her eyes in the mirror. The Virgin Guadalupe altar stood to one side of us on top of the vanity. 'Like when you squeeze a limón between thumb and forefinger back and forth and back and forth. The way a Teatláneca squeezes all the juice out.' I pinched an imaginary wedge of limón between the fingers of my left hand.

I combed her wet hair straight and then pressed it in my fist to put the curl back. 'Curls are muy sexy,' I told her.

'Don't say sexy!' Robert stood in the door.

'Hijo de la chingada.' I patted my chest. 'You gave me an attack of the heart.'

'Don't say that either.' Robert turned. 'She's five years old, for Christ's sake.'

These scenes came to me after the trouble had ended. They played clearly as movies in my mind, and I would think, *Ay, sí. I should have seen it.* But then, then I was focused so hard sharp on my job that I could not soften my vision to see what danced in the periphery.

About a year before I left Idaho, Robert said to me, 'Sometimes I don't know if we can work through our cultural differences.' Just like that he said it. Sitting quietly in a chair, without any warm-up words. That's

204

the way he talked, and I sometimes liked that about him, his straightforward gringo way, but when he said that caca about the cultural differences, I wanted to slap him.

I thought, *Go to the fucker place if you don't want me, Robert.*

But I did not speak my mind. I spoke my job as wife, I spoke to divert the trouble that retumbaba my panza.

So even though I was saying *Go to the fucker place* in my head, what I said aloud was, 'What do you mean, chiquitito?'

I stood behind him, massaging his shoulders, 'There is something stronger than culture,' I said, but his shoulders did not yield to me, his voice did not soften.

'Not everything can be repaired with sex, Maggie,' he said. 'Not everything is about sex.'

'Of course,' I told him. 'You're right.' But what I thought was *Passionless pendejo. Name something.*

Our house was modern and open. We had a kitchen, dining, den room called 'the great room.' Light and bright. High, angled ceilings with windows in the roof for more light.

'I'll prepare some chilaquiles and we can talk,' I told him. He loved my chilaquiles.

'Food's not always the answer, either.' Robert stood. His voice was too loud. His mouth had gone to upset mouth, a subtle straight zigzag like the rickrack his mother liked to sew on the hems of Martina's little dresses.

Tell the hungry ones that, I thought, but I didn't say that either.

Robert's mouth was easier to read than his eyes. Just like in Mexico when certain words have the hand motion that accompanies them – a tight, quick wave toward one's own mouth when saying comer, to eat; or the horns formed by folding down all fingers

205

but thumb and pinkie, tipping the thumb toward the mouth to mean to get drunk – Robert had a certain mouth for his moods and actions. Rickrack mouth was for when he was feeling like a woman does and mad about it. He had an about-to-orgasm mouth – tight and jutting at the chin, a rectangular opening – and even a wipe-his-nalgas mouth – stretched down at the same side of his butt that was lifted off the toilet seat – but rickrack mouth, his hurt-and-angry-and-fighting-the-two-inside-himself mouth, that was the most difficult to work.

I said, 'Sí, mi vida. Sí, mi amor, chulo, chiquitito . . .' Nothing worked.

Robert with his upset mouth blinked at me. Tears heavy in his eyes. Sometimes I thought Robert was more woman than man. He said, 'When I return from this fishing trip, we have to talk. Something has to change.'

There was enough danger in his sad and serious tone to make my nalgas clinch and my belly nauseous.

My Virgin Guadalupe and my milagritos had come with me to cold Idaho. Robert said that he felt uncomfortable with Lupa next to our bed, and I found a small private place for Her.

On velvet that draped with my suegra called the vanity that was Guadalupe's altar in the small room Suegra called the powder room, I set Lupa and the milagritos. Banana, leg and heart. They are solid gold, not gold plate. It is important not to be cheap when you are showing gratitude. All three milagritos shone at Lupa's feet beside a tiny pyramid of masa. Beside broken eyeglasses of my mother. Near apron strings of Chucha. Next to the bathroom sink.

Color gives Guadalupe much pleasure, so I painted Lupa's room. Blue. Not the blue of sky or sea, but blue of crystal bleach añil. The rest of that house had beige walls. Robert did not like walls with color. Something about light. Something about elegance.

Then, as now, I held each milagrito. I lit candles to the powers beyond me, to the things I could not understand. They say, with the Virgin, not so close with the candle as to burn the saint or so far that the saint has no light, but I ignored that advice. Some candles I lit almost close enough to scorch Her, others too far to illuminate Her.

Then, as now, I said my thanks. I asked for guidance – *Show me how to make my gringo desire me again, Lupa.* I held my face close to Hers. I kissed the Virgin's mouth.

Robert took us to a counselor woman.

Dr Johnson had a white sectional couch in her office and she sat on one leg of it, Robert and I sat around the bend on the other. No practical woman would have a white couch. The edges of the cushions were graying. Among her framed degrees – doctor of psychology, masters of arts, cross-cultural counseling – masks hung, the cheap ones I recognized that were made for tourists in México, ugly devil heads with long painted tongues, jaguars with laughing dentures, pigs with fangs.

Dr Johnson was dressed in yards and yards of material – a skirt that hung to her ankles, a blouse that hung to her knees. It reminded me of the marital sheets in Teatlán, the sheet with the embroidered-edged hole in its center that some couples used on their wedding nights, and others used all their marriages to lay the wife and the modesty beneath the sheet with the hole centered over her cosita, except that, of course, there was no hole over Dr Johnson's cosita.

Sitting on her white couch, I smoothed my tailored skirt over my thighs, pressed my knees together, and

207

tucked my ankles at an angle just as my first mother-in-law taught me.

This Dr Johnson under her sheets said that I was a survivor. She taught Robert and I how to fight professionally.

I feel X when you do Y in situation Z.

What I heard you say was . . . you feel X when I do Y in situation Z.

Robert was not much better at professional communication than I. He faced me with unmanly sincerity. Held my hands inside his. 'Magda, I feel confused when you act one way and I know you're feeling another.'

The therapist said, 'That's good, Robert. Now see if you can be more specific, more concrete. Exactly what do you feel when Magda does what specifically?'

I practiced silently. *I feel embarrassed, Robert, when you talk tonterías in front of this pendeja stranger.*

Robert blinked at the doctor. 'This feels unnatural, doctor,' he said. 'What I want to say is that Maggie is dishonest. She doesn't trust me. She manipulates me.' He turned to me. 'You don't trust me.' His voice rose. 'Why? I never know what you're thinking.'

I did not respond.

While I counted the minutes before we could rise from the white couch, Robert and Dr Johnson spoke the hungers of the rich. Robert cried his favorite words, honesty, trust; intimacy was Dr Johnson's favorite. I could eat none of them – not trust or intimacy – could hold none of them in my open palm. And more than that, I knew that in trust, there is danger.

'Practice, Magda,' Dr Johnson turned her attention to me, only she said, 'Practica, Magda,' rolling her single r like a Russian, trying to get on my good side with her bad Spanish.

I would not like the meddlesome stranger.

And I didn't like the professional fighting. In fighting, though I rarely allow myself, a person sometimes needs to scream and call names, to send her opponent and all his relatives to the fucker place, to slam doors.

I concentrated on the Virgin, her palms together, her eyes to heaven, and my own reflection in the mirror behind her was hazed. Beside Guadalupe, no bigger than my face, I seemed a large child looking into a dollhouse. If I looked beyond the Virgin, through the gazebo into the mirror, I could see only my eyes. She blocked the reflection of my nose and mouth, and with my self in focus, I could no longer hold her image clear. I shifted my focus from self to Virgin, Virgin to self, trying to hold both in focus at once, but I could not.

I kneeled before Lupa and practiced. It was important to 'work' on the marriage, the doctor and Robert said. Working on our marriage. What they didn't understand, what Lupa knew: I was always working on my marriage.

'Robert,' I said right through Guadalupe to the mirror, 'you seem upset. Would you like to talk about it?'

Then I spoke my anger. 'What kind of dead fish are you? You are not having an affair. That, I would know. Have you turned joto, Robert?'

Guadalupe's eyes remained to heaven.

'This professional communication just civilizes, converts emotion to lies. You understand, Lupa. I feel encabronada angry beyond English and frightened in my cells when my pendejo husband acts like a cold red snapper.'

'Mami?' Martina stood in the doorway in her flannel nightclothes, then came to my bench and sat beside me before Guadalupe. Hair in wild fluff, eyes sleepy, Martina lightly touched the leg, the banana, the heart, and I took her hand and stroked her fingers open with the tips of my own, pinched the tiny golden leg from the velvet and placed it on the center of her puffed palm. Martina blinked down at the milagrito, then slowly, seriously, folded her fingers to fist.

From the quietest place within . . .

Love is birthed by burros. That is the excuse of most, but it cannot be mine. I've said it before that mine was no Pedro Infante swooning lose your reason kind of love. My pendejado error was in not losing my reason, but in keeping it. There are times when our own beliefs fail us. It is the worst betrayal que hay.

So many years with a full belly and a sound roof, I almost believed that I had risen above my beginnings, above the shame and pain of my mother and my aunt. I had eleven years living in Idaho, eleven years married to my Robert, nine years with my hija, Martina, eighteen years away from the go-go cages of Tijuana, fourteen years away from the arid expanses of Monterrey, thirteen years with the stolen money of Julio. All the years, the fruit of my esfuerzo.

But nothing saved the marriage – not my own tested techniques, not conversations with Guadalupe or conversations with the counselor woman, not sexy clothes or XYZ – and Robert left me. I say that smoothly now, Robert left me, as if it were easy – tan tán. That is the only way to think of things that will not change. Tan tán.

Thirteen years ago.

Vows of love and chimney smoke.

I remember it sharply. I see it now.

Robert calls me from a telephone booth at a gas station near the Clearwater River, where he camps and fishes. It is a Saturday in March of 1987. Too early for fishing. In the background, there is the *ding ding* of the black tube as cars roll over it. Hoods slam shut over motors.

From our Idaho home, standing in the room called the great room, I speak to him of family things – his mother's cold, tamales, Martina's art.

With the phone pinched between my shoulder and ear, I finger the soft paper of Martina's drawing and describe it to him. The colors are strong – red and green and purple, some black. Child simple. A woman in a box. Three people, two large and one small. Everyone floats along with objects in the air – a yellow crescent, one running leg, a dripping heart. 'It looks like a dream. I think it is Lupa's altar,' I tell him. 'Martina calls it, "Family." Her teacher put three gold stars on the top.'

My voice is all-is-well-cheerful. Robert has not looked for me in bed for weeks. He has talked too much of our differences.

'I'm making tamales,' I say. 'Carnitas and some sweet pineapple.'

'Maggie,' he interrupts. 'I've been thinking a lot this week.'

I squeeze tight the telephone receiver to cut off the message.

Don't.

'I'm thinking that it might be best if I take some space.'

Space.

I see him tumble through the air like an object in Martina's drawing. I see him in the wilderness. Lying on his back, envying the stars, the planets.

Have it, cabrón. Have the Milky Way.

'Don't you have a lot of space there, mi vida?' I say.

Robert inhales a big breath and speaks in its exhale. 'Maggie. Don't be difficult. You know what I mean.'

The space in the hollow of my chest closes and begins to draw against the rest of my organs.

'Excuse me one minute, vida,' I say.

I take large steps to the bathroom, grateful that the carpet absorbs my footsteps, grateful that the baño is so near. I close the door, kneel before the toilet, lift the seat. My force erupts into the bowl so fierce, and through tears, I see waves rocking up the porcelain sides. Again a tidal rolls through me and another blast of my guts pushes through. I fold my elbows across the cool porcelain, lay forehead on forearms and convulse like the dogs in the Teatlán streets. Again and again to bring up the day's poison. Again after there is nothing left. The convulsions that roll through me slow. The vomit waves that ride up the sides of the bowl gradually calm to center. I am near blind. My nose runs slick salt. My mouth is stretched wide in a silent wail that pulses at the back of my throat. There is no sound or substance that can come from me.

Gripping the sides of the toilet, I arch my back and raise my head. There are only blurred pastels of the wallpaper through my lashes. Snot runs into my mouth stretched so wide that I feel the skin split, and the waves roll through roll through, but I cannot make a sound, and I finally suck a breath and curl down fetal onto the oval of pink nylon fur.

The calm lady on the phone says, 'If you'd like to make a call, please hang up and try again. If you need help, hang up and dial your operator.' A beep alarm sounds like emergency testing on the radio.

On the other side of the door, Martina places the phone in its cradle and silences the beep. Martina. I

213

can feel her standing at the door. I feel her ear to the wood. I think I hear her breathing.

When the phone rings again, Martina answers. I imagine her, how big the receiver is in her small hand, against her young ear.

'She's in the bathroom,' she says.

I bite the meat below my thumb. To bring me back. The skin gives. I hear the littlest snap and taste my thick blood.

'Yes, three golden stars,' Martina says.

I push myself to sitting, stand, bend over the sink. Water on the face. I must control this. My life. My home. Robert. Martina. More water on my face. Colder.

At the counter, I signal Martina to hand me the phone.

'Mami?' she questions, but I take the receiver before she can give me away.

'Robert?'

'Where did you go, Maggie?'

Martina presses into my thigh and hip.

I grip the receiver to cut off the message. It cannot pass through my fist.

'Maggie,' Robert says, 'I need to get this out. I've rented an apartment.'

'Sí, mi amor,' I say. How to know the truth he speaks when I cannot see his eyes.

'I need to think, Maggie.'

'Sí, mi vida.'

I draw from my first mother-in-law the distance, the dignity of Monterrey. 'I'll set out some things for you,' I say. La señora de Aguilar.

'We'll talk,' he says. 'I just need to gather my thoughts.'

'I'll call before I come,' he says. 'Maggie, are you okay?'

'Sí, corazón.'

I press my thumb over the little holes of the mouth-piece. Blood from my arm drips onto Martina's curls. Robert is quiet.

'I'm sorry, Maggie.' Robert's voice is so close. Inside me. I sense him lean into the black box and fold himself around the receiver. His lips must nearly touch the little holes in his phone.

I remember the therapist. Robert's how-to-communicate books. I hope I get it right.

'I feel . . .' I search for the therapist's formula. Press my thumb again over the microphone and try to regulate my breath. Lift my thumb, then cover the mouthpiece again and try to focus for the right words. Nothing comes.

'Maggie.' It is not a question or an answer. It is only my husband saying my name. Saying the first good-bye.

I take my hand from the mouthpiece and let it rest atop Martina's head. Stained curls push between my open fingers.

It was a promise I had made myself and the Madrecita de Dios years before Idaho when I pushed the tejuino carts through the streets of Teatlán. I saw more often than I wanted a señora making herself a fool. I saw more than once a woman run after her husband, begging, crying, her hair oily and tangled, then collapse and beat her fists in the dirt. I saw a woman limp and despairing just inside her doorway, heard another shrill with anger. 'I smell her on you, hijo de puta. I can smell her!' Even so young I knew that madness and excess worked against the women's desires. Their mistake, I calculated, while pushing my cart and rehearsing for life, was in expecting too much from the men. These señoras expected their men to see beyond the two eyes swollen with weeping, beyond

215

the tight and down-turned mouth, to hear something deeper than the high-pitched nasal demands, to understand the truth and reason beneath their pain.

No, Madrecita, I swore to her as I pushed the cart through the streets and witnessed the same domestic indignities again and again. If ever a man is to leave me, to disappear for days without explanation, to bring the scent of another woman to my house, I will smile and say, 'Que te vaya bien bonito,' and my punishment to him will be in how I maintain myself beautiful, in my good manners, in my clever cool heart. And in my mind, I practiced – I rustled my pretend skirts like María Felix, I lifted my eyebrows and smiled coolness and pride to the offender.

The young Magda had no idea how difficult an act that would be.

After Robert called, I assessed. Robert was mi esposo, padre to Martina. We lived in a big clean house in the United States of America, there was food in my belly and money, and though I had depended on my smarts and my long legs for much of my success, I could not depend too much longer on my looks. My chichis and belly were marked by motherhood. There was a roll over my waistband. Men still looked, but it was mostly the spark in my eye that fired them, that smoked over my flaws. I had almost forty years, enough to be called doña in México and I thought that Robert might be mi última camión, my last bus.

I prepared for the future, making piles of mine and his – house, cars, furniture, child – checking titles – mine, Robert's, mine and Robert's – checking accounts, counting the cash I kept in a Whitman's sampler box taped under Lupa's vanity, cash in a shoe box in the laundry room, cash in a dress box high in the closet. I had saved part of the grocery money every week, written checks for spending money never spent. And hidden the cash. Every time we had sex, I had slipped money from Robert's wallet – twenty or thirty or fifty dollars – depending on the sex. Depending on how much would go unnoticed. For more than ten years. Then there was the money left from Julio.

It added to twenty-six thousand, seven hundred and forty dollars. I still remember the amount. I still remember dry paper between my fingers.

I walked through the house and measured in my mind what would fit in a car, what would fit in an apartment, what mattered. I made plans with check-lists to meet the possibilities: if Robert was unsure, if Robert had a woman, if Robert wanted a divorce, if Robert wanted to take Martina, if Robert wanted to come home. I could be a waitress, buy a restaurant – I was not afraid to work – get my GED, go to college, pack money, take Martina and run, get a facial, fix my hair, seduce Robert. Between making plans, I lay on the cool kitchen floor and tried to remember un-believable things, scientific and historical facts that Robert had told me – that glass is liquid, that meteors are garbage and ice, that dogs can mate with wolves, jackals, coyotes, foxes, that Babylonian men painted their lips red before battle. I lost weight. Robert liked a slender woman.

With Guadalupe, the picture of the man in flames, milagritos, money, and clothes too warm for Teatlán, I returned to barrio Rincón. I returned without the usual bulging duffel bags. Not the big shot from America smiling too sweet with too many gifts. I had used all my strength to say a dignified good-bye to my husband and to my child, to drive from Idaho to Teatlán.

South on black asphalt through Idaho and Utah

toward Arizona and the border with one hand loose on the steering, Lupa secured in the seat belt next to me. I remember little of the trip except that each night from atop the stiff cover of a bed in a tidy hotel room, I called Idaho.

Martina answered most nights.

'Tell your papi that I am safe,' I would say.

'When are you coming home?' she'd ask.

'Soon,' I'd answer. 'I'm going to see your tía abuela, my tía. And your abuelita, my mother. I'm going to rest.'

Only her breath into the receiver.

The same question and same answer every call. As if the information could not stick inside her.

Before I had backed out of our white cement drive-way, Robert said, 'Remember to call every night. You promised, Maggie.' He stood beside my car window with Martina.

Bouncing the back of her head against his panza, she said, 'Bring me dulces de leche, Mami.'

I nodded to both.

There was a blush beneath Martina's dark skin. The hair around her temples, damp.

'Dame un beso – kiss me, hija,' I said.

Martina leaned into the window. 'Dulces de leche or coco mounds,' she whispered close to my face, and pressed her lips hard and long to mine, an old-fashioned fake movie kiss.

'Martina.' Robert said. 'My turn. Let your mother and me speak in private for a moment, please.'

Martina pulled her mouth from mine and studied my face – a child's close, open gaze. 'Don't forget,' she said, pressed her forehead to mine for emphasis, then turned and walked toward the house.

Robert bent and leaned into the car window. 'Sure you don't want me to drive down with you?' he asked.

He made me tired.

On the porch step, Martina sat rocking slowly, with her arms straight and each hand tucked under her pompis.

Robert's open palm on my forearm.

'Think about what I've proposed, Maggie.' His fingertips tapped my arm lightly. 'Go to Mexico. Rest. Remember what you love. Think about what is best.'

How civilized, this separation. How unsatisfying.

Perhaps the women in the barrio knew. That it was better to pound fists into dirt, tear hair and blouse and scream pain. They say death met without resistance is an offense to life. Perhaps separation met with such calm was an offense to our family.

I let the car roll backwards onto the street and beeped twice the horn, our good-bye habit. Martina stood and ran down the porch steps and across the lawn, one hand raised waving above her head. 'Hasta luego.' She stopped at the curb.

'Soon, hija,' I called out the window.

'Bye, Mami.'

Six days later, I arrived to the house of Mami.

For years, when I had visited the narrow dark home of my childhood, I had felt suffocated. Repulsed. The stale manteca choked me. Made me sick in my tripe. I could not stand to sleep there.

My barrio home had not affected my esposo or hija the same way. Robert had been charmed by the attentions of Chucha and Mami. He sat happy in their dark house eating tortillas and machaca, taquitos de marlin, smiling and nodding at Spanish he barely understood.

'Buenísimio,' he repeated as he ate. 'So good. Muy good.'

Mami would pat masa until a tortilla was complete and then offer it toward Chucha. Chucha would pinch an edge, peel it from Mami's palm and lay it tenderly to cook on the comal. Each woman worked steady and smiled her amusement toward the stove as Robert spoke his Spanish.

Martina would run up the circular stairs in bang and rattle and call to the children of the barrio from the rooftop. '¡Ahorita, vengo!' She helped her uncles grind sprouted corn, she stood on her toes to stir tejuino.

She sat in Chucha's chair.

Still, I had insisted that we stay in a hotel during our family visits. We stayed in the golden zone in white hotels with crisp sheets. Taxis had brought us to visit el barrio Rincón.

This time when I arrived alone to el barrio, I did not care about the smell of my mother's house. I longed for a cot in the darkness. I needed stale air and dirt. Something I cannot explain. To lose my faith.

For days I lay in someone's cot. Papi was dead. Abuelito dead. Mami and Chucha, hermano Rigo and primo Rafa with their wives and children – all lived pegado juntos in the houses of Mami and Chucha.

Their lives continued around me. I lay still, and they spoke of me as if I were not there.

'Not so rich and important now, is she, Mami?' hermano Rigoberto called to her from the table. 'Todavía puta, pero no tan trucha, ¿Eh?'

Still a whore, but not so clever. Rigoberto altered the little summary of me.

'She'll be pushing tejuino carts down the malecón next week.' Rigoberto needed to prick until someone winced.

Mami was full blind and sat long hours at the window as if she could see.

Everything spoken came to me through a long tunnel.

'Te-jui-no.' My brother imitated the sexy way I had

called it. 'The cart is in the alley, Magda.' He laughed. 'You'll have to sell more than tejuino to live the life you have lived. Do you believe that you can fit yourself into the short shorts?'

He set his beer down hard on the table.

'Vain puta,' Rigoberto said under his breath. 'You'd think something terrible had happened. How many men has she abandoned?'

Sucede que me canso de ser hombre. I remembered bits of Señor Neruda's poem. *It happens that I am tired of being a man . . . tired of my feet and my nails and my hair and my shadow.*

'Her daughter,' Rafa's wife said. 'How can a woman leave her child?'

How can a woman leave her child?

I had not left my child.

Can't a woman rest a little to regain her reason?

Neighbors talked through the open window to Mami. 'Is it so bad, Maria? Bad enough to lie in bed during daylight?'

I remembered Robert's proposal in bits and pieces. 'Leave Martina with me during the school year, Maggie,' he had said, 'and all vacation times and summers with you.'

He talked about education. Opportunity. Confidence. Something about Martina knowing her Mexican roots.

Robert had said, 'Make a home for Martina to know in Teatlán, Maggie. That way she will be with me totally when she is here, and with you totally when she is in Mexico. Let her know her grandmother and her great-aunt before they die. Not for a week, but for months.'

And he had said, 'Think about the Barrow children next door.'

The Barrows. The divorced woman and her

confused, part-time children haunted my brain. They seemed always nervous in their limbs. Going somewhere. Three children who spent four days with father, then four days with mother, and never knew where homework or favorite sock or toy was. There was a rare look in the eyes of those children. 'You and your mom and dad live here every day?' I heard one ask Martina. Then, 'Can I spend the night?'

I heard a neighbor of Mami say, 'Ay, lying alone on a cot like a spinster with no one to dress but the saints.'

Another, 'Our children are not strong like we are. Are they, María Cande?'

I heard the words of Pablo Neruda: *I want only a rest of rocks or of wool.*

I heard the words of Robert: *What's best for Martina may not be what is easiest for us.*

'Magda has become spoiled in America,' Rafa's wife said.

My sister, Rosa, came. I heard her speak to Mami. 'Is she talking yet? Does she still have money?' Manuel. Trouble.

Children sat on the edge of my cot. They whispered questions I did not answer. They touched my cheeks and eyelids lightly to see if I were alive. My nephew, Little José, carefully unfastened two buttons of my blouse before I caught his wrist and squeezed it firm in my fist.

If I had listened carefully, I would have heard Mami's silence loudest. It roared in reply to the stupid talk, circling each tonto in the room and pulsing at my temples.

But then, lying in the cot, I thought myself abandoned, and I wished for a sweet story: that Mami protected me from cruel and simple relatives and neighbors.

She did not.

I wished that Chucha spoke to me a gentle, simple and healing truth.

She did not.

The women waited.

They could not save me. They did not try.

Chucha brought lime water for me to sip. From a chair beside my cot, she wiped across my forehead with a wet cloth, circling my face, squeezing the rag into a bowl of soapy water on the floor. Down my neck, over my chest. She pressed into my armpits. 'Ya, hija. Open your sobaco. I cannot stand your stink longer.'

I could smell my own staleness, but it did not seem to belong to me. With my focus to the gray ceiling, I spoke for the first time since laying myself down. 'Tía, the counselor woman told me . . . If only I had . . .'

Chucha stopped my words with a hard thump on my clavicle. A low and hollow sound. 'Stop. Now,' she said. 'Do not torture me or yourself with tonterías. What if, if only, if, if . . .' She washed me roughly, scraping the tender skin high inside my arm.

I closed my eyes.

While the lives of my family continued around me, I had lain and relived my own. Scene after scene, I had revised my behavior with Robert and imagined the results – if I had been more subtle, more sexy, if I had not played man/woman games, if I'd played them more skillfully. What if I had teased and cajoled my husband to happiness? What if I had spoken perfectly the X, Y, Z of the situation? Had I spoken trust, honesty – Robert's favorite words . . . I revised the life again and again, trying to fit a different ending: Robert smiled, Martina took my hand. We lived together every day.

'What if . . .' Chucha spoke a nasal mimicry. She rinsed the rag and brought it to my skin with too much water, scrubbed high on my chest and my shoulders as she would a floor, then balled the rag and slapped it on my ribs. 'If my abuelita had had wheels, she would have been a bicycle.' The force of her breath cooled my wet skin, the smell of her aging gums blended with lye soap. 'There is no what if. There is only what is. The stink of your sobacos. The stink of your cosita.' The legs of her chair scraped the floor as she stood. 'Which you, hija apestosa, will have to wash yourself.' And Chucha left me.

One morning Mami was sitting in a chair next to my cot. The house was still, only the two widows moving in first light. She whispered her breath against my cheek. 'Lean over torment and listen,' she said. 'Listen, hija. The hardest failure is when you fail yourself.'

'What, Mami? What tonterías do you wake me with?'

She sat in silence for a moment, then continued. 'Fail yourself, hija, and you fail your daughter.'

I wanted no mysterious dichos, no filosofía, no advice for life so early in the morning.

'How helpful, Mami. Por favor, let me sleep.' I rolled to my side, turning my back to her. She understood nothing.

'No, hija. You'll have to find another cot.' Mami pinched the back of my arm hard between her fingers. 'Get up,' she said.

It was a mean, sharp pain that made coraje rise in me.

I brushed her hand away without turning. 'Take your dichos to your window, vieja.'

She pinched me again. 'Get up from this cot. Take Chucha some coffee.'

Ascending the circular metal stairs, I felt pressure heavy against my chest. Still, it was good to move.

Just before my head rose above the roofline, Chucha called to the still air. 'Pocha.'

I set Chucha's coffee on a small crate beside her seat,

224

then stood behind her, gripping the back of the chair with both hands.

'Eres tú, Magdalena?' she said without turning to me.

'Almost.' I lowered myself to my knees and sighed long and far. Chucha's hair needed washing.

'Qué suspiro tan lejos,' she said.

Tiny pebbles pressed into my knees.

'Have you finished with las tonterías of the should have and the if only?' Chucha asked.

I spoke into the swollen creases of Tía's neck. 'Almost.'

Our voices as long and far as my sigh.

'I have fought a lifetime of battles with ifs and onlys.' Chucha's words were slow and even, filled with pause, in rhythm with my sadness 'They only serve to hurt.'

With one cheek pressed against the top of her back, I could hear Tía's heart push blood. 'Do they hurt more than what is?'

Chucha tilted her head as if listening for the answer, her focus toward the ocean she could not see. 'Perhaps not more,' she said. 'But for longer. Much longer. Because they keep us from the truth.'

On the roof next door, a little girl squatted to piss. Her mother shouted to her from inside their house.

'Do you remember how Abuelito yelled to me from his window below?'

I nodded against the fabric of her dress.

'I hated him,' she said.

There was a small hole in a seam at the collar of her dress and I worked the tip of my little finger inside it. 'What made him so crazy?'

Tía lifted her chin and cupped her neck between her thumb and fingers, stretching the skin down its length. 'Sometimes I did,' she said. Her breath rose high in her chest to meet her hand. 'How I miss him.'

Farther down the row of roofs, a grandmother nudged a sleeping dog with the straw of her broom, then a quick short strokes swept dirt and trash and dried shit toward the edge.

The wind caught the grandmother's dust and blew it into our faces. She waved an apology, and there was a tear in the underarm of her black dress.

'Tía . . .' My cheek still pressed against her back. I did not want to move. 'I have lost myself. No me conozco.' Chucha's dress fabric was worn rotten soft. I could have torn it with my cheek. 'And my daughter . . .'

How can a woman leave her child?

Cup trembled against saucer as Chucha took it from the table.

Beyond the grandmother, a man stood on his toes atop a crate, stretching himself long over the roundness of his water tank, pushing the heavy circular lid to one side. He pulled himself up so that his feet hung limp and his head dropped inside. Curses echoed against the concrete walls of the empty tank. He emerged, dropped back down to his crate and called to the sweeping woman. 'Doña, do you have water?'

'No, joven.' She continued to sweep. 'Not for days.' She called over to us. 'Is there water in your tank?'

'Not for a time,' Chucha answered though she never looked their way.

The business of water mattered none to me.

After long silence, Tía spoke. 'Was she wise?'

'Who?'

'The American curandera, the consejera.'

'Her. The counselor woman was not a practical woman,' I said. 'She had a white couch, and she liked to talk about intimacy. She never talked about anything that you could hold in your hand or put in your belly, and I could not tolerate her.'

'Intimacy.' Chucha looked into her open palms on her lap.

'Once your belly is full, you discover that there are many kinds of hunger. Each more complicated than the one before it.'

The water tank echoed deep empty as the man banged the lid in place.

'And why did you speak of her yesterday?'

I did not want to answer.

'Chupita?' Chucha insisted.

'Ay, Tía. It is because the doctor woman said one thing that I have only just heard. She said it in the same even tone, in the way she always spoke without passion: "Sometimes old strategies no longer serve us, Magda."' I imitated the doctor. '"Sometimes we have to develop new ways to see and to be in the world." I dislike her even more, her making a consejera's dicho saying from a truth that tears my life.'

I felt weary again after the surge of anger. 'Can you see it, Chucha? That hateful ironía. My woman charm, the same focused will and harsh fire that liberated me from the barrio – that saved my life – they were the skills that both brought Robert to me and that drove him away. My own rules, my reglas for living have crumbled, y no me conozco. Here I am with forty years and without husband or child or dog to bark for me.'

'Así es.'

'En serio, Tía. I don't know what to do. I could steal Martina and keep her here. Cooperate with Robert's plan. Return to Idaho and share Martina like a pogo stick toy bouncing between two houses.' I thought again of those Barrow children. Wondered if I could

227

explain them to Chucha so that she would understand.

'Do you remember when Martina was last here?' Tía asked. 'La reina took possession of this chair as if it were hers.'

I nodded my head against her shoulder. 'La reina,' I repeated.

'You sat in this chair like that when you were young.' Tía stroked down both thighs with her hands. 'Queen Magdalenita.'

I raised my head and looked over Chucha's shoulder to see her view. The air became suddenly still, and laundry on close and distant roofs dropped to hang without life.

'Josita? Where are you?' Rigoberto's wife called below. 'José! Ven. Come. Now!'

'When was the last time you sat in this chair, Chupita?' Chucha asked.

I could not remember.

Chucha and I stayed together in silence until she sipped the last of her coffee. Noise rose from the street as the light became harsh; sweat pooled in the bend of my knees. Tía pushed with her hands against the seat of her chair to stand, and walked stiffly across her roof toward the metal stairs. Still kneeling behind her chair, I watched her calves and hips, then torso disappear. Chucha descended one step at a time, holding the iron rail firmly. The sound of each step down vibrated to completion before the next began. Just after her head lowered out of vision, Chucha stopped on a stair and said, 'One week more. Then you must leave this house. Make a life for yourself, Magda. And, si Diso quiera, maybe for Martina.'

Martina. I imagined my hija's name carried the thousands of miles to tremble within her slight body.

The stairs rattled again, then stopped. 'Some

questions, Chupita, have no answers. Some questions take a lifetime.' Chucha answered the question I had not spoken aloud.

Chucha's last step faded. From the base of stairs, she spoke softly. 'Eres tú, Magdalena?' To herself. Perhaps to me.

'Almost,' I whispered against the skin of my arm. To myself. Perhaps to Tía.

When I came down from the roof, there were sacks of corn kernels stacked atop my cot. No matter. I had no ganas to lie there longer. Though I felt as if those sacks of corn pressed my chest, my legs vibrated with the need to move more. I felt at once heavy and nervous, slowed and agitated. Thank Lupa the condition was not reversed, that it was not my legs that were heavy. My legs, at least, could transport my heart.

I took my purse from its hiding place and walked out into the barrio. Walking. Walking. Past the homes, past the stinking alleys.

I heard myself muttering the names of families as I passed their houses just as Mami had. 'Rodríguez, Ramos, Trujillo. García, the fisherman, Montevilla, the ill-breds, de la Cruz, those huevones.'

I walked into barrio Juárez, into barrio Golondrina, past the Pacífico beer factory into barrio Puerto, the fly colony – so many flies from the guts of so many fish – past seafood carts and taco stands. I thought to buy a taco de carne asada for strength, but my panza rejected the idea.

In the Central Market I squeezed between car bumpers. The *bee-op* whistle of traffic policía. Competing music – mariachi and Sinaloense, salsa and canciones de amor. Scent of guava, color of mango. Bump and push of warm bodies.

I passed Cine Maravillo. 'Bless the heart of Gordo

Chuy, that old hijo de la chingada,' I said, but did not stop walking. A Chinese karate man kicked his leg high in the poster.

I walked in dullness, but some place deep in my panzita, I recognized the sound and color of my beginnings. The path I had known from juventud took me. Movement took me. Knowledge that had no words or reason moved my heavy corazón through a route that was pressed into my cells.

I was in Teatlán and it was loud and dirty. I had loved Idaho for its tidiness, its cleanliness, smooth black asphalt, white curbs, rolls and rolls of toilet paper in shining public baños. I am crazy for clean. But I had missed the noise and life on the streets. Moscow, Idaho, was a town of ghosts quiet inside their homes.

It was when I reached the malecón and hailed a pulmonía taxi that I knew where I would go. 'A la zona dorada,' I heard myself say. The golden zone.

Sea air whipped my dirty hair and cooled the sweat on my arms and legs, and it was with that sensation that I remembered. It had been days since I had changed my clothes or washed myself.

'Where in the golden zone?' the taxista yelled through wind back to me.

'To the miracle Jesusito.' I leaned forward to speak loudly in his ear.

'He's closed today, señora.'

'That's not important. I just want to ride through his neighborhood.'

Robert had his proposal.

My plans began to form.

I would use Robert's own plan to have my hija live with me in Teatlán. With a month left before Martina's school year ended, I began my search for a home.

Robert had proposed it: I was to have her during summers and vacations; he, during school time. My plan was a little different. My plan was to take Martina for the summer and never return her to Idaho.

That first summer in Teatlán with Martina, the first time I hailed the telephone repairman down from a pole near my house, I smiled, handed him a sweating glass of limonada, and tucked a napkin folded around bills into his shirt pocket. 'A little something for more refrescos,' I said. Then, 'Might you make me the small favor of cutting my telephone line?'

'Perdón?' he said 'Cut it?'

'Yes, joven.' I waved to Martina, who was playing with a neighbor. 'Yes, cut it, please.'

'Muy bien.' He shrugged his shoulders.

'Muy amable.' I returned to my house.

I reasoned that more time without her father's voice would help Martina separate from him, but it seemed to work in the opposite way. Martina picked up the phone receiver all during the day and night. 'Can't you fix it, Mami?' she asked. 'Can't we go to a public phone?'

'Sí, hija,' I assured her.

Martina spoke more and more of her father. 'Papi says . . .' 'Papi took me . . .' 'Papi wants me to . . .' 'When can we call him, Mami?'

There was war inside me that summer. With a heart pressed heavy and a mind insisting on survival, I fought. To be a good mother. To protect my hija. To know what was best for her. I fought through hurt and anger and plans of vengeance, I fought my own self-ishness. I fought fear.

I talked at the window with Mami, on the roof with Chucha.

While Martina played with her cousins, I asked

231

my mother and aunt too many times, 'What should I do?'

'Lean over torment and listen,' Mami said.

'You'll know what to do,' Chucha said.

But con tanto miedo, la intuición no sirve.

With so much fear, intuition does not function.

The sun grew hotter, canary and apple mangoes fell from the trees, the burning jellyfish filled the ocean, and my plan dissolved.

When again I saw the same telephone repairman in our neighborhood, again I hailed him down the pole.

'Joven,' I waved to him. And when he stood on the ground, I picked pretend lint from his shirt and slipped more bills into his pocket. 'I appreciate your service,' I said. 'Now I have a more difficult request, but one I know that you are capable of completing.'

'Dígame, señora,' he said, muy serio.

'I need you to keep my phone working properly. Always. No importa how.'

Sometimes the only way to have a phone line in Teatlán is for someone else to lose one.

'My neighbors may sometimes go without, but their children and the fathers of their children are not so far away.' I raised my chin to point toward Martina, who watched us. 'If you complete this great favor, señor, I imagine that the Virgin may smile on you, and I know that you will never lack for refreshments.'

'Bueno, señora. Para servirle.' he said. 'Anything for a child.'

After that, Martina talked to her father on the telephone every few days. He was no father to abandon. Robert was a father that taught his daughter to catch fish. He kissed her wounds. Joined the organization of parents at school. He wanted everything for her. Even Mexico. Even Magda.

*   *   *

At the entrance for foreign flights, at the Teatlán airport, I kneeled on the floor before my hija so that my face was level with hers. Passengers walked around us to present visas and place belongings on the conveyor belt. There were few tourists in the heat of August. Mostly there were Teatlecos who carried in cardboard boxes tied with rope the Mexican treasures that their relatives in the United States of America hungered for – smoked marlin, ranch honey, good masa.

Robert stood to one side of the entrance, allowing other passengers space to go ahead of us, and to give Martina and me privacy, he watched the boxes and purses pass through the rubber slatted curtain.

Robert and I had already said our good-byes.

The air conditioner was not functioning, and hot wind blew through open windows. Gotitas of sweat stood on the upper lip of my hija. Her face glowed not just from sweat, but from months in humid Teatlán, each cell plumped full of moisture, as it should be. I wondered how long before those cells dehydrated in the north, and if Martina would notice, if she were more de Idaho or de Teatlán. If her cells yearned more for cool and dry or for warm and moist.

Martina fanned her beach dress to cool herself. 'Teatlán Beach Bum' was printed on the front. She lifted the hem and pressed the cloth against my damp forehead.

'No need for that, hija,' I could not resist a lesson. 'Remember that Teatlán is a place to sweat bien bonito. A place with beautiful, moist heat that lets you sweat so that the wind can cool you.'

Martina wiped her own face with the dress, and I could see her tiny nipples and near black belly. I tried to ignore Robert's discomfort that I felt tugging my sleeve, the other passengers, the heat. For one small moment more, I wanted only my hija and me to exist.

'Bueno pues, hija.' I said.

'Bueno pues,' Martina repeated.

This was our first real adiós. I had no plan brewing. No secret hope to steal her. Only the hope for our next meeting.

I smoothed the dress over her panzita. 'Más que mis ojos, hija,' I said.

'I love you more than my eyes, too.' Martina kissed my face in her own version of the sign of the cross, four quick kisses – lips, forehead, one cheek, the other.

'Adiós, hija,' I said.

'Que te vaya bien, Mami,' she said, proud of her Spanish, then turned and took her father's hand to pass through customs aduana where I could not follow.

The times between fall and Navidad, between Christmas and spring vacation, between spring and summer were long. Longest.

But it was only pain. Pain is not so bad when you expect it.

In the end, I cooperated with Robert's plan because I could not imagine a better one. There was much logic, much reason to support it. Robert had made a column of pros and contras to show me. In the pro column there was education, confidence, the opportunities of America, the soul of Mexico. We could give Martina the best of two parents and the best of two worlds without bouncing her between two houses every week he said. But a logic column hasta la chingada could not add to total a satisfying answer. Every reason seemed too cheap, too common, too easy an explanation. How could Guadalupe Magdalena Molina Vásquez leave Martina Guadalupe Jones Molina for months every year? Some questions have no clear answers. Some answers take all of a life.

*   *   *

In the days and months and years that followed, as I scrubbed shining clean circles in counter and chrome of the golden zone restaurant I leased, the whispered syllables ricocheted against my ribs and then left me to travel toward my hija. *Mar-ti-na.* I wondered how long before she really understood the plan, how long before sadness became anger, and if she would forget me from one season to another, how long before she would forgive me. I wondered how I had left my child. But all wondering and all remorse cannot change a pecado sin. The syllables of my hija's name stretched from my lips north across mountains as I served juices and food and 100 percent purified water to Americans, as I smoothed their fears and built a business: Lupa's Juices. Her name stretched over plains as I purchased my restaurant in the golden zone. The sounds of my hija's name traveled over deserts as I bought a small house in Olas Altas, then the fine 30 Ibis house beside the miracle Jesusito. As I gathered riches, her name stretched north to Idaho on the moisture of my breath.

Mar-ti-na.

It was the holy chant, the promise that saved me.

I thank my own coming blindness . . .

Abuelito used to say that con azúcar, hasta la mierda sabe a buena – with sugar, even shit tastes good. The sugar disease has come to me, though later in my life than to Abuelito's. I inject myself daily, a needle piercing into my too-sweet thigh.

I must be tasty now.

Perhaps, like Abuelito, I'll have my legs removed. I'll grow three bellies and be unable to inch my way up the circular stairs to my roof, and so I'll howl out to men as they pass my window. Though there is not so much movement in the street here in Las Gaviotas as there was in my barrio Rincón, I'll wait for the neighbor men and call out to them, 'Ay, chiquitito . . . pelón . . . nalgón.' Baldy, big ass. I'll call them as I see them. What a big tennis racquet you carry, I'll say. How sharp the crease in your slacks. What a large and squeezable ass . . . Qué bueno estás.

The doctor assures me que no. My worry, he says, is my vision. Dr Lancaster explains how my eyes are crazy for more blood. More oxygen. How they are growing too many little blood vessels and covering my retina like the madreselvas vine on my garden wall – starving, crazy growing too much too fast. I imagine myself peering from behind the tangle of madreselvas. Don Manuel comes every week and trims the vine back so that the plumeria can bloom. Old as he is, he can be as brutal with his machete and that vine as he is tender with seedlings. So silent, so steady, he repeats his tasks each week, but the vine, in the end, will win. The hungry vine, I call it, will always win.

On my roof, I close my eyes and practice blindness. Mine is the house just next to the miracle Jesusito, the one I first passed walking behind Mami and Chucha on their knees, the one with the iron gates where the clean dog with the long combed fur barked, where the servant girl stood and crossed herself as we passed while the jefa's daughter called to her from the window, 'Berta, did you iron my dress? My yellow dress, Berta?' I close my eyes and see details then and now. Berta's solemn mouth, the single lavender-blue petals of plumbago, fuchsia hibiscus blooming outside my bedroom balcony, shining marble floors and good beds with fresh white sheets, and the rooms for every need – three baños and recámaras, a sala room and kitchen and laundry room and eating room with a polished wood table. I see it all, and I pinch myself a mean pain to recognize me.

In blindness practice, I sometimes wish for the noise of barrio Rincón. Money hushes, and the people of the golden zone starve my ears. Their lives do not push and squeeze out onto the streets for all to see and hear, a sadness for me now. Though I never want to return to barrio Rincón – those who know poverty do not have nostalgia for it – I long to hear lives: a señora scolding her daughter, a drunk singing his lost love, a fight between brothers, a wife weeping, radios. Good or bad, cruel or kind, barrio Rincón is always with noise. Thanks to Guadalupe for the children. Even in the rich Las Gaviotas, the children cannot be enclosed or silenced, and I hear the bells of their bicycles, their quarrels and dramas and games. Their rehearsals for life.

There are Sunday pilgrims who come from my own barrio Rincón and shuffle past my house just as I once did, but they do not visit, and I no longer call to them. Señora León passed one Sunday, Doña Montevilla another. From behind my iron gate, when I called to Señora León, she nodded a greeting and hurried past. 'Señora León, soy yo,' I called after her. Her big chichis and belly bounced under her dress with her quick pace. Doña Montevilla, she seemed embarrassed that I recognized her. I know that people from my barrio talk about Guadalupe Magdalena Molina Vásquez, who escaped the barrio to live in this fine house, but they cannot understand that she is the same Magda that fought with them for talking of chiles and cositas and changuitos in the street, who sold tejuino in short shorts. I am lost to them.

From barrio Rincón, only Afilado Bustillos walks my Gaviotas neighborhood with confidence. Gracias a La Virgin that he knows that I am still myself. I hear the squeak of his bicycle wheel blade sharpener, and his aging voice yell, 'Scissors. Knives. Everything sharpened.' And I make my way to the gate. Afilado is sassy with me as if I am still young and full of fire and sex. 'Que guapa,' he comments after he is inside my courtyard and away from neighbors' ears. 'A new dress?' He connects the sharpening strap to his bicycle wheels, pumps a pedal with his foot so that the wheel and strap spin, then pushes the blades of scissors and knives and cleavers at an angle against the spinning leather. He spins memories of Magda's youth that are the ugly rumors of my neighbors, memories that are fire and laughter to me. 'But ay, the tejuino outfit . . .' he says, and he smiles a wicked manly smile and grinds metal to his strap. Metal singing. Old Afilado so comfortable in his manliness. Sunlight sparks on metal and he works proud of the finesse of his skill. He sharpens. He tells me news of the barrio. Doña Josefina near death. Don Xavier a father at his age. A fiesta, a fight. A child dead before her time. He flirts. And with Afilado I remember, though I am not tempted, that age doesn't stop sex.

Ugly doesn't either. Beneath the ashes, the coals burn hot.

Last January, just after la Martina left Teatlán and returned to Idaho for her final semester at the university, while I was serving lunch to two sunburned gringos, there was an explosion. It was silent and tiny inside my left eye, and I gripped the tray while dark liquid, oil on water, pooled slowly over the red table-cloth, over the faces of the gringos, over the poster hanging above the table to cover the torso of Cortés and the breast of Malinche. I set the nachos and tall glasses of the plátano smoothies too firmly on the gringos' table, made my path to a stool in the kitchen, and sat staring at the mosaic floor tiles as the dark pool swelled and blacked them from sight.

That was the first time. It seems the crazy vessel vines are weak by nature, and they break, they leak.

Blood blinds me.

The blood slowly drained away from my eye, absorbed by and hidden in my own spongy organs. The opaque wash gradually became more transparent, then veins of black threaded my vision. When blood fibers dissolved, my sight was restored with tiny flecks of darkness, debris left behind.

How different than I imagined, this sight, when as a child I put my mother's thick glasses before my clear eyes. Then, all was blurred to beauty; bare lightbulbs stretched to twinkling stars. Now my pools of darkness portion and separate my sight. Pedacitos of debris dance across my vision like the floating back ash of burned paper. Ragged pieces of a life. My friends, I call them. My sins. I live with my friends who come and go, black flecks that dance around inside my eyes, briefly blocking a portion of a customer's face, the tortilla I am frying, Isabel's small finger. And there is my constant friend, the black dot that sits firm in my right eye. Se burla de mi.

In March, after the third explosion hemorrhage in my eyes, I went to the clinic in Houston – all chrome and marble, clean and shine – to my Dr Lancaster for the laser treatment.

With antiseptic hands pink and rough as a washer-woman's, Dr Lancaster stretched my eye open and gelled what looked like a jeweler's loop right onto my eyeball so that I could not close my lid. One at a time. All the while his mouthwash breath puffed my cheek as he explained every move, and I was reminded of Chucha explaining the world to Mami. As if nothing existed until she called it into being.

'I'm going to drop three drops into your eyes,' he said. 'One . . .' He counted before releasing each gota into my eye. 'Two . . . three . . .' It was good that he talked. 'You'll feel a prick behind your eye . . . the worst will soon be over. I'm going to place this like a contact lens right against your eye.'

The chair leaned back like the recliners of American fathers. 'Let me set my aiming beam,' he said. 'I am partial to this lovely blue.'

I was blinded to all but his silhouette. His voice.

'Magda, are you okay?' Dr Lancaster did not allow silences. 'I'm a damn good aim,' he said. 'How's your daughter?'

'Graduating from college soon,' I answered. 'Yours?'

'I'm considering tying her to a tree until she's thirty.'

His medical smell was close again. 'Here are some drops so that your eyes won't dry.'

I felt nothing.

'Now rest your chin here, Magda.'

I pressed my chin into a pad, put my head on display.

Dr Lancaster fired the sharpest, most directed rays to and through the surface of my eye to my retina. One by one, the doctor zapped a beam to the vessels and meat of my eyeball. He worked from the periphery inward, and again and again he explained that sometimes he cauterized the bleeding vessel – which makes sense – and that sometimes he killed the meat of my retina so that the vines would stop growing – which does not. It is perverse, that theory of his: kill the good to prevent the bad. Dr Lancaster explained all that was accomplished by the rays again and again, but I just imagined my garden vines. Don Manuel would never remove the soil to kill the vine. I imagined Dr Lancaster, like Don Manuel, striking the vessels, the vines, again and again. The doctor sat close behind the machine that looked more like something in a dentist's office than in an eye doctor's, all swivel and rotate and shining enamel in front of my face. Though I saw nothing, I heard the machine's low hum and knew that a beam too tiny to perceive blasted forth into my eye. One hundred, two hundred, one thousand, two thousand points, two thousand rays.

'Yes,' Dr Lancaster said. 'We got 'em, Magda. That's one. Another.' He chuckled. A boy with a video game.

Each zap freed me, burned me, each hurt me more than the previous, but each one released my sight for a small while longer.

Dr Lancaster gave me one year of sight. I gave me more. I thought of all the invisible beams I had aimed

241

from Chucha's chair to the Sea of Cortés, and I imagined them turning and coming back to me right in the doctor's chair.

Dr Lancaster aimed, he fired, he chatted, and when he ran out of words, he whistled. It was a long process, though it lasted for only twenty minutes. The numbness dissolved to a burn, the burn to hot piercing needles, and then the constant ache of healing wounds in my eyes.

Pain is not so bad when you expect it.

When Dr Lancaster was done, I sat back in the chair, and in the dim room, I blinked Christmas ornaments of light above his head, over his face to the ceiling. My eyes had no control of movement for a while after the treatment, and until he patched over my eyes, one circled independent of the other.

Dr Lancaster spoke from the wheeled stool at my side.

The breath of his words.

'You must consider the operation, Magda,' he said. 'There is blood that has hardened on your eye. It could cause your retina to detatch. The laser cannot correct that.'

I blinked beneath black patches.

After my laser treatment and before my operation, I traveled to the graduation ceremony of the University of Idaho. The Class of 1999. My hija's graduation. We sat in a row on the bleachers – Robert, his mother, his wife, me – in the warm spring sun. Always his mother and wife accompanied and separated Robert and me. There were things I needed to discuss with him. Our daughter's future. Things for private. But privacy between us had not been found.

Robert has grown into himself the way men do in middle years. More meat. More substance. It had been four years with only talking on the telephone, without seeing him – since Martina's high school graduation – and when he answered the doorbell that morning, I had wanted in a flood and mezcla of emotion to stroke his thinning hair, to suck my panza tight, my posture tall, to spit on his porch that was mine, to sit on our steps and trace the veins on the top of his hand while I told him simple details of my life.

I dressed to make Martina proud, to make Robert and his wife suffer a little. In the elegant style of la Señora de Aguilar, silk draped loosely over my bosom, linen slid freely over the smooth slip and my round pompis. And my legs, freshly shaved and softened. Only the best silk stockings. Heels high enough to flatter my ankle and bulge my calf slightly, but not so high to tilt me forward into what la Señora de Agular had called 'unnecessary weakness.'

Robert and I had only minutes seeing each other in full-meaning gaze alone in the foyer of my old home that morning before his steady wife, Linda, had hurried to the door to welcome and embrace me. Hers is always the see-how-civilized-mature-and-good-I-am show. She has much pride in her maturity, her solidity, her ability to be above petty jealousy, but she almost never allows Robert and me time alone.

Linda held me, and over her plump shoulder, I tried to tell Robert everything in one private look: *That I had brought Martina's gift. About Isabel. That he will always be mine.*

'Martina Jones Molina.' The president of the university pronounced each of her names evenly as if in a solemn unrelated list.

With the milagro of laser and thanks to the good aim of Dr Lancaster, I saw my hija move across the stage. A gold tassel swinging from her cap. White tennis shoes shining from below her long robe. She probably wore her too-big shorts beneath, her belly button ring erect at her ombligo.

Robert, his mother, and his wife clapped loudly, but two palms together was not enough to express my joy.

I could not contain my heart Idaho style. With my jaw clenched to control the release, the emotion squeezed through my teeth. 'Hijita de la chingadita, ay, queridita putita mía, come te quiero.' I wanted to run to the stage, to lift my child into the air, her entire length and weight stretched and balanced on my two palms at her belly, her legs and arms flying free just like when she was an infant.

Robert stood and reached over his mother and Linda to touch my shoulder. 'Maggie?' He laughed. 'Shush the swearing, Maggie.'

Without taking Martina from my sight, I kissed Linda, even kissed my ex-suegra, stretched one hand to Robert. 'Y tú, chiquitito, mí hijoto de la chingada . . .'

Martina shook the hand of the dean, took her diploma, and walked to take her place with the other graduates.

Dios mío, how beautiful she is.

Under the noise of applause, Robert said, 'Look what we made, Maggie.'

'Mira lo que hicimos, Robert,' I repeated, and lifting both hands above my head, arching my neck back, I could feel the weight of infant Martina in my palms.

Seated with Martina in the great room of the house where I once lived, I opened my purse and reached across the low coffee table to hand my hija the envelope that was her graduation present. I had planned a private brunch – just my Martina and me – for the following day, not knowing that Martina and her friends were leaving that morning for a raft trip. Poor planning. It was against my reason to give her the gift in that moment, but Martina teased and begged, and I lost my sense.

She opened the envelope carefully and unfolded the stiff paper that was inside. Blinking. She let the paper lay open on her lap. 'I don't understand, Mami.'

'It is a deed, hija. For one-half of Lupa's Juices.'

Martina folded the deed and returned it to its envelope. 'Thank you, jefa.'

'I thought, hija . . .' I leaned forward and spoke quietly '. . . that you could learn the business and run it as my partner. The business thrives, hija. You could be a wealthy woman if you're lista.'

'That's what you thought.' She inhaled deeply and then held her exhale in bloated cheeks before puffing it out at once.

Dream of a Sunday Afternoon in the Alameda, a framed poster of Diego Rivera's mural hung above Martina. It was a gift from Robert that I had left behind. An angry-faced Mayan woman dressed in high-heeled button boots and a yellow dress. Young Diego in knickers and striped socks holding the hand of a skeleton wearing a bonnet. Dark flecks danced over the images. To keep my silence, I noted the details with sight and memory – a black dog with a bone, a white child with a doll, an angel holding the Mexican flag.

'Mami, I was thinking of joining the Peace Corps,' Martina said.

'The Peace Corps,' I repeated.

'Of going to Africa, Mami. Maybe Rwanda. To help the orphans there. I want to make a difference. I want my life to mean something.' She chewed her lip for a moment. 'Tell me, Mami. Who is this gift for?'

What she might think, what anyone might imagine, was that I wanted my hija to come to Teatlán to care

245

for me if I lost my sight. No. There was money enough to hire the help needed. I wanted no pity or charity from my hija. For thirteen years, I had lived with my daughter during Navidad and summers, and I thank Lupa and Robert for that, but it was never enough time to settle and rest into the habits of family. My best hope was to have Martina near me for a while so that together we could know each other as women, so that together we could teach Isabel.

'It is for both of us, hija, and for Isabel, too.'

Robert came in from the kitchen with beer bottles laced through his fingers. Linda followed with a bowl of tortilla chips.

'Is that your graduation present?' He set the bottles on the table. 'What do you think?' he asked.

'You knew.'

'It is a generous gift, Martina.' Robert said. He crossed his leg and his bare heel slapped the sole of the chancla, his foot still slender, clean and clipped. 'And complicated.'

In divorce, I had learned much about la amistad. When I no longer worried about losing Robert, when I stopped working my wife job, we became friends. Without sex, friendship comes easier. Not to say that the conversion from wife and lover to friend came easy – tan tán – or that I left behind all flirting and teasing with my once husband, but to raise a daughter together while living apart, to do that, I had to learn to talk truth more straight and serious.

'Martina is young for such a responsibility,' Linda said.

'Martina is capable,' I said.

In our telephone talk, Robert had warned me of Martina's response. 'You don't want her to think you needy or manipulative,' he advised. 'Let the choice be hers. Hold your temper and your lectures. And Maggie, don't use any aphorisms.'

I focused the intimacy of my native Spanish on my hija. 'Piénsalo bien, hija. Think about this well, daughter. That is all I ask. I don't want to argue with you. If you decide not to accept, I will tear the deed and honor your decision without argument. You are intelligent and independent. I want you to be your best. You can travel to Rwanda and help the children there. You can travel many places. But where can you go, hija, that you are worth more?'

Martina and I locked ojos as if no one other existed. Perhaps it was anger that swelled her eyes with tears. Hatred or fear. Perhaps it was love.

The laser treatment is not always sufficient. Sometimes the effects are not lasting. The blood, Dr Lancaster has explained, when it does not drain from the eye, hardens and scars, and the scars pull against the retina until it detaches, and then: blindness. Blindness sooner.

That is when surgery is necessary. Surgery to remove the hard tissue.

On July 15, 1999, the surgeon friend to my Dr Lancaster filleted the thinnest membrane from my eye. He put me to sleep in the clean Houston hospital and he filleted away old blood. Scars.

At the ombligo de mi hija . . .

These are the words that accompanied me out of anesthesia.

At the ombligo de mi hija . . .

I lay in darkness, and brought my fingertips to the hard black plastic ovals over my eyes.

Martina in the waiting room.

Magda in recovery.

'Is anyone there?' I tried to ask.

I moved without moving. Someone wheeled my bed through antiseptic air to a new room.

At the ombligo de mi hija pulses a small silver ring. As I rose from the anesthesia drugs, as my senses slowly returned, that is what my mind reached toward. Who can explain what sticks on a mind?

It is an ordinary ring. That conservative women wear in their ears, that rebelde children wear in the wet, soft tissue of their noses, tongues, even chiles and cositas.

So fierce is their need for pain, for suffering.

Gracias a Dios that Martina's ring is not in a nasty place with too many germs breeding.

I lay in darkness in the hospital bed and envisioned the small ring shining just above her sloppy one-sex American pants about to fall off her pompis.

Muy rebelde, she believed herself.

Muy sexy, I thought her.

Who can explain what sticks on a mind?

Mine fixed on Martina's ombligo, on the ring that hung from the rubbery edge of her beginning place.

It fixed on home and on a place on my altar below La Lupa, beside the little golden running leg and plátano, below the golden heart, where a gift waited for my Martina: a small gold ring for her belly button.

Solid soft twenty-two-karat gold, the gold of my milagritos.

Before leaving Teatlán, I had stood at the altar in my home, set Martina's gift inside my mouth and held it there, pushing the pink meat of my tongue to mound through the gold circle for a moment before replacing the ring on the velvet among the milagritos to await my hija.

I thank mí hija, bien trucha . . .

Let the child grow, and she will say who her mother is.

When Martina and I reached the winding roads of
Durango, I wanted to put a little Guadalupe on the
dashboard – a special Lupa in my purse with a suction
cup just under Juan Diego. Just for this part of the long
ride from Houston to Teatlán.
   'Ay, Mami, you're smarter than that,' Martina said
while La Lupa was still in my hand.
   This was a familiar route that I had traveled
with Julio the marijuanero. I knew its narrowness, its
dangers – curves too sharp, boulders in the road,
animales – but I returned La Lupa to the purse. Though
I could see the form of my hija, her face was lost to me.
American music played softly. My senses confused,
sound pulsed behind my wounds, smells brought
color to my mind's eye.
   We had traveled in three days across the flat hot
plains of Texas over the desert to Chihuahua, and we
made our winding descent down the Sierra Madres
Occidentales. I closed the lids over raw eyes to better
see what I remembered.
   The hard black patches had been removed from my
eyes by the chapped hands of the good Dr Lancaster
the morning we left. Light stabbed my eyes, and only

with near black lenses before before them could I tolerate the day. My vision, he said, would be weeks returning. 'The blood will drain, your vision will improve,' he had said, 'and with corrective lenses, you will see.'

As she drove, Martina talked to me about books she was reading, about La Raza movement in the United States of America, about pollution and the environment, about the total vegetarian vegan who eats no animal thing. No egg or milk or mantequilla. The world was dark watery blur.

'They'd starve in Mexico,' I said.

'We could create a vegan section on LJ's menu,' Martina said.

I loved the sound of her voice even when she spoke tonterías. Martina swayed with the car as she drove too fast around the road's curves.

'You take the cheese, the meat, the sauce from a tostado and you've got lechuga on a tortilla with maíz. Who will eat that?'

Isabel would eat nothing but hot dripping carne every meal if she could. She and the Lupa's Juices' cook were probably eating just that in my house in Teatlán as Martina drove and planned a new meatless menu. I almost saw the red rock wall rise from where the road had been cut, the tops of conifers that were level and below the narrow shoulder on my side of the road.

Martina slowed, then braked the car to stop.

'The road is blocked, Mami.' Her voice had lost its play.

'Tell me everything you see, hija.'

'A truck. Across our lane.'

'I cannot see, hija. Tell me more. Now.'

She spoke quickly in a breathless whisper. 'Two men standing in the bed of the truck with rifles, four approaching our car, some in brown uniforms, some not. Rifles.'

Forms of men moved toward us, two toward each car door.

A brown flesh blur tapped the window of Martina. She lowered it.

'Muy buenas tardes,' he said.

His voice was sticky sweet with danger and ironía, his head too close to my hija's.

The little I could see and what I felt in my tripe blended with memory. I knew what surrounded my hija and me: oficiales, policía, a pack of lobos. On the streets they say that if you must choose between a police or a cholo thug, safer the cholo. The two top oficiales were at our windows, lower lobos stood at a distance behind them, the lowest forms stood with guns in the bed of the truck.

'¿De dónde vienen?' he asked.

Martina was silent.

'Houston, joven,' I answered, but I had no way to know if I had deflated or inflated his power by calling him young man. I could see only the shadows of his most obvious movements – when he bent at the waist to peer into Martina's window, when he stood. There were no subtleties that I could read – no twitch at the corner of the mouth or slight narrowing of the eyes, no relaxation of his forehead, no softening at his lips. My heard pounded behind the wounds of my eyes. Scent and sound did not give me the immediate information I needed to manipulate these men, to see what moved them when. All I knew was that these men could be dangerous, that Martina's fear or her anger could guarantee her harm. The key – had I told her this? – was not to show enough strength to challenge or enough fear to bring out their need to smash weakness. A delicate balance.

The official tapped the door of the car. 'I asked *you*,' he said to Martina. He spoke only Spanish.

'No hablo español,' she said.

'Una pocha,' he said. 'Una pochita,' he repeated this bit of information over his shoulder to the men as if announcing the kind of prey. I could feel them in my tripe, knew that they were pacing in place, pulling nervously on their chiles, anxious for scraps.

Martina had attempted to pass for Anglo, but with her dark skin and mine, she could not. Failed, she sat in silence.

'Is la pocha too good for Spanish?' He used pocha the new way, to mean Mexican American, for disdain.

I heard the angry exhale of my hija.

'Stop your tongue,' I said to Martina in English.

There was a tap at my own window. I lowered it, and the official pushed his head through to look at Martina's things in the back. Stale beer and cigarettes, dirty hair, raw onions on his breath. The unwashed sourness of his pants.

'Step from the car, ladies,' the offical at Martina's window said. 'For inspection.' There was dangerous politeness in his voice.

I gripped Martina's leg to keep her seated.

'Ay, señores,' I said. 'Let us pass. I am recovering from eye surgery and my daughter worries for me.'

The man at my window said, 'Two beautiful morenas. One blind. One mute.'

His partner laughed without humor. The other forms lurked at the front and rear of our car like the black flecks that pulsed in the periphery of my eyeballs before creeping over my vision.

Martina sucked her breath.

'What is happening, hija?' I asked in English.

'He's running his thumbnail up my arm,' Martina whispered.

'Smile and gently remove his hand,' I instructed. 'And don't speak English more. It makes their paranoia rise.' I could smell Martina's fear, acid pinching high and metallic in my nostrils. So could the officials.

A lesser lobo on Martina's side waved one arm above his head, and a car rolled slowly by. I thought I saw a smear of a child's face pressed to the back window. I imagined the parents on the front seat with faces forward, blind to offenses so that they might protect their own. My mind ran over strategies. How to offer money, how to measure my fierceness.

The official at Martina's side moved to the rear windows. 'What contraband have we here?' he said. 'Marijuana? Cocaína?' He tapped the glass with his fingernails. The back door latch clicked.

Martina's words broke out of her. 'Deja la puerta cerrada, señor.' Loud, too loud. Cracked with fear and effort.

'Ay,' Martina's official spoke over the roof to mine. 'The pocha speaks Spanish. Pero muy mal hablada es.' He imitated her accent, making it stronger and uglier to hear than it was. The man had the instincts of an animal or crazy person. He knew too quickly my hija's rawest sores – pocha, accent.

'¡Ya!' the official at my side spat. 'Inspection!' He opened my door and pulled me from the car in one movement too quick to prevent.

'¡Déjame, apestoso malcriado!' I yelled in panic, and the man pushed me against the closed door of the car before ill-bred was complete from my lips.

Behind me, the electric windows closed, all locks clicked.

I stretched my neck long to take small sips of air. The official stood inches from me. *Be still*, I told myself, but my whole self trembled. *Still.*

'Not bad, mamita.' The official was blur and stink.

253

Menace. 'Look what I have,' he called to the others but his breath remained on my face. 'Contraband. Well-bred chichis.'

The official gripped my wrist in his fist and knocked my knuckles twice against the window glass behind me. 'Tras, tras.' His voice was a mean song. 'Knock, knock, hija. Let me in.'

My hija had locked herself inside. My eyes throbbed to see, but I could only smell the mongrel pressed against me, hear the other men agitated.

Behind me, the official at Martina's window tapped on the car roof. 'Hallo? Hallo?' He imitated English. 'Is anyone home?'

Though I tried to make myself still as stone, my heart pounded deep inside me, vibrating from bone to skin.

'Now the rica is silent,' my official said. 'Now that her pocha daughter has closed the door to her.' He pushed his knee between my legs, pinching the skin of my thigh.

The car horn exploded constant and loud, and I startled just as the apestoso peligro did. My official pounded the roof of the car with his fist.

The horn stopped. The brief dragging buzz of a back window lowering.

'¡Atención!' Martina shouted.

The official at her window was yelling.

Martina pressed the horn again, then lowered a different window. 'Listen, pendejos,' she called.

Martina used a moment of shocked quiet to speak quickly. 'Somos hija e esposa del vice consul del consulado del Los Estados Unidos en Teatlán.' We are daughter and wife to the vice consul for the American consulate in Teatlán.

She blew the horn again, then lowered what sounded to be her own window a little.

'Did you hear me, sir?' she asked her official, then raised her window glass.

My own official still held my forearm tight, but I felt his breath and body move their attention to Martina. I heard Martina lower her window again, a long dragging moan all the way down.

'He is the vice consul in charge of American visas.'

There was silence, and I imagined the official and my hija to be evaluating each other in steady stares.

'Were you able to hear me, sir?' Martina's voice had transformed to cool and formal confidence.

'Sí, señorita,' he answered. 'You were speaking of your father.' Martina's official then called over the roof in a low and private voice meant only for my official. 'Leave her.'

My official closed his fist tighter around my forearm. Mean silence.

'Leave her,' Martina's official repeated.

I heard the click of my lock and felt the door push against my nalgas. 'Mami. Now.' Martina spoke with the same authority as the official.

Inside the car, my lock clicked. I heard my own ragged breath, smelled the sour acid of my own fear.

Martina gripped the steering wheel in one fist and pressed her arm near straight, pressed her back more erect against the seat, seemed to be driving away, though the engine was not running. 'Usted most likely has no interest in traveling to the USA, or I imagine your visa is current, but . . .' she said to her official.

These men had no hope of ever attaining a visa. All under forty. Uneducated. Poor.

'As for our belongings,' she said. 'We carry with us, only personal possessions and gifts for my father – books, chocolates . . .' Her list faded to disinterest. She turned to face the windshield.

'Perhaps you will share your gifts,' my official said.

He stood and pressed his body close to my window door, allowing a car to pass on the narrow shoulder of our side. Careful crack of dirt and stone beneath the tires.

'Shut up!' Martina's official said.

Martina continued, 'Perhaps you will meet my father the next time you go to renew your visa.'

She opened and dug in her purse, ignoring how the men stiffened at her movement. 'Papi is the new Vice Consul Robert Jones at the American consulate – in charge of the American tourists and American visas.' She clicked the end of her pen in the air, ripped the paper quickly from a metal spiral. 'Here is his name and mine.' Martina pushed the paper toward her official. 'This should speed things up when you go to renew your visas.' Her Spanish was clear and formal. She did not acknowledge all that had passed before; she no longer acknowledged their danger.

Martina is my child.

Her official took the slip of paper, unsure whether to believe her, unsure not to believe words written, reluctant to spoil a chance for a visa.

My official held no paper. He was suspicious. 'Your father allows his women to travel alone?'

Martina lowered my window and leaned toward it so that she could see my official. She seemed to consider his words in calm silence before speaking. 'My mother could not fly after her operation,' she said. 'There is something to fear, señor?' My daughter's hand rested on my seat while she waited for my official to respond.

He did not answer. He did not step away from the car.

Martina slowly straightened to her seat and then pushed the control to raise my window glass.

Her official stood and stepped away from her

window. 'There is nothing here to inspect,' he mumbled to the others. He tapped twice atop our roof, then held one arm straight up to the approaching car and waved us away with the other.

Slowly, evenly, Martina pulled away from the disappointed men. Their bodies rotated to follow our escape and they stepped closer to our car to sniff the meal they had been denied. The lobos standing in the road by the truck barely left enough room for our car to pass. Martina drove with one arm on the wheel, and maybe from outside, she looked relaxed, but inside the car, the air was stiff, it trembled as metal brushed the dirty pants of the wolf soldiers. I felt guns at my nape, at my back.

Martina maintained that slow speed long after the officials were behind a bend in the road. All my senses screamed to press the accelerator pedal to the floor and flee the danger, but Martina continued an aching, even, slow speed long after we passed the dangerous men. She was frozen in her stiff posture, one arm on the wheel. She did not lift a hand to pinch the mocos from her nose or wipe tears from her face. My hija drove slowly down the mountain, the only sign of her weeping the small cracks of moans that escaped from deep in her throat.

I knew that conifers and rocks pressed on either side of us, that occasionally the shoulder dropped away to the long view of rolling mountains. What I had always felt with Julio and felt on the same path with my hija was an urgency to return to the wetlands, to the Sea of Cortés. My body stretched toward home, longed to skip this tortuous slow descent. I wanted the road to flatten, the skies to open. I wanted to latch the iron gates of Ibis 30 behind my Martina and my Isabel, myself, to smell charred tortilla in my kitchen, to smell the rotting sea from my roof.

When my hija's tears seemed to have stopped, I said, 'You were clever, hija.'

She said nothing.

It is important to tell the story of a danger escaped – to tell it again and again. The men with guns. What one said. What another said. What you said. How they smelled. What you thought. How it could have been.

' "Gifts for my father . . ." ' I quoted Martina to initiate the telling. 'How did you think to make him vice consul?'

Martina gripped the wheel with both hands. 'I lied,' she said.

'You saved us,' I corrected her.

'Sí, Mami. Just the way you would have.'

Martina lifted her chin and sobbed loud. Undisguised. She choked and wailed words wet and deep in her throat, words I could not understand. I leaned to my hija and touched the top of her hand, but she did not release her grip to press her palm to mine. Her hand tightened around the wheel and her knuckles rose from her hard fist, and Martina drove slowly down the mountain, leaning forward against the wheel as if blinded by hurricane rains.

I kiss the Virgin's mouth . . .

I practice blindness. Though my vision is near good with my glasses, I remove them and make my way through my home. Three stair steps down – the cool slick of marble against the smooth soles of my slippers – five steps normal in length – a rough plaster wall. Isabel follows behind me whispering my path and hers: 'one stair, two stair, three stair, one wall, two wall . . .' The moist soles of her feet stick and release on the marble. Right turn and then four quiet steps over the wool rug to the sala and the altar of Guadalupe. La Virgin. My Lupa.

In my fine house on 30 Ibis in the golden zone of Teatlán, La Lupa doesn't hide in a powder room as she did in Idaho. Here She stands in full color on her own table, a mirror behind her. I bend to the small Virgin. Her palms together, Her eyes to heaven.

'Soy yo, Lupa,' I introduce myself as if She cannot see me.

I run my finger against the grain of the plush velvet draped beneath her. Scrape a long match along the side of its box so that I can light many candles. Stand in the amber light and finger Chucha's apron string, lift the broken arm of Mami's eyeglasses, press my thumb into the small pyramid of masa, lift the shining stone of my old engagement ring to the candle fire.

I know that Isabel's eyes peer just over the burgundy velvet, that her fingertips hang just at the table's edge.

Filled with the gratitude that saves me, I place each milagrito – sacred heart, plátano, Robert's ring, piernita – one by one in my mouth and press its shape on my tongue. With the golden heart on my tongue, I light a candle for Mami and Chucha; with the banana, I light another for the education of Isabel. With the ring sharp against the roof of my mouth, I light a candle for Robert. For all that has been gained and all that has been lost.

Prayers most large come last.

Mi hija. She is not the same since the day of the dangerous men on the highway. When I remember her cleverness, it is in a mezcla of emotion that spasms my heart. Though Martina resists me, she has learned my lessons. I celebrate. I grieve. My heart opens with pride only to feel salt thrown into it. This is something I know well – what gives pride also gives shame; what brings happiness, sadness – but concerning my hija, philosophy does not soothe me. I cannot tolerate to watch her suffer.

With the officials at the roadblock, my hija was forced to make a deal with a danger, to make a deal with the way of the world. She holds it as a shame she cannot touch, one that she cannot admit. So magnificent, my hija, so fine in her righteousness, so fierce in her beliefs, but she wears that day like a dark and heavy shawl. And she is diminished. Martina will not speak of the day of the dangerous men, and yet I know she turns it over and over in her heart.

What Martina talks about is change. How to make Lupa's Juices what she calls a business of conscience. Pay profit sharing, counsel the women about sexual politics, make a vegetarian menu. She wants to take down the picture of Orozco's naked Cortés and

Malinche to replace it with what she calls an old-fashioned feminist poster, Rosie the Riveter, a woman baring her biceps, a red rag around her hair.

A mother is not spared one cell of her daughter's pain, yet in a rare way, I welcome Martina's fall just as Mami and Chucha must have welcomed mine. When I returned to barrio Rincón without husband or hija or dog to bark for me, I thought my mother and aunts without hearts. So cool and smug. Now I understand from skin to bone that they were both heartbroken and relieved. Heartbroken for my fall, relieved that I had survived it. Así es. That is the way it is. A daughter will be humbled. A mother hopes for it and dreads it, knows it must come, prays that it may not.

I place the golden leg on my tongue, light a candle for Martina, and speak inside my heart. *I see you, so proud in your struggle, so fine in your desire to change the way things are and I want to apologize. For the pain and the cruelty, for the ways of the world, the ways of men and women . . . But I cannot.*

I remove the golden leg from my mouth and set it near Lupa. With milagritos shining wet on velvet, all returned to their places, each candle lit – not so near that the Virgin is burned, not so far that She is not illuminated – I bend so close to Guadalupe's brown face that my breath fogs Her.

'Lupa,' I tell her, 'I'm neither virgin nor santa.'

Then I part my lips and press them slowly, carefully against Her small cool ceramic mouth, and I linger.

I pull my lips from Hers. Stand. Finish my confession. 'Solo mujer, Lupa,' I whisper.

I am only a woman.

The daily ritual continues. With my syringe of insulin, my razor, the Barbasol, a bowl of warm water, I climb to the roof. Isabel follows behind, carrying our thick towels. The railing still holds the night's

261

coolness. Diamond metal mesh presses through the thin cloth of my slippers.

'For Christ's sake, Mami, put your glasses on.' Martina scolds me from her plastic lounge chair on the roof.

'In a small moment, hija.'

I want to see. Her. Isabel. The world. But I make myself practice.

Martina's head is featureless, only smears of brown, darker at the eyes, darker still on top of the head, a mauve blush at the mouth. Only two thin strips of yellow interrupt the brownness of her near-naked body. Below, in the gardens of my neighbors, I see smears of young green – bougainvillea just budding. All is blurred save the black dot that is constant in my right eye, all but the black flecks that sprinkle and dance across my sight. My sins, my friends, I call them.

Standing with one foot balanced on the seat of Chucha's chair, I apologize to my long limb before injecting into my sweetness.

'Perdóname, piernita,' I say, and prick my thigh.

Pain is nothing when you expect it.

Running my hand over my calf, I feel that I have waited too long to shave. Already, the hairs have pushed through the skin.

Isabelita walks along the roofs edge calling forth the world below. 'Some are walking on their knees, Tía. One woman pinched her little boy and made him cry. Adolfito has a new red bicycle. His toes barely reach the pedals.'

The Sunday pilgrims pass below on their way to visit the miraculous Jesusito. Isabel calls me tía though I am not.

While Isabel describes the world to me, Martina sits near. I know that her legs straddle her lounge chair to make room for the notebooks and numbers spread across it, that the tops of her shoulders are near black from the sun, that she bends intently over her open books to write in them, then sits back a little to contemplate what she has written. She invents a world. In one journal, she calculates business plans for Lupa's Juices; in another, she plans menus; in another she writes her observations, her complaints about me, weighing again and again the pros and contras of a life in Teatlán, a life with her mother. She writes about leaving. About staying. Sometimes she reads to me.

In the good light of the morning sun, I shave my legs. Always the same. Just after time with Guadalupe, after Isabel calls forth the world. Just before I send my thanks west to the sea. Isabel comes to me, and we stand on either side of Tía Chucha's chair toe to toe with each other, each with her leg extended and her foot pointed atop the wooden seat. Martina does not join us.

'These legs have brought me things you cannot imagine, Isabel, and I thank them by treating them well.'

I touch my legs and remember the blue veins like jellyfish tentacles pushing to surface, the dimples of the good life at my thighs, the coarse stubs pushing through my brown skin in a thousand blue points – things that I can tolerate not seeing. But the new silk hairs on the leg of Chucha's granddaughter, Isabel . . .

I teach Isabel about the power of legs, about the necessary strength of heart.

She covers her legs white with the Barbasol.

'Always use shaving cream to keep the legs soft, smooth.'

Isabel's attention is absorbed in the white foam.

I teach her even though she has only six years, just as I did my Martina.

'Always a new blade.'

263

Isabel scrapes the empty razor in a mostly straight path from ankle to knee.

'Use the tools you have, Isabelita. I had great legs. I used great legs.'

'Oh, pl-ease,' Martina says under her breath.

As we shave, I sing the song that Isabel will never hear her great-grandfather sing, 'Dónde estás, corazón? Ya no te oigo tu palpitar.' Where are you, my heart? I cannot hear you beating.

When I pass my best blade over the cream, it reminds me of the snowplows in Idaho. I know that my brown skin shines up in the sunlight in a path cleaned by the razor, and there I am. There is my once-beautiful leg revealed. Isabel, smart child, learns quickly, and she sings with me, 'Quisiera llorar y no tengo más llanto.' I would like to cry, but I have no more tears.

All the time while cleaning the razor, dipping it in a bowl of hot water,

I thank the dark virgin, Guadalupe, morena like me.

And while I smooth in lotion afterwards, making my skin shine even browner, *I thank the blindness of my mother, the prisoner who set me free, the power of sex . . .*

I have no rosary, but I understand the wisdom of beads knotted together, the razón of repetition, the same words mouthed without sound. Mami and Chucha would roll each bead between thumb and forefinger, scarfed heads bowed, a moan or mumble sometimes escaping. Dry lips moving moving. One bead linked to the next – *Hail Mary full of grace* – one prayer to the next – *Blessed art thou among women, and blessed the fruit of thy womb . . .*

My own litany is my life that rolls silently through me, each word and phrase blending,

Las promesas, los pendejados, my own blindness . . .

Each event, lesson, story and person knotted to

the one before and the one after it. All of the same strand.

I whisper my own silent prayer. From the quietest place within me, the place where pain births gratitude, *I thank the women who still whisper in my ear.*

Isabel returns to the roof's edge. I sit in Chucha's chair. Close behind me, the miracle Jesusito lies in a glass case among too many toys. South and east behind him, egrets strut the shallow waters on skinny legs with eyes sharply focused for the movement and shadow of snake and eel, and farther still, beer factories and canning factories and concrete box houses crowd out all green and breeze. All this pushes from behind me, pushing west. I sit and aim to Cortés, pushing my lives to sea, beaming memory and gratitude over the terra-cotta roofs of the rich.

Isabel knows that my ritual is complete. She says, 'Most of the worship people are waiting on their knees at the gate of the tennis club. May I ride my bicycle with Adolfito?'

'Sí, Chula. Vete.'

I inhale little girl musk as she brushes past me. The iron stairs rattle with her quick steps down.

Martina stands and swings one leg over her lounge chair full of notebooks, then walks to the roofs edge.

A sea breeze joins our silence.

'Tell me what you see, hija.'

Looking down to the street, she says, 'Put on your glasses, Mami, and come see for yourself.'

The front door slams, then the iron garden gate. The bell of a bicycle.

I push the lenses before my eyes and join my hija.

Below us, Isabel stands and pumps the pedals of her bicycle. Her braid bouncing against her back. 'I'm coming, Adolfo. Espérame, Adolfito.' Pink and yellow streamers fly out from the ends of the handlebars, and she squeals like a dolphin as she pulls alongside her friend.

The last of the Sunday pilgrims walk on knees toward the miracle. Some are gathered at the gate. I strain to see if blood stains the asphalt just below us. So clearly as if today, I see Mami and Chucha walking the rough road on torn knees toward Jesusito. Though we cannot see it, the blood of Chucha and Mami is sealed there beneath years and layers of tar and rock. Adolfo and Isabel race past the last pilgrims, past the house of Jesusito. In the garden across the street, a servant holds two corners of a small rug, turns her head hard to one side and snaps the rug in the air.

Beside me, Martina in her bikini shines from oil and sweat. The yellow gold ring in her ombligo erect against her darkness. She stands strong with her legs straight and feet apart, observing the world below.

'Kiss me, hija,' I say.

Martina blinks to the street, then slowly turns to me. Both eyebrows are raised and she holds an arrogant half smile.

'Kiss you,' she repeats, revealing nothing.

Mi hija stands watching me for a long moment, sighs long and far, then, with eyes open, she bends to me, parts her lips, and presses them lightly, carefully to mine.

The pain is no less than the joy, and both are near unbearable.

Gracias, I whisper.

THE END

My own litany of gratitude . . .

Gracias a Doraluz Villazón de Loustaunau, Josefina
(Kyky) Ramos, María de Gútierrez, Cristina Iñiguez y
todas 'las Mamis' por abrir de nuevo los ojos y el
corazón.

To Guadalupe Ixtlixochilt Bustillos Valdez, who
insisted that I know the old songs and the old movies
– por enseñarme algo de lo mero mero Mexicano,
gracias.

I light candles to the generosity and smarts of the
mentors and students of the creative writing program
at Warren Wilson College, especially Kevin McIlvoy
(who praised me off the cliff), Pete Turchi and Wilton
Barnhardt (each who dusted me off, hauled me back
up to the top and pushed me off again), Andrea Barrett,
Richard Russo, Pablo Medina, C. J. Hribal, Marjorie
Hudson, Cindy Eppes, Veronica Patterson, Kathryn
Schwille, and Susan Kelly.

To Mike Pompe: for your eloquent and patient
e-mails describing retinopathy from the inside, thank
you.

Besos and abrazos to the people working in the
Colorado Council on the Arts. Your recognition and
support fortified me.

And to the folks associated with the Bellwether Prize
for Fiction, especially Barbara Kingsolver, Terry

267

Karten, Grace Paley, Ruth Ozeki, and Frances Goldin, I cannot say it enough: THANK YOU THANK YOU THANK YOU. I'm jumping up and down. I'm hollering.

Doble gracias a Terry Karten, kind editor, for her attention and smart insights.

Gratitude to Jean Naggar, advocate and agent.

Praise for my sweet Pumpkin, Dawn Marie Rowe, my consultant and conscience, for her plucky, straightforward intelligence. Brava, Punk!

For my dead daddy, H. R. Hinton, Jr., who taught me about backbone, and for my mama, Marie C. Hinton, who tells me stories, my deepest love and respect.

And always, always, immense gratitude to my best, Mitchell, who believes.

Bless y'all hearts.

THE HOUSE OF
THE SPIRITS
Isabel Allende

'A GENUINE RARITY. A WORK OF FICTION THAT IS
BOTH A LITERARY ACCOMPLISHMENT AND A
MESMERIZING STORY'
Washington Post

Spanning four generations, Isabel Allende's
magnificent family saga is populated by a memorable,
often eccentric cast of characters. Together, men and
women, spirits, the forces of nature, and of history,
converge in an unforgettable, wholly absorbing and
brilliantly realized novel which is as richly
entertaining as it is a masterpiece of modern literature.

'EXHILARATING . . . POSSESSED BY AN IMMENSE
ENERGY, A FECUND IMAGINATION . . . AN
ELEGANT WAY WITH LANGUAGE'
Newsweek

'THIS IS A NOVEL LIKE THE NOVELS NO ONE
SEEMS TO WRITE ANYMORE: THICK WITH PLOT
AND BRISTLING WITH CHARACTERS WHO PLAY
OUT THEIR LIVES OVER THREE GENERATIONS OF
CONFLICT AND RECONCILIATION. A NOVEL TO BE
READ FOR ITS BRILLIANT CRAFTSMANSHIP AND
ITS NARRATIVE OF INESCAPABLE POWER'
El País, Madrid

'ANNOUNCING A TRULY GREAT READ: A NOVEL
THICK AND THRILLING, FULL OF FANTASY,
TERROR AND WIT, ELABORATELY CRAFTED YET
SERIOUS AND ACCURATE IN ITS HISTORICAL AND
SOCIAL OBSERVATIONS'
Die Welt, Berlin

0 552 99198 8

BLACK SWAN

LIKE WATER FOR CHOCOLATE

A Novel in Montly Instalments with Recipes, Romances and Home Remedies

Laura Esquivel

'THIS MAGICAL, MYTHICAL, MOVING STORY OF LOVE, SACRIFICE AND SIMMERING SENSUALITY IS SOMETHING I SHALL SAVOUR FOR A LONG TIME'
Maureen Lipman

The number one bestseller in Mexico for almost two years, and subsequently a bestseller around the world, *Like Water for Chocolate* is a romantic, poignant tale, touched with moments of magic, graphic earthiness and bittersweet wit. A sumptuous feast of a novel, it relates the bizarre history of the all-female De La Garza family. Tita, the youngest daughter of the house, has been forbidden to marry, condemned by Mexican tradition to look after her mother until she dies. But Tita falls in love with Pedro, and in desperation he marries her sister Rosaura so that he can stay close to her. For the next 22 years Tita and Pedro are forced to circle each other in unconsummated passion. Only a freakish chain of tragedies, bad luck and fate finally reunite them against all the odds.

'WONDERFUL . . . HARD TO PUT DOWN . . . IT IS RARE TO COME ACROSS A BOOK AS UNUSUAL'
Steve Vines, *South China Morning Post*

'A TALL-TALE, FAIRY-TALE, SOAP-OPERA ROMANCE, MEXICAN COOKBOOK AND HOME-REMEDY HANDBOOK ALL ROLLED INTO ONE . . . IF ORIGINALITY, A COMPELLING TALE AND AN ADVENTURE IN THE KITCHEN ARE WHAT YOU CRAVE, *LIKE WATER FOR CHOCOLATE* SERVES UP THE FULL HELPING'
Carla Matthews, *San Francisco Chronicle*

The worldwide bestseller – now a major film

0 552 99587 8

BLACK SWAN

LA CUCINA
Lily Prior

'WONDERFUL. A FESTIVAL OF LIFE AND ALL ITS
PLEASURES'
Jane Harris

A delicious début novel set in Sicily about a shy librarian
with a broken heart whose passion for cooking leads to an
expected love affair.

La Cucina combines the sensuous pleasures of love and
food, simmering in the heat of a Sicilian kitchen. Rosa
Fiore is a solitary middle-aged woman who has resigned
herself to a loveless life, and expresses her passionate
nature through her delicious cooking. Then, one day, she
meets an enigmatic chef, known only as l'Inglese, whose
research on the heritage of Sicilian cuisine leads him into
Rosa's library and into her heart. They share one sublime
summer of discovery, during which l'Inglese awakens the
power of Rosa's sexuality, and together they reach new
heights of culinary passion. When he vanishes
unexpectedly, Rosa returns to her family's estate to grieve
for her lost love only to find a new fulfilment, as well as
many surprises, in the magic of her beloved Cucina.

A love song to Italy, *La Cucina* is a celebration of all
things sensual. It spills over with intense images, colours,
fragrances, and exuberant characters, all reflecting the
splendour of the Sicilian countryside in which it is set.

'A HEADY CONCOCTION, BY TURNS FUNNY,
FRIGHTENING, SAD AND JOYFUL'
Valerie Martin

'SWEET, NAUGHTY AND IRRESISTIBLE'
Harpers & Queen

0 552 99909 1

BLACK SWAN

A SELECTION OF FINE NOVELS
AVAILABLE FROM BLACK SWAN

THE PRICES SHOWN BELOW WERE CORRECT AT THE TIME OF GOING TO PRESS. HOWEVER TRANSWORLD PUBLISHERS RESERVE THE RIGHT TO SHOW NEW RETAIL PRICES ON COVERS WHICH MAY DIFFER FROM THOSE PREVIOUSLY ADVERTISED IN THE TEXT OR ELSEWHERE.

99588 6	THE HOUSE OF THE SPIRITS	*Isabel Allende*	£7.99
99313 1	OF LOVE AND SHADOWS	*Isabel Allende*	£7.99
99946 6	THE ANATOMIST	*Federico Andahazi*	£6.99
99921 0	THE MERCIFUL WOMEN	*Federico Andahazi*	£6.99
99618 1	BEHIND THE SCENES AT THE MUSEUM	*Kate Atkinson*	£7.99
99619 X	HUMAN CROQUET	*Kate Atkinson*	£7.99
99860 5	IDIOGLOSSIA	*Eleanor Bailey*	£6.99
99917 2	FAY	*Larry Brown*	£6.99
99687 4	THE PURVEYOR OF ENCHANTMENT	*Marika Cobbold*	£6.99
99979 2	GATES OF EDEN	*Ethan Coen*	£7.99
99686 6	BEACH MUSIC	*Pat Conroy*	£7.99
99692 0	THE PRINCE OF TIDES	*Pat Conroy*	£7.99
99836 2	A HEART OF STONE	*Renate Dorrestein*	£6.99
99587 8	LIKE WATER FOR CHOCOLATE	*Laura Esquivel*	£6.99
99910 5	TELLING LIDDY	*Anne Fine*	£6.99
99827 3	IN COLD DOMAIN	*Anne Fine*	£6.99
99721 8	BEFORE WOMEN HAD WINGS	*Connie May Fowler*	£6.99
99851 6	REMEMBERING BLUE	*Connie May Fowler*	£6.99
99893 1	CHOCOLAT	*Joanne Harris*	£6.99
99800 1	BLACKBERRY WINE	*Joanne Harris*	£6.99
99859 1	EDDIE'S BASTARD	*William Kowalski*	£6.99
99959 8	BACK ROADS	*Tawni O'Dell*	£6.99
99864 8	A DESERT IN BOHEMIA	*Jill Paton Walsh*	£6.99
99909 1	LA CUCINA	*Lily Prior*	£6.99
99865 6	THE FIG EATER	*Jody Shields*	£6.99
99673 4	DINA'S BOOK	*Herbjørg Wassmo*	£7.99
99825 7	DINA'S SON	*Herbjørg Wassmo*	£6.99

Transworld titles are available by post from:

Bookpost, PO Box 29, Douglas, Isle of Man, IM99 1BQ

Credit cards accepted. Please telephone 01624 836000
fax 01624 837033, Internet http://www.bookpost.co.uk
or e-mail: bookshop@enterprise.net for details

Free postage and packing in the UK. Overseas customers: allow £1 per book (paperbacks) and £3 per book (hardbacks).